Kath inspired by memories

Of old-fashioned Christmases at the Taylor mansion, frost lacing the windowpanes, the snowy landscape glittering like diamonds. Of Grammy Taylor making cocoa in the big, comfortable kitchen. Of Lydia's face lit by the glow from the fireplace, her eyes starry as she spun fantasies of her future.

Of Taylor House as it was—warm and welcoming and filled with love.

She wanted to honor those memories and to preserve a tradition... To find that someone who would know that she was fighting for more than a house, more than wood and nails... To find that someone who would understand that Taylor House was about happiness and security and love.

It would all happen... if Katherine's dream came true.

ABOUT THE AUTHOR

Leigh Anne Williams, a successful writer of
screenplays and song lyrics, found it a
natural progression to move from writing
popular love songs to writing romances.
Recently Leigh's most challenging project
has been the writing of a musical. She
makes her home in Manhattan's Greenwich
Village.

Books by Leigh Anne Williams

HARLEQUIN AMERICAN ROMANCE
232–GOLDEN DREAMS

Katherine's Dream
Leigh Anne Williams

Harlequin Books

TORONTO • NEW YORK • LONDON
AMSTERDAM • PARIS • SYDNEY • HAMBURG
STOCKHOLM • ATHENS • TOKYO • MILAN

Published October 1988

First printing August 1988

ISBN 0-373-16265-0

Prologue

Grammy Taylor squinted in the sunlight, staring up at the worn and weathered door frame that had just showered her with flecks of ancient paint and crumbling wood. "Just because you're older than I am doesn't mean you have to be so disrespectful," said the elderly woman, vexed. "After all, I didn't slam it, I closed it."

The house, of course, did not respond. Mute, it merely took in the sun, complacent and proud in spite of its undeniably rundown appearance. A century and a half had taken its toll on the moss-covered back wall of stone, on the ever-leaking slate roof, the slowly disintegrating foundations. Mrs. Taylor saw that the wood above the door was rotted clear through, and had to allow that the house wasn't being willfully mean to her.

Shaking her white-haired head, she brushed the offending bits from her calico shawl, muttering a conciliatory "Oh, well." Then she turned, cane guiding her down the stone path to her vegetable garden, which no doubt needed attendance. Emily always missed something when she weeded it, and the arugula lettuce, if Grammy remembered correctly, was in danger of parching.

En route, she stopped to gaze in anticipation at the sunlit display of her beautiful yard. A scant month ago, the carpet of green grass had been edged with flowering bulbs, tulips and hyacinths planted among the forget-me-nots. The bleeding hearts had come back, hardy things that they were. Soon the summer flowers would be in bloom, but even in the in-between there was a suitable symphony of scents in the air. Mrs. Taylor closed her eyes, inhaling, immensely pleased. Then she turned back toward the house.

"I've done you a good turn, here," she reminded it. "Never had a garden like this in your youth, did you? No." The back windows of the house twinkled, glimmering in response, and a soft sigh of breeze-ruffled leaves from the sheltering elms that hovered round it seemed to whisper approval.

Grammy Taylor listened to the spring sounds, head cocked to one side, and for a moment imagined she could hear the high-pitched laughter of a happy child in the wind. The children that Emily cared for weren't here today, she knew. How long had it been since the house had resounded with the noise of Taylor children? It was something she sorely missed, she realized. That had been the happiest of the times they'd shared, she and the house—when her daughters Katherine and Lydia were little girls.

She remembered Edward, the proper professor, giving them both piggyback rides on this very lawn, alternately oinking and braying like a mule to their screams of delight. Grammy smiled. Little did the academic world know the fond and rustic creature her dear husband had really been, here at home. But she knew, she and the house. "We've had some fine times, haven't we?" she murmured, still smiling at the glinting gables in the warm, warm sun. "Fine times, indeed..."

Suddenly she was dizzy and couldn't catch her breath. She thought she might sit down. Right here on the grass? Well, why not, after all, what better place?

With difficulty, clinging to her cane for support, the old woman slowly lowered herself and sat then, cushioned by the soft, long grass. There was a strange tightness in her chest as she gazed at the vines twisting round the shutters of he kitchen's open window, where the blue of her glass bottle collection sparkled in the sun.

Dizziness was still clouding her vision, and she fantasized she saw Edward striding out the back door toward her, a smile lifting the ends of his gray mustache. Such a handsome man. Such a handsome house.

The children...

The cane slipped from her slowly unclenching hand. Grammy Taylor closed her eyes.

Chapter One

It was one of those gorgeous Massachusetts mornings in early June when every visible living thing for miles around still practically screamed "Spring." But Katherine could only see a little piece of it from her seat in the chapel pew. Outside the narrow window, bees buzzed, birds chirped, monarch butterflies did impromptu air ballets in a sky so brilliantly blue as to defy any painter's palette. With so much life in bloom out there, it felt even more awful to be sitting in this quiet semidarkness waiting for a funeral to begin. Especially since it was her mother's.

Katherine looked down at the little card she'd been fidgeting with when she'd taken her seat. The card had accompanied the bouquet of flowers from the Atchins family. Katherine glanced at it again before putting it in her bag: "In loving memory of Grammy Taylor."

They all called her Grammy, even Katherine. She'd called her Mother when she was growing up, of course. But when Katherine's daughter Clarissa had started calling Mrs. Taylor Grammy almost as soon as she could talk, the name had stuck. The Greensdale children Emily looked after at the house every week called her Grammy, and that was how the town knew her now, after years of her having been "the professor's wife."

And that was how she'd be remembered, Katherine thought, but the idea of "remembering" disquieted her. She'd sat through her share of funerals, but that didn't mean she'd ever be used to the experience, especially the air of unreality that always went with it. What had Grammy herself said to her only a few years ago, at Jeffrey's service? "Death has no manners."

How true. Death had its own perverse logic, played by nobody's rules. In a better world, death would have waited at least one more day for Grammy Taylor. It would have at least waited for Katherine to come down to Greensdale, as she'd been planning to for weeks. A mere sixteen hours might have made all the difference. By then she would have been there, at her mother's side, and she might have been able to, well, do something.

Not fair, not fair: the singsong litany echoed through her mind again for the umpteenth time. Katherine sighed, pulled a strand of honey-blond hair from one eye and opened her purse to take a look at Jeffrey's old brass pocket watch within. A few minutes past eleven. Time to get on with it, as Grammy might say. She could hear the husky warm quaver of her mother's voice as clearly as if she were sitting right beside her, instead of lying stretched out in that box up here. She half expected Grammy to knock impatiently on the lid. That would be just like her.

Katherine shook her head ruefully. She was suddenly seized by an urge to laugh or cry, but she took hold of herself and chose neither. Katherine had never been one to display her emotions, and years of marriage to Jeffrey Addison Cartwright had tempered her already undemonstrative demeanor even more. As wife of a great American man of letters and university professor, one wasn't expected to "let it all hang out," not even as his widow.

But her insides were in turmoil. Katherine stole a glance at her compact's mirror. Curious to see what feelings showed, she contemplated her face as if it were a strang-

er's. Soft blond hair swept back from a high, smooth forehead above dark brown eyebrows and gray-green eyes that
were troubled now. The nose was long and slender, com-
plexion fairly pale but starting to show the few freckles
summer brought out. The full lips were set tightly, the chin
jutting upward defiantly.

At forty-three, she still looked to herself like an attractive woman, but one who was daring the world to cross her
again. Deliberately Katherine relaxed her features, the lips
sagging, and long lashes drooping over her eyes. But now
she looked absolutely miserable, and that wouldn't do.
Grammy would—would have—poked fun, chucking her
under the chin with a bent and shaky forefinger. "You'll
break my mirror," she'd have laughed, "with a monkey face
like that!"

Once again, Katherine felt the irrational urge to laugh.
Hold on, she instructed herself. Lack of sleep and the ever-
present grief could easily breed a bout of giddy hysteria, and
now was not the time for it. She had a daughter and a sister
to look after.

Clarissa was still sniffling quietly at her side. Katherine
took one of the extra handkerchiefs she'd brought along out
of her bag, one of Grammy's, with its antique embroidery
on the corners, and pressed it gently into her daughter's
hand. The tip of her pert nose was reddened from a seemingly endless supply of tears. Katherine stroked Clarissa's
tousled blond hair as she nodded her thanks.

Clarissa was taking it hard. She'd grieved when Jeffrey
died, but she'd always been much closer to her grandmother. The two of them had had a special relationship,
faithfully exchanging letters, phone calls, holiday visits. Just
this past year, her daughter had spent the whole summer at
the house in Greensdale. At times it seemed to Katherine
that Clarissa confided more easily in Grammy than she did
in her own mother.

Clarissa was staring at the simple coffin now with a look of disbelief, and Katherine understood. She gave her daughter's shoulder a comforting squeeze, and looked past her to see how Lydia was holding up. She was slumped forward, her long fine hair falling around her face like a veil. Katherine wanted to give her little sister's back a consoling pat, but it was too far to reach.

Little sister! Lydia would bridle at the phrase. But to Katherine, it didn't matter that Lydia had recently passed her thirty-second birthday. She'd always be The Kid, even though at five feet and ten inches she seemed to tower over her older sister. She'd grown into a beautiful woman, and Katherine wondered idly why she'd made no mention of a current man in her life when she'd arrived at the house last night.

Her eyes returned to the front and to the floral arrangement Lydia had created out of flowers picked from Grammy's garden. That was a nice touch, and Lydia had done a beautiful job. The stands of golden forsythia behind a palette of violets and pink Jacob's ladder made a much more appropriate, meaningful display than any formal wreath the local florist might have come up with.

Oh, it was all too solemn, too still in here! Impatiently she drummed her fingers on her black knit skirt. Once again she felt a surge of irrational anger at the unjustness of the event. They should have been celebrating Grammy's seventy-first, not suffering through this! If you had to have a heart attack, Grammy, she thought, carrying on another in a lifetime's series of friendly arguments with her—Grammy loved a good fight—why couldn't you have had the decency to wait until I got there? And the day before your birthday! How rude!

That was the voice of Grammy, wasn't it? Katherine had never thought about how much she'd miss her mother, but only because she'd never imagined life without her. She felt the sadness welling up within her, too big to handle. She closed her eyes and forced the feeling back.

Not now. No, there were so many arrangements to take care of, funeral things, graveyard things, wills and legalities, things of stone, wood, paper that had little to do with emotion and human weaknesses. And she'd have to be strong. It was something she'd been forced to become good at.

HERE THEY ALL WERE. There was the coffin. Hard as it was for Lydia to accept, there was no denying that Grammy Taylor had passed away. Passed away? Too passive for Grammy.

Lydia was used to such gentle euphemisms in her work, as the "passing on" or "leaving" of many a beloved dog, cat or bird brought their bereaved owners into Lydia's Pet Sanctuary, hoping to replace the irreplaceable. But such phrases didn't seem to go with Grammy. And you couldn't replace her, could you?

Lydia's hair was in her eyes. She brushed the bangs aside, not that it made her tear-clouded vision any clearer. She straightened in her seat, absently smoothing back the blond tresses that fell a full foot past her shoulders. Her long hair had been her most prized possession since childhood, when large eyes and the long, thin Taylor nose had combined to make her quite the ugly duckling. She still found it hard to believe that she was now considered pretty.

But at the moment she was sure her eyes looked saucer-shaped and red-rimmed from mourning. Remembering that Grammy had loved to brush her hair for her—"A hundred strokes!" she'd always insisted—was enough to bring tears into them again. Clarissa was already nudging a handkerchief into her hand. Lydia took it, and knowing that it came from Katherine's apparently bottomless purse, shot a wan smile in her sister's direction.

Katherine smiled back, looking pale but opaque. She was a rock, Katherine was, a lovable rock, yes, but every now and then Lydia wished she could see her crack open a bit. After all, Clarissa was sitting there blubbering like a baby, she herself was a mess, but Katherine seemed almost serene.

Well, that was Katherine, the eternal big sister. And far from resenting her for her composure, at the moment Lydia felt grateful. At least one of them was holding things together. Because, when you thought about it, fate had dealt the Taylor family a pretty bad hand over the years.

First there were Grandmother and Grandfather, who'd passed away within a year of each other when she'd been in her teens. Then Dad, half a dozen years back, not entirely unexpected after all the operations, but he'd still been hale and hearty in his early seventies. And then her brother-in-law, only three years after that. Jeffrey had been a mere fifty-five. For Grammy, who seemed ageless, to follow Katherine's husband so soon—well, it just seemed perverse, somehow.

Grammy had been the one dependable Taylor over all those years. Even though she knew it was fantasy, Lydia had somehow assumed the old woman would live forever. And now that Grammy was gone, so suddenly, she felt as though the family had been dealt a terribly disorienting blow. *Was* it a family, just the three of them?

Lydia bit her lip, staring at the flower she was twirling in her hand. Well, the house was still there and all the grounds. That was something to hold on to. She'd have to see to it that Grammy's garden got attended to properly, no matter what else might happen.

The garden had been Grammy's pride and joy. Once a haphazard motley pattern of wildly growing perennials in the main backyard of the Taylor house, Grammy had gotten seriously involved in cultivating it after Father's death. Its centerpiece was a bed of lettuces, vegetables and mint from which she proudly produced delectable salads, though it was Emily who really did the work.

Emily Atchins was a girl from town—girl? Lydia thought, amused, for after all Emily was thirty-six, only four years older than herself—who looked after Grammy, having taken on the job of cook and housekeeper. Though Grammy's eyesight had been failing, legs weak and fingers stiff from arthritis, she'd always treated Emily as a visiting friend who insisted on doing chores she could very well manage herself.

Lydia remembered the feast they'd all attended for her seventieth birthday party last year. The elderly woman had bullied her way into the kitchen, inadvertently creating a number of culinary disasters that Emily had thereupon miraculously turned around into a well-cooked meal—and then Grammy had complained, eyes twinkling, that she could never get any dishes prepared without Emily getting in her way!

Emily was seated at Lydia's side, noisily blowing her nose into a lace handkerchief. It struck Lydia suddenly that one of the only men in attendance at the moment was the minister, a properly serious-looking but incongruously tanned young man who was hovering by the mahogany coffin, waiting politely to see if there would be any more people from town attending.

Lydia doubted it. Emily, Grammy's one close companion from Greensdale proper was already here. And at this late date, one could hardly expect the boundaries that had always existed between the Taylors and the town to evaporate, no matter how significant the occasion. The minister was clearing his throat, evidently having reached the same conclusion. At last the service seemed to be about to begin.

Clarissa was blowing her nose again. Lydia patted her knee fondly, a little concerned about her niece. She seemed more scattered and spacey than ever, depressed beyond the immediate, sad circumstances of this visit. She'd cut her hair dramatically short, had broken up with a current boyfriend and apparently switched possible careers in midstream again.

Lydia knew that most women in their early twenties went through this sort of thing. She herself had somehow avoided the worst of it, knowing since childhood that she wanted to work with animals. But Clarissa had always been impulsive and unfocused. When would she settle down? *Would* she ever?

Still, it was really none of her business. Lydia turned back to face the minister.

SHE COULDN'T STOP. That was all there was to it. It was physically impossible to stop crying, so she might as well just get used to it. Clarissa blew her nose again and saw the minister wince slightly. Had it been that loud? Yes. *Sorry*. She averted her face, embarrassed, as both her mother and Aunt Lydia simultaneously put supportive hands on her shoulders.

Their sympathy unfortunately only brought a fresh torrent of tears welling to her eyes. Clarissa shook her head and crumpled up her handkerchief. It was hard to concentrate on what the minister was saying, but she supposed that was okay. He didn't know Grammy as well as she had, and reciting platitudes right now didn't matter. Grammy was gone. What could you say that really meant something?

This was a problem, she mused. Words were changing meanings on her this morning. People said they were sorry, and "sorry" didn't seem even vaguely adequate. Then there were other expressions that suddenly seemed bizarrely appropriate. "Heart attack," for example. It *did* make sense in a weird way. Your own heart attacked you, of all the unjust things, and then, well, if no one was there to fight back for you in time...

That's what had happened to Grammy. And if only she'd been there! She'd have fought for Grammy tooth and nail.

But no, she'd been all caught up in her own dumb little dramas, breaking up with Nick and figuring out where to move to and trying to sell that old painting for some extra cash—

No. She couldn't blame herself. She knew instinctively that Grammy wouldn't have approved. In her last letter, she'd even told Clarissa she'd understand if she wasn't able to come to Greensdale for her birthday, not that Clarissa would've even considered missing it. But Grammy was like that. *Was.*

Clarissa lifted the handkerchief to her nose again as quietly as she could. This wasn't going to be easy, this switch from present to past tense. The idea of beginning the adjustment, thinking Grammy used to, Grammy did, instead of *Grammy is,* refueled her sadness all over again.

Clarissa stole a look at her mother, imagining it must be harder for her. After all, Grammy was Mom's mother. Mom looked stoic, but Clarissa knew how sad she was. She knew how to read her mother. She remembered that even at Dad's funeral, Mom hadn't cried, not because she hadn't been devastated. Boy, had she ever! But crying just wasn't something she did in public. Well, try as she might, Clarissa sure wasn't taking after her.

Aunt Lydia didn't have her older sister's reserve. Clarissa could hear her quietly weeping even now. But then, Lydie—her mother's pet name for Lydia—always had a wide open heart. To see her with those rabbits of hers, or any of the animals she delighted in nurturing, was to see love in action. Everything about her aunt seemed warm, from her open affection to the foods she loved to bake at a moment's whim.

I wish I was grounded like that, she thought. *Earthy.* Lately she'd been feeling absolutely ground-less. Giving up the sculpture studio in Berkeley, coming East again after she'd sworn she didn't want to live there . . . and now this. Losing Grammy felt like losing some sort of human anchor she'd been depending on for years.

She blew her nose, gently, gingerly, and then tried to focus on the minister. Grammy would've been bored. She was too full of life to want to dwell on death. She wouldn't have wanted to see them all there in a stiff-backed pew, stuck inside on such a heartrendingly gorgeous day.

Clarissa was feeling lost, but even as she registered the sensation, her mother's hand reached for hers. Instinctively she put her other hand out to find Aunt Lydia's. Now the three of them were connected, facing forward but linked by a current of love beneath the skin. This, she imagined, was a picture Grammy would've enjoyed.

PETER BRADFORD HATED FUNERALS. Ten years in a New York law firm hadn't softened his resistance to suits and ties. This stiff black suit was truly a pain, especially since he wore it so rarely. Putting it on this morning, it felt both outgrown and never grown into in the first place.

For another thing, this funeral was on a Sunday morning, which meant he was going to be late for his jam session with the Screaming Honkers over in Plattesville. This was annoying because the boys in the Honkers (they were all a dozen years or more younger than his thirty-nine) had been practicing tunes from the old Stones albums he'd lent them the week before, and Peter was dying to hear which ones they'd mastered. He'd been wanting to play lead guitar on "Satisfaction" since high school. And a long week of town council meetings had really doubled his impatience.

He played guitar on the weekends to blow off steam. A couple of hours with those butt-kicking young rockers was better than three sets of tennis. He scowled at his reflection in the mirror above the sink as he fussed with the knot in his tie. One of the advantages of having returned to Greensdale to take up his law practice was a tacit lack of strict decorum here. He often spent days in the office in blue jeans and a jacket, and none of his clients minded. But for this funeral, propriety was important.

Peter ran a brush through his chestnut-brown hair, which looked neat enough, and stepped up his momentum. He only had a few minutes to get over to the church. Bounding downstairs he realized he was still scowling, which was a bad sign. That was how he used to be only a few years back, when the pressures of New York City life had made his nervous system short of combustible. *It's just a funeral,* he told himself, but that was no help, and he knew why.

It was a funeral that had brought him back here four years ago, when Dad died. He remembered disliking each and every aspect of the thing, the pomp and circumstance of it, especially since Dad had never been one to stand on ceremony. He still missed his father more than anything, and was only now beginning to realize that there were some things in life you just might never quite get over. This was a fact of adulthood he didn't enjoy contemplating, and today's funeral was certain to engender such contemplations.

If Dad had been around, he'd probably have talked Peter into sneaking off to fish for catfish in Carson's Lake off Route 9. Peter had tried it on his own only once since Dad's death, but the fun seemed to have gone right out of it. Peter shook his head, slamming the door to his bachelor quarters above the Wilkinses' tackle shop. See? The morning was turning maudlin already.

Striding toward his gleaming silver BMW, the one sign of affluence he'd allowed himself while retrenching in Greensdale, he noted the spectacularly cloudless blue sky and the fine weather. Well, at least they wouldn't have to stand in the churchyard in the rain as they had that last time. Funny thing, that. A storm had cut loose just as they carried the coffin out, with serious lightning and thunder when it was lowered into the grave. Mom had said it was Dad's final protest at the conventional rituals of daily life.

Inside the BMW he felt a moment of calm. Sitting at the wheel of this prize possession, bought in Manhattan when he'd still thought he might make a go of it as a member of

Howard, Howard and Holmsby, always had a soothing effect on Peter. Easing down the driveway, windows open, he was able to think about what lay ahead with a more detached feeling. He was going to have to deal with the Taylors, so he needed to get over his prejudices toward them and his resentment at having to do this thing—fast.

The Taylors had never really been a part of Greensdale. They lived here, yes, but they hadn't been born here, as much of the town's bedrock citizenry had. Edward Taylor had bought that old mansion in the hills—no local could've afforded it—with money earned by the written word, that in itself the subject of much perplexity. The old scholar, a highbrow from his mustache to his oxfords, had moved in with his wife and enough books for a public library at least forty years ago, but even to this day there was a sense that the Taylor clan was a town unto itself. They had airs.

Old Mrs. Taylor was well liked, to a degree, and Emily Atchins swore up and down that she had been the sweetest, albeit stubbornest woman ever to grace God's good earth. But the Taylor children and grandchildren had spent only a modicum of time at the local schools before being flown off to private ones, and this was perceived as snobbery. Too good for Greensdale High?! Edward and the Mrs.—in town she was known as Grammy—socialized with Greensdalians only on the most public occasions, and they were always receiving citified visitors in expensive cars, which did not promote great camaraderie with the likes of say, Luke Wilkins.

From his seat behind the counter at the tackle shop, Luke was a sort of unofficial mayor here, with a horde of relatives who'd lived and died in Greensdale, and to Luke the Taylors would always be "summer folk," whether they'd lived here over four decades or not.

Of course, Peter reflected, he, the local-boy-made-good, was driving just the kind of car that offended Luke. But then he'd never been as anti-Taylor as Luke. Peter thought them snobbish, sure, but he saw nothing wrong with academic pursuits and making money in whatever way you knew how to. He'd also had a secret crush on Grammy Taylor's oldest daughter when he was in junior high.

He'd never even spoken to her, that was the funny thing, because she'd been years ahead of him, a senior when he'd been in the eighth grade. But there was something about Katherine Taylor that had fascinated him. She was a beautiful young girl but beyond that, there was a quality to her sleek blond looks, a touch of class, that did something to his adolescent heart.

Peter had one particular memory of Katherine Taylor that hadn't quit, not in the twenty-odd years that had intervened. He'd been walking by the school grounds one Saturday afternoon and noticed her up ahead. Just then the outdoor sprinkler system had gushed on, startling both of them. He saw Katherine dance away from the spray of water, laugh—he could remember vividly the throaty, uninhibited sound of that laugh—and then turn back for a moment, smiling in the sun, to let some spray splash across her face.

Then she was striding away with perfect posture, her alluring air of cool back in place. She hadn't seen him, yards behind her, and he had the distinct impression he'd glimpsed the "real" Katherine Taylor in that playful moment. She'd left their high school for some Eastern boarding school only a month later, never to return. But that image of her private smile in the sun and spray, and the sound of her laugh had stayed with him ever since.

She wouldn't be smiling this afternoon, he thought grimly. And most probably she wouldn't look anything like his cherished memory. Time could be unkind to pretty high school girls. It was this thought, and the even uneasier thought that Randy Morgan wanted him to talk business to Katherine Taylor and her sister this week, which nearly made him turn left instead of right as he got to the fork on Bridge Road. But dutifully he drove toward the church.

Many cars were parked outside. In fact he wondered where he might find a space. He'd spied one small one behind a battered Volkswagen and was carefully maneuvering into it—a challenge—when he noticed that people were coming out of the church's side door, slowly moving onto the cemetery grounds.

Peter hurriedly jockeyed into position, checking his watch. Was he that late? Looking at it again as he climbed out of the BMW, he realized the watch had stopped. And there was the coffin procession already! Now he was going to make the worst conceivable impression on the Taylor sisters, being late for the funeral.

He trudged up the walk to the cemetery's low gate and hurried through. Maybe if he caught up with the tail end of the procession no one would notice. He mingled with the last stragglers, nodding a hello to the few people he knew from town. Apparently the funeral of the Taylor matriarch hadn't drawn a capacity crowd of locals. Even death didn't resolve old differences.

Satisfied that his late arrival wasn't affecting the proceedings, Peter made his way slowly to the site itself, anxious to get a glimpse of the Taylor women. In a moment he saw the three of them, clustered not far from the Reverend Bailey, with Emily Atchins at their side. His heart gave an unsteady lurch as he saw the woman closest to him, because it was difficult to believe his eyes. Katherine Taylor hadn't aged a day! In fact...

It couldn't be Katherine. Squinting to get a better look, he surmised it could only be her daughter, who resembled the Katherine he remembered in many ways. Though her eyes were red-rimmed with tears, they were pretty, intelligent eyes of a similar hue, and the nose had the same slender perfection he'd admired in his youth. When they'd gone over things after the town council meeting Randy had mentioned a daughter but Peter couldn't remember her name.

To her left, in gray, with hair down to her…long hair, that had to be Lydia Taylor. He'd never met her, as he'd already graduated from college and moved to New York by the time she was in her teens. He could see the family resemblance in her solemn face, too. Curious, he looked past her to the figure in black.

There she was, standing straight and tall. Her eyes were clear, face expressionless as she listened to the minister, gazing down at the coffin now within the open grave. If anything, age had only enriched the classic beauty of her profile, he decided. She still exuded that air of coolness and intelligence, so much so that he found himself wondering why she wasn't showing the grief her sister and daughter were exhibiting.

Lydia was gripping Emily Atchins's hand, and Emily was snuffling loudly, Katherine's daughter also crumpling a handkerchief to her own tear-stained cheek. As Peter watched, the minister handed Katherine the little hand shovel used to pitch a ceremonious bit of dirt into the grave. Katherine stepped forward. She looked down, her lips moving silently for a moment.

Then she quickly, elegantly, he thought, turned the shovel over. They heard the fall of the dirt onto wood in the sudden silence. Katherine handed the shovel to Lydia, gave her shoulder a steadying squeeze and stepped back. Then, to the surprise of all in the vicinity, she kept going.

Peter watched Katherine stride away from the grave site, other mourners and curious onlookers turning to see her go. Then, remembering themselves, they turned back respectfully as Lydia continued the final rites. But Peter kept his eyes on Katherine's receding figure.

"Strike up a conversation somehow, I don't care how," Randy had cajoled him. "But move fast, will you? Say hello and broach the subject as delicately as you can. We don't know how long the two sisters will stay in town.''

Peter remembered those words, but hesitated. It didn't strike him as appropriate to go barging into Katherine Taylor's private world at a moment like this. So he merely stood, watching her leave the cemetery, wondering what exactly might be going on behind those strawberry-blond tresses right now. Had she quarreled with her mother? Or had they never been that close to begin with? She certainly wasn't acting the part of the bereaved daughter.

Or perhaps, he mused, she was feeling similar to the way *he'd* felt at Dad's funeral, not wanting to grieve in public and bitter at the grim finality of it all, a little mad at the world at large. He liked to think that was the case with Katherine, as he watched her get into a Volkswagen and gun the motor.

She was certainly in a hurry to get out of there. The car jerked forward, then lurched back. There was the unpleasant sound of metal butting metal and scraping. Peter smiled ruefully. Pity the poor sucker who'd had the misfortune to park behind her this morning. She was still maneuvering her way out of the tight space and didn't seem to care what damage she did.

Then the smile froze on this face as he realized just who that poor sucker was—and whose BMW had just had a fender dented. With a strangled cry, Peter took off down the lawn.

Chapter Two

Katherine had already had about as much as she could take of this whole business.

She was used to being in control. It was a role she'd grown into at an early age, the big stretch between her and Lydia casting her immediately as the Big Sister Who Knew Better. She'd helped out her mother after Dad was gone.

Raising Clarissa, born when she was still a young coed, and years of fighting her way through the bramble bushes of male-dominated academia had forced her to hone her leadership skills. Assuming Jeffrey's work load after his death had made her, finally, an absolute management wizard. She was the woman who could do it all.

But three days of mourning in Greensdale were fast transforming her into the woman who couldn't do anything, and Katherine was unnerved. Commiserating with Lydia, who seemed to be taking it the hardest, coddling poor Emily, who was a walking wreck, and consoling Clarissa, who had single-handedly bought out Martha Gibbons's dwindling Kleenex supply at the little variety store nearest the house, had taken its toll. Katherine had turned snappish, listless, forgetful and unorganized, all of these qualities she deplored in others, let alone herself.

Even the simplest things, such as getting out of a parking spot, seemed impossible right now. She was aware that she'd inflicted a little damage on the car behind her, but was cranky enough at this moment to blame it on that car. After all, she was doing the best she could, and she didn't remember the spot being quite as tight when she'd parked earlier.

"Hey!"

There was a man running toward her waving his arms. Katherine had both hands tugging at the recalcitrant wheel, so she merely shot him an annoyed look, grimacing with the effort of turning against the curb to eke out another inch of space.

"Hey, wait—look—Miss Taylor!"

He was actually knocking on her window. With a sigh of exasperation Katherine put on the brake and rolled the window down, frowning at the man, who seemed unduly distressed. He seemed to know who she was, but she didn't recognize him, and she wasn't in the mood for conversation.

"Can I help you?" she asked, brittlely polite.

"You certainly can," he said, returning her frown. His eyes were a piercing blue beneath dark brows and a somewhat unkempt thatch of brown hair. His full lips beneath an aquiline nose didn't seem used to frowning, and twitched excitedly as he spoke. "I'm sorry to bother you at a time like this, but you're in the middle of trying to total my car."

"I am not trying to 'total' your car," she returned, glancing back at the gray BMW that had been giving her such a hard time with increased irritation. Total? People who used nouns as verbs grated on her nerves. "I'm simply trying to get out of this space—a space that *you've* made impossible to get out of."

"Impossible?" he said. "Look, if you weren't in such a hurry—"

"But I *am* in a hurry," she said, and, anger flaring up again, she gave the wheel a last vehement twist and stepped on the gas forgetting she was still in reverse. As she lurched backward there was a squeal of rubber that was followed by a musical tinkling of glass. Katherine stared at the rearview mirror, her face reddening in embarrassment.

The man who owned the BMW hadn't said anything, and in the uneasy silence she chanced a look at him. He was looking back at his newly decimated headlight in clear disbelief.

"How did you do that?" he murmured, transfixed.

"How?" she echoed, irritation helping to mask her guilt. "What do you mean, how? You just saw it, didn't you?"

"Yes, but the front fender's supposed to guard against this kind of thing," he said slowly, moving back to inspect the damage. "Unless... Oh," he finished, and folded his arms.

She'd been meaning to have the back of the VW Bug worked on for a few months now. A little scrape with a Chevy on the Hampshire College campus had twisted its fender out of shape, and apparently higher powers had calculated that the protruding metal's height would be perfectly scaled to punch out BMW headlights.

With a sigh, Katherine opened her door and got out. "Look, I'm really sorry," she said, joining him by the rear of her car. "Why don't I give you my phone number and I'll pay the bill, okay?"

He nodded absently, seemingly in a state of shock. How could anyone get so wrought up over a bit of broken glass? As she watched, he gingerly brushed a shard from the shattered light, and squinted at her twisted fender end, which was still stuck there. "That fender looks lethal," he muttered. "Is it registered?"

"No," she answered, unamused. "But as I said, we're in the local directory, so if you call tomorrow..."

"What's a woman like you doing driving a heap like this?" he muttered, more to himself than to her.

"What sort of heap am I supposed to drive?" And what was "a woman like her"? she wondered. Katherine folded her arms, prepared to dislike the man in earnest.

But he ignored her, trying to free her fender and not having an easy time of it. Katherine shrugged, then walked back to her open door. The engine was still idling. "Here, why don't I just move it up for you a little bit?"

The man glanced up with a panicked look. "No!" he cried, and simultaneously she heard a loud ripping of fabric. In his hurry to dissuade her he'd lifted a warning arm, but it seemed his jacket sleeve had caught on the fender, and it was now neatly split right up to the shoulder. Katherine and the man looked at the ruined jacket, then at each other.

She was steeling herself for some kind of outburst, but as he held her gaze, little laugh lines appeared in the soft skin around those bright blue eyes. He was grinning and shaking his head, and as she looked on, confused, he chuckled. "Thank you," he said.

"Excuse me?"

"I've always hated this suit," he said. "Now I won't ever have to wear it again."

"Oh." She didn't know what to do, really, feeling terrifically embarrassed by the whole gruesome incident, and wanting more than ever to get away, fast. But at least the man was being good-natured. "Well, I . . . as I was saying, I could move—"

"No, no," he said, a little too quickly, though smiling still. "Don't you move, please. I'll be glad to get my car out of your way." She nodded, mortified that he was assuming, on account of one very understandable mishap, that she was a menace behind the wheel. "Just pull forward a bit and then wait right there," he said, adding, "please," as he caught the look in her eye.

Katherine nodded, got in, shut her door and waited, fingers drumming on her steering wheel. She was feeling even more annoyed with herself for sniping at the man. The whole situation was just intolerable. In a moment, though, he'd backed up for her, and she shifted into reverse again, ready to spring forward.

But the BMW pulled up alongside her as she started pulling out, and the man gave his horn a quiet little toot. Katherine braked, looking over at him as he leaned across his seat and rolled down the passenger window. She gazed at him expectantly, and for a moment he just looked back at her.

He was a handsome guy, whoever he was, high-cheekboned and healthy-looking, with a ruddy tan. Not the kind of man she'd ever been attracted to; he had the broad shoulders of an athlete and she had a sense he wasn't used to being stuffed into suits. He looked as if he wanted to tell or perhaps ask her something. There was a boyish perplexity glimmering in his eyes that nearly drew a smile from her tightened lips.

"Miss Taylor," he said. "My name's Peter Bradford."

Katherine nodded. On her campus she was still known as Mrs. Cartwright, but she'd always be Grammy Taylor's daughter here. "Nice to meet you," she said cordially. "Again, I'm sorry about your car."

"That's okay," he said, and his bright blue eyes seemed to peer right into hers for an instant. "I'm sorry about your mother."

It was a simple statement, one she'd heard so many times over the past few days that she nearly didn't hear it anymore when it was said. But somehow, coming from Peter Bradford's lips, it sounded genuine and heartfelt. Katherine stared at him, surprised and alarmed to feel a knot tightening in her throat.

None of that. "Yes," she said. It was all she could manage just then. Embarrassed, with a quick little nod, she turned her eyes back to the road, and pulled out past him onto the quiet street. As she drove away, she imagined she could feel him watching her, and sure enough, when she glanced in the rearview mirror the BMW was still there, not

moving. She wondered idly who he was. Well, she'd probably find out when he called about the bill, not that it mattered. She had to get back to campus tomorrow.

"IT's ABOUT TIME you showed up." Lydia's chin was
streaked with flour as she gave Katherine a welcoming smile.

Clarissa rose from her seat at the kitchen table as Katherine came in. "We were ready to start worrying!"

She gave her mother an arms-only hug, hands still extended outward, sticky with pie dough.

"But you're just in time to cut up a few extra apples,"
Lydia said, inspecting the bowl on the counter. "Nutmeg,
nutmeg... where did she keep it?"

"Top shelf to the left," Katherine said, admiring Clarissa's crust in the making. "Nice job."

"Nice? This pie is going to be a work of art," her daughter announced, sitting down to apply some finishing
touches.

"I'm sure." Katherine caught the apple Lydia threw to
her and went to get another knife from the wooden rack.
She might've known she'd find her sister in the kitchen on
her return. To Lydia, cooking was therapy. During or after
any emotional crisis, her immediate impulse was to make
and bake a pie from scratch.

"Where did you go?" Clarissa looked up as Katherine
took a seat beside her, apple, knife and cutting board in
hand.

"Nowhere," Katherine told her. "I drove around."

Daughter and sister nodded, and all were silent a moment, intent on their respective tasks. Katherine was filled
with a sudden pang of fierce affection for them as she
looked from Lydia to Clarissa. Anybody else, she knew,
would have badgered her with all kinds of questions after
her disappearance before the end of Grammy's funeral service. But Lydia and Clarissa knew her well enough to let well

enough alone. If Katherine wanted to say anything else, she'd say it.

And thus, feeling secure in their understanding, she did. "I couldn't handle standing around there in that grave-yard," she explained, slicing the green apple with deft, quick strokes. "So I drove out to Naidisch's apple orchard."

"Pick any apples?" Clarissa queried.

"Too late to add 'em to this pie," Lydia joked.

"I just strolled around," Katherine said. "Did I miss anything while I was gone?"

"Nope," Lydia said. "A few people came by after to say some nice things, that's all."

"She's leaving out the most important part," Clarissa said, smiling. "There's a young doctor who treated Grammy who has the hots for Aunt Lydia."

"Clarissa!" Lydia frowned, vigorously shaking spices into her bowl. "Your imagination—"

"He's actually Grammy's old doctor's son, you know," Clarissa continued, licking her fingers. "Jacob. And apparently he was asking Emily all kinds of questions about Lydia."

"He was only being nice," Lydia sighed. "Wanted to make sure all of us were okay."

"Oh, sure," Clarissa said. "Did he ask Emily about me? No."

"Do you know him, Lydie?" Katherine asked.

"We met once a long time ago," Lydia said. "Hand me that piecrust masterpiece," she went on, in a tone that forbade further discussion. "Kath, what time is Mr. Stuart coming over tomorrow?"

"First thing," Katherine told her. "Which means nine, I guess." She was going to ask her more about Dr. Harrison, intrigued by her sister's avoiding the subject, but Clarissa interrupted.

"What are you going to do with the house?" she asked, then looked abashed as both Katherine and Lydia fixed her with narrow-eyed gazes. "Well, come on, we all know what's in the will. You don't need Mr. Stuart to tell you."

"We'll discuss it when he's here," Katherine said uneasily. She had only half-formed thoughts about the future of the Taylor mansion, not having wanted to deal with the whole business. In her long drive through the Massachusetts greenery, she'd settled on only one conviction: no matter if it meant spending the whole inheritance to pay property taxes and maintenance, she wasn't going to sell if it meant having Grammy's house torn down. And she knew Lydia would agree.

"Let's have those extra slices," Lydia said, and Katherine rose with the cutting board. In a moment, the work of all three Taylor women had been deftly combined by Lydia's practiced hands into a confection that rivaled anything from a professional bakery. "Seems a shame to eat it," Lydia said, as she put the last decorative indentations in the crust with her knife.

"I'm dieting," Clarissa announced.

"Are you kidding? You're a scarecrow," Katherine began.

"Emily will be having a bunch of those kids she takes care of over tomorrow. I'm sure they'll polish off whatever we leave," Lydia said, looking down on their creation with justifiable pride. "Then there's Mr. Stuart, of course. Maybe I ought to make two?"

"DELICIOUS," the portly elder gentleman pronounced, setting down his now spotless china plate with a regretful sigh. Mr. Stuart, of balding dome, great girth and bifocals, had been the Taylor family lawyer since Katherine was a child. She even had dim memories of him with a full head of hair. "Now, where were we?"

"You said we'd have to stay an extra day or two," Lydia prompted.

Mr. Stuart pursed his lips, looking through the bottom half of his thick glasses as he picked up a sheaf of papers. They were seated, Katherine, Clarissa and Lydia, in the Taylor house sun parlor, since the attorney had been nice enough to conduct this little meeting there instead of at his office in town. Dappled sunlight bronzed the unpainted wicker furniture in the long room. Katherine noted that Grammy's sewing kit was still in place by the wicker rocker just beyond Mr. Stuart.

"Yes. You see, the will is perfectly in order," he declared, "and as all of you Taylor women seem to be in acceptance of its terms, my advice is that you stay put for a day or two so that I can move the necessary paperwork through, with your signatures..."

He droned on in his low-key, methodical way, but Katherine had ceased listening. If Mr. Stuart needed her and Lydia to remain another day to get the last legalities taken care of expediently, so be it. That pile of term papers back in her campus office could wait. Anyway, she needed an extra day to collect her wits. She was suddenly the co-owner of an ailing mansion. And what was she supposed to do with it?

Lydia and Clarissa, she saw, were paying attention, so she didn't have to. Katherine let her mind wander around the house as she sat there, remembering wallpapers, beds and bits of bric-a-brac. She followed familiar creaky floorboards down sunny halls, peeped into closets scented with Grammy's sachets, and corners Katherine had played with dolls in. There was so much of Grammy in every room.

Now it was all hers and Lydia's, but it would always be her mother's. The thought of selling it to another family disturbed her. The thought of living in it—by herself?—seemed daunting, somehow, and how could she, without switching colleges? It was at least an hour drive from here to the town of Amherst, where Hampshire College was.

Once again, distressingly enough, her famed organizational skills were failing her. When it came to things *in* the house she couldn't even imagine where to begin. There was silver Grammy left to Clarissa among many other prized and precious objects. There was Grandfather's library, which Mr. Compton at Hampshire had already made discreet inquiries about. That pillow Grammy had embroidered for the guest room bed, with her own and her husband's initials woven within a heart of red yarn in one corner—no mention of it in the will, of course, but Katherine wanted it, and no one else had better get in her way.

Her sudden fierce desire to possess that pillow actually got her to her feet before she quite realized what she was doing. Mr. Stuart stopped in mid-discourse. Lydia and Clarissa looked up at her, surprised. Katherine gazed back at them, self-conscious and perplexed herself, but mercifully the front doorbell chimed at just that moment.

"I'll get it," she said. "You go right ahead." She smiled at them all and left the parlor.

Emily, who had refused to take leave of the house just yet, met her in the hallway, coming from the kitchen, but Katherine indicated she'd answer the door. Emily smiled, retreating. There were sounds of children laughing in the kitchen and Katherine wondered which of Emily's rotating brood they were as she entered the little foyer, and pulled open the massive front door.

There was a man standing there who looked vaguely familiar. "Hello," he said. "I know I should've called, but I was in the neighborhood, so I thought..." He stopped, taking in her expression. "Peter Bradford," he said. "Yesterday? Your car?..."

"Oh!" She felt the heat rising in her cheeks. "I'm sorry, I'd completely—"

"It's all right," he said, and smiled. He had a nice smile. It seemed to spread like a sudden bloom of light on his handsome face. Out of context, his appearance didn't in-

spire the irritation she'd felt yesterday. He was also, she saw
a few inches taller than herself, which she hadn't noticed in
their first encounter. Katherine was so used to men being
just her height or shorter—even Jeffrey had been under six
feet—that looking up at a man was a bit refreshing.

"How are you?" he was asking.

"Oh, fine," she said automatically. "And you?"

"Fine," he said. It was the oddest thing, really. She was
momentarily content to just stand there looking at him, and
though any intelligent lines of conversation vanished right
out of her head as she gazed up into his bright blue eyes, he
didn't seem to mind, gazing silently and thoughtfully right
back at her.

"They're different," he said quietly. "I hadn't noticed."

"Hmm?"

"Your eyes," he said. "The left one's definitely greener."

"Oh." She nodded, noticing the way the sun brought out
the lighter brown highlights in his hair. "Yes, it is."

He cleared his throat. "Hope I'm not intruding."

"No," she said, and then realized she was making the
man stand outside. "Oh, I guess you'd—" She stopped,
glancing back into the darkness of the parlor. She just didn't
feel like going back inside and getting involved with Mr.
Stuart and all of that again.

"Maybe I should have called," he began again, seeing her
hesitation.

"No, no, it's fine," she insisted, and stepped into the
sunlight, quietly shutting the door behind her. "Listen, I'm
really sorry about the way I acted yesterday."

"No big deal," he said. "You've been under a lot of
stress."

"I guess," she said, blinking in the bright light. He was
acting as if he understood her, and she didn't know if she
liked that, but at least he didn't seem to have any hard feelings about the snafu with his car. At the moment he was
looking quizzical.

"You were on your way out?"

"No."

He nodded, cleared his throat. "Then where are we oing?"

"Oh!" Where was her *mind* going was a better question. "I've been cooped up inside for a while," she explained. "So if you want to talk..."

"Sure. Well, I don't want to take up too much of your ime, Miss Taylor—"

"Katherine," she corrected.

"Katherine. But if you do have a minute—"

"Here, why don't we walk around to the back?"

Peter Bradford nodded, and fell into step beside her as she tarted down the slate path that wound its way around the ide of the house. She felt a little warm in her white sweater nd tan jersey pants, but there was a cool breeze rustling the lms and it was good to be outdoors again. She hadn't re-lized how claustrophobic she'd been starting to feel in the ouse.

"Quite a place," Peter said, looking up at the vine-overed stone chimney as they passed it. Compliment or ig? She couldn't tell.

"Yes," she said absently. "I suppose I should go inside nd get my checkbook," she began, as they turned the cor-ier. "But if you'll just give me the bill, I'll put something n the mail."

"Oh, I don't have it on me," he said.

"No?" She paused in midstride. "But I thought..."

"Don't worry about the car." He shrugged. "Actually, here's something else I wanted to talk to you about."

She gazed at him, confused, about to ask what that could e, when a movement beyond him in the vegetable garden aught her eye. "Hey!" she cried, striding past him across he lawn. "You—stop that!"

There were two large rabbits in the garden, the white one hewing happily on her mother's prize arugula. "Shoo!"

she cried, waving her arms at them. The rabbits froze, then hopped quickly back to the corners of the little wire pen Lydia had apparently fixed up for them at the corner of the garden. Katherine saw the hole they'd managed to nudge open in the wire as she knelt to inspect the damage. "Of all the nerve," she muttered. "Grammy's going to—"

She stopped herself, staring at the half-eaten leaf in her hand. She could feel Peter Bradford watching her in the sudden quiet. Quickly, with as much dignity as she could muster, Katherine stood, brushing her hands on her pants. "Sorry," she murmured. "I . . ."

Her voice trailed off lamely, but Peter didn't seem to notice. "We don't usually see rabbits that fat and healthy around here," he said. "Yours?"

"No, they belong to my sister," she said, glancing back at the house. "She brought them here from California." He followed her gaze. Lydia and Mr. Stuart could be glimpsed in the sun parlor. They were probably wondering what she was doing with some strange man in the middle of Grammy's garden. "So, Mr. Bradford—"

"Peter," he corrected.

"Peter," she said. "What was it you . . . ?"

He suddenly seemed singularly uneasy. "Nothing important, actually," he said. "It can wait. Nice garden."

He was looking around him with the strangest expression, like a man who both wanted to be there and didn't. "Maybe you should tell me what's on your mind," she suggested.

"Maybe another time," he said, avoiding her eye.

"Is it . . . the suit?"

He stared at her blankly, then smiled, shaking his head. "Oh, no, I meant what I said before. Goodbye and good riddance to black suits, really."

"You do look better in jeans," she told him, because she couldn't help noticing this was true. Wait, that sounded a little . . . "I mean, more comfortable," she added quickly.

"Oh, thanks," he said. "You look better when you're not in such a hurry to leave the scene of a crime."

"Thanks," she said wryly. Then he looked away with an oddly pained expression.

"Well . . . I'll be on my way."

"Peter, what *is* it?"

He looked up again at the sound of his name, pursed his lips, shook his head, then gave a little sigh. "Oh, hell. I might as well get down to it," he said, looking thoroughly ill at ease. "I feel bad about bringing it up at a time like this, but I'm supposed to talk to you in person, while you're still here in Greensdale . . ."

"Yes?"

"Well, it's about the house. I understand that your grandmother has left the property to you and your sister?"

Word certainly traveled fast in a town the size of Greensdale. "That's true," she said warily, her guard up now. "What of it?" The sharpness had returned to her tone, and she saw he could hear it. He was looking at her oddly. "Yes?" she said. "Go on."

"Excuse me, but—hold still," he murmured.

"What?"

As she stared at him, uncomprehending, he stepped right up to her, his face suddenly quite close, his fingers brushing her hair. Startled, she stared at him, then looked down to see the little furry strip of green on his forefinger.

"Someone about to visit your left ear," Peter said softly, with a faint smile.

Katherine bent forward to look at the beautiful tiny thing. The caterpillar was all fuzzy stripes and wiggles, turning about on Peter's finger in confusion. She'd probably accidentally whisked it off a leaf when she'd bent over the arugula.

"Didn't mean to upset you," he murmured, seeming to address the agitated little creature. But Katherine sensed an apology hovering behind those playful words that was directed at her. She couldn't help the smile that tugged at her lips.

When she looked up, Peter's eyes seemed perilously close, their soft velvet depths glimmering with gold flecks of inviting warmth. She felt a little tremor go through her as he held her gaze. Strange. He wasn't being flirtatious, but she couldn't help feeling a subtle pull when he looked at her, a flicker of warmth that seemed to rise within her.

For a moment time was suspended again as their gazes locked. Then she remembered what he'd been talking about and took a step back. "You were saying?"

"Right." Peter's reluctance was apparent. He knelt to put the caterpillar into the grass, then straightened up again, his forehead creased. "Well, I represent—that is, I'm a lawyer here in town, and I'm also a member of the town council, and there's been a lot of discussion recently about a business concern that's interested in setting up a plant here. So we were wondering if you'd thought over your plans . . . for the house?"

Katherine folded her arms. "Go on," she said, whatever warmth he'd stirred up within her rapidly chilling.

"Well, what I'm trying to say is . . . do you think you might be planning to sell?"

Peter knew as soon as the words were out of his mouth that he'd said the wrong thing. But then the whole thing was wrong, and he knew that. He'd sensed from only a minute's conversation with Katherine Taylor yesterday that she wasn't going to want to deal with this. Hadn't he called Randy Morgan that very morning, practically begging him to lay off the Taylors for the time being, or, barring that, to get someone else to break the ice with them?

But Randy had stood firm. "You're good at this stuff, that's why I asked you to help us out," he'd countered. "These guys from ConCo are frothing at the mouth to get that plant built. You wait another week and they'll go play ball in another county, Pete. I don't want to lose this op-

ortunity, and damn it, you're a Greensdale boy—don't you
want the town to be in clover, for once?"

Of course he did. But at the moment the interests of the
community at large were not weighing on him as heavily as
the look in Katherine Taylor's eyes. He'd never seen aqua-
marine fire before, but it was there, flashing from beneath
her long lashes. "I realize my timing isn't the best," he began, "but you see—"

"Your timing is downright insulting," she said coolly.

"I don't mean to offend," he hurried on. "It's just that
this thing's happened to come up...when it did, and we
thought, well, rather than bother you at work, later in the
week—"

"You'd come swooping up here like a vulture," she said
dryly. "Who's 'we'?"

Peter cleared his throat. "The town council's been ap-
roached by a firm called ConCo, with a plan to build right
here in this county. If we could work out a way to bring
them to Greensdale, it would really be a boost for the town.
You know, there've been a lot of layoffs at the auto plant in
Jefferson—"

"Stop right there," she interrupted. "Let me get this
straight. You don't want to buy the house? You want to buy
the property?"

"Well, yes," he admitted uneasily.

"So you'd just tear the house down."

Peter opened his mouth, then shut it, thinking it best to
merely nod. He was ruing the day he'd taken on this job.

"Did this bright idea just come to you overnight?
Or...no, don't tell me you've had your eye on the property!—"

"No, of course not," he said hurriedly, though it was true
that one of the ConCo contractors had gone over maps of
the area only a month ago and pointed out the Taylor
property as choice. The sudden death of Grammy Taylor
had then looked extremely serendipitous to the other coun-

cil members, hence Randy's zeal to feel out the Taylors with all due haste. "Look, I'm sorry," he began again. "It wasn't my idea to—"

"I'm sorry we've had this conversation at all," Katherine said, starting to stride back across the lawn. "Send me the bill for your car and I'll take care of it."

"Katherine—" She turned, looking back at him with as much friendliness as a woman of stone.

"Yes, Mr. Bradford?"

The shift in their just burgeoning relationship, if you could call it that, was painful for him to contemplate. And try as he might, he couldn't help thinking that she was extraordinarily beautiful as she faced him in the bright sunlight, chin raised defiantly, golden hair cascading over squared shoulders.

"Honestly, I'm aware that this is a sensitive time for you. I want to apologize for bringing up something that's obviously touched a raw nerve . . . and I hope you won't hold it against me," he finished, though that wasn't what he'd thought he was going to say.

"I won't hold anything against you, Mr. Bradford," she said evenly. "Because I won't be thinking about you. Good morning." She turned away again.

"Wait," he said, before she disappeared into the house.

"My lawyer's name is Gerald Stuart." She tossed the name over her shoulder. "You've just missed him, but if you insist on pursuing this thing, I'm sure you can catch up with him in town. You're fast on your feet." And with that parting shot, she went into the house. Peter was left in the sunlit garden under the baleful gaze of a pair of rabbits, who seemed, he imagined, to hold him in the same contempt that the mistress of the Taylor house did.

THE PARLOR WAS EMPTY when Katherine strode in, fuming. She paced the length of it, her mind still brimming with scathing remarks. Once she was satisfied that Peter Bradord had left her in peace, she left the parlor for the kitchen, where Emily was cooking something that smelled wonderfully of apples and cinnamon.

As she drew closer she could hear raised voices in there ow. Emily, catching sight of her approaching through the pen doorway, hurriedly turned to this unseen chorus and hushed them. So when Katherine walked into the sun-filled itchen, she saw five cherubic faces gazing up at her in ushed silence from around the kitchen table.

"Hello, Katherine," Emily said brightly, busily stirring p a pan full of melting apple slices. She had her dark hair inned up into a bun. With apron on and sneakers, spatula a hand and ruddy cheeks, she looked to Katherine like some aaster cook from an old Dutch painting transported to aodern-day Massachusetts.

"Hi," she replied. Nary a peep sounded from the three irls and two boys seated at the table. Their eyes followed er every move with great interest as Katherine bent over to aspect Emily's applesauce-in-the-making. "Heavenly," atherine noted, then turned back to the children. "Hey, ids," she said. "I don't think I met you the last time I was ere. I'm Katherine."

Giggles and whispers were the reaction. Emily cast a reroving glance over her shoulder. "No manners. Well, that's 'icki, who's not going to get any applesauce if she keeps aising a ruckus—" A little girl who looked about four romptly hid her face behind her hands. "And her sister 'rish, who still hasn't washed up and better hop to it oon..." The girl next to Vicki, who might have been her win, rolled her eyes dramatically and scrunched back in her hair, avoiding Katherine's curious gaze.

"I'm Mike," piped up the boy with a cowlick next to her. 'he boy on his right elbowed him indignantly. "No, *I'm* Mike," he said. "That's Gary!"

"I'm Em-il-y At-chins!" crowed the last little girl excitdly, and this sent the whole table into gales of giggles.

"Isnot! Isnot!" the boys were bellowing, as Emily left the stove to stand over them all, spatula raised in a mock-threatening manner.

"Pipe down, I mean it!" she said, and a hush descended once again. "This is now Miss Taylor's house, I'll have you know. So if you don't want her to kick your little fannies right out the back door, I'd suggest you behave," she said calmly, and all five children looked to Katherine, wide-eyed.

Their solemnity brought a smile to her lips that was impossible to repress. "Don't worry," she assured them. "It takes a lot to make me start kicking."

The children nonetheless sat still as statues, watching her again. "There's coffee," Emily said, indicating the stove.

"Thanks," Katherine said, and went to fetch a cup. It hadn't taken much to start her kicking at Peter Bradford, she thought ruefully, pouring coffee. Well, it served him right—even though, she allowed grudgingly, he was only doing his job. It seemed the two of them had gotten off on the wrong foot on first meeting, and at this rate they were fated to stay that way.

Not that they had anything in common to begin with. But there had been a moment, when he'd found that caterpillar in her hair and she looked at him and felt... Nothing important, she assured herself. Anyway, the man had a lot of gall to have come up here the day after her mother's funeral!

The children were whispering behind her, but as Katherine turned to face them they clammed up, the twins making a great show of being good by clamping hands over their mouths. The Mike-who-was-Gary, however, spoke up boldly. "I thought this was Grammy's house."

"She's Grammy's daughter," Vicki whispered loudly.

The two boys exchanged a look and sat back, digesting this information. Katherine moved back to Emily's side, her curiosity piqued. "Where are yours?"

"Willy and Lois are over at Betty Tyler's today," Emily old her, shaking a bit of freshly ground cinnamon over the ubbling apples while she stirred with her other hand. "It's oo bad. I know they'd like to see you."

Katherine nodded. She knew all about Emily's little sysem from earlier visits. Times had been hard in Greensdale or a while now, and in most of the local households both arents worked. The auto factory in Jefferson, the nearest arge town, had closed down a few years ago, putting a lot f Greensdale men out of work. So more and more women ad taken on jobs while their husbands began commutes to obs farther afield. At the moment there were almost three reschool children to each working mother in Emily's little lique of friends, and so the town wives pitched in and took urns taking care of their children, babysitting for them in roups at various houses and places of work wherever it was ossible.

"These are Sadie Travis's and Barbara Wainright's," Emily went on. She continued rattling off unfamiliar names, apidly detailing a system that to Katherine's mind seemed Byzantine, but had a logic her organizational mind could ppreciate.

"I've been meaning to talk to you about this," Emily aid, portioning out her applesauce on plates for the chilren. She straightened, addressing the table. "Now anyody who burns their tongue gets no sympathy from me! You remember what happened last time, right?" Five heads odded vehemently. "Okay. You let it cool, now. I'm going o be right outside the door with Miss Taylor, so no funny tuff."

Katherine followed Emily out of the kitchen and onto the ack veranda. "I know this isn't the time to be asking you," he began apologetically. "But as it is, we've been relying on he Taylor house for some time now. You know your mother oved to have the children up here twice a week, and I was vondering—"

"Don't even worry about it for a moment," Katherine interrupted. "Nothing's going to happen to this place immediately, and I'm sure Grammy would want you to go on just as you were before."

"Thank you," Emily said. "We'd appreciate it."

"Our pleasure," Katherine assured her. "They seem like a sweet bunch of troublemakers to me."

"That they are," Emily said wryly, automatically turning to give a reproving yell at Michael, who was making Indian war-whoop noises inside. "I better get back in there..."

"I don't know what's going to be done about the house ultimately," Katherine told her honestly. "But in the meantime, please bring the children up here whenever you like, really. I'm sure it's fine with Lydia."

"You know they never go beyond the kitchen and the backyard."

"Yes, I remember Grammy's rules," Katherine said, smiling. The last time she'd come down for a visit, a four year-old girl had been momentarily misplaced, then discovered hiding under the dining-room table by Grammy, who'd followed her trail of muddy footprints. As penance for this trespassing, Grammy had solemnly instructed the girl in the proper care and feeding of a cabbage patch.

As Emily hurried back into the kitchen Katherine looked out at the garden, half expecting to see Grammy there, with her funny, bee-bonnet type hat on. But of course she wasn't. Katherine allowed herself a little sigh and went into the kitchen.

Emily had her whisk broom and pan out, muttering under her breath as she cleaned up a pile of plaster near the stove. "One of these days that ceiling's going to fall right on my head," she said. Katherine glanced up. The plaster was indeed precariously peeling, and a goodly chunk had spattered the top burners and the counter with white grit.

"We'll do something about that," she said absently. "Do you need anything from town, Em? I'm going in."

"Paper towels, if you happen to run into any," Emily said.

"You missed a spot!" This from the little girl who had claimed to be Emily. Katherine left Emily making dire threats at the giggling kids, which she clearly never carried out, and went off to see if she could find company for the trip to town.

"I LIKED HIS LOOKS, from what I saw," said Lydia.

Katherine shrugged. "Well, I didn't like what he was saying, so I told him to take a hike. We're not having Mother's property turned into some kind of industrial complex. Are we?"

"Of course not."

Katherine had been telling her sister the story of Peter Bradford's visit that morning as they strolled down the aisle of the grocery store on Elm Street, Lydia munching on honey-roasted nuts from a bag they'd indulged in at the Carters' candy stand around the corner. "I should have gotten a big cart," Katherine added, finding the basket on her arm about to overflow with purchases.

"But what *are* we going to do?" Lydia queried.

Katherine shook her head at Lydia's proffered nuts. "According to Mr. Stuart's figures, we can keep the place up as is for another six years at least, if we use the money Grammy left."

"But for what, or whom?" Lydia popped a can of olives into the last free corner of Katherine's basket. "I'm not about to change coasts. Clarissa doesn't even know what country she wants to live in at the moment, and you're not about to move to Greensdale."

"I wonder if it could be declared a historical landmark."

"Not old enough, I don't think," Lydia said. They were nearing the cash register. Katherine noticed that both the women behind the counter and her customer, a young woman, were staring at them. They looked away as Katherine put the basket down.

"I'll see you later, Sadie," the younger woman said, departing. The woman behind the counter nodded and Katherine suddenly made the connection. This was the Travis Grocery, so the woman had to be Sadie Travis, one of the working wives Emily had spoken of earlier.

"Hello," Katherine said. Sadie Travis gave her a perfunctory nod, beginning to unload the basket.

"If you can handle this, I'm going to the drugstore," Lydia said. "I'll meet you at the car."

Katherine nodded, watching Sadie. She was short, with a full figure and braided hair, and nice eyes that were averted right now. She had an aura of being all business but Katherine decided to take the plunge. "I believe I met your two children today," she said. "Vicki, and . . . ?"

"Trish," Sadie said, her features relaxing in a brief smile.

"Yes, and they're both adorable," Katherine said. "I'm Katherine Taylor, and Emily—"

"I know," Sadie interrupted. "I hope you don't mind the children being up there."

"Not at all," Katherine said, aware that the woman was being only marginally friendly and not sure she understood why.

"Too many kids not in school yet and not enough of us at home to look after 'em," Sadie muttered, more to herself. "Sorry to hear about your mother," she added. "That'll be twenty-nine dollars and seventy cents."

Sadie was already gazing past her to the window. Katherine looked down at her stuffed bag of groceries and suddenly felt supremely self-conscious. She and Lydia had stocked up on what were essentially luxury items, she realized. If unemployment was as bad in Greensdale as Emily and that Peter Bradford had indicated, no wonder a working woman like Sadie Travis was a little standoffish with one of the Taylors.

She'd almost forgotten that sensation of being an outsider in her own hometown, familiar from her youth and her visits over the years. But it came back in full force as she hurriedly got the money out of her wallet, feeling her cheeks redden. She was at a loss at how to pick up the already terminated conversation. "Well, if there's anything I can do," Katherine said, though even as the words were out of her mouth she felt her embarrassment increase. Sadie was giving her a blank look, and why not? What was she saying? "I mean, about the children," she went on lamely.

Sadie shrugged. "Oh, we manage."

"I told Emily she's welcome to keep babysitting at the house, if she needs to," Katherine ventured.

"That's nice of you," Sadie said, and handed her the change. "You take care now," she added, but Katherine sensed it was a routine salutation said purely by rote. She nodded, smiled awkwardly and gathered up the shopping bag. She hurried through the door to the street, feeling more upset than she should've been, no doubt. But then, she was oversensitive to everything since the funeral.

Automatically she avoided thoughts of Grammy, which always hovered gray-cloud style in her mind, and thought of Emily and Sadie and all the other local women she'd never even met. Sadie was probably Lydia's age. If Dad hadn't gone along with Grandfather's insistence that the girls get "a good education" elsewhere, she and Lydia might've made a lot of friends here. But they never had. The reality of it was saddening.

And if the Taylor house was sold, it would almost be as if the whole family had never been here, she mused, moving slowly down the sidewalk. She pictured that bunch of Greensdale cherubs Emily had introduced her to in Grammy's kitchen. Well, they'd remember Grammy fondly when they were older. Wouldn't they?

Where had she parked the car? She blinked in the afternoon sunlight, then caught sight of the trusty Volkswagen across the street, where her sister was engaged in conversation with three men in suits. One was Mr. Stuart, she saw as she crossed, the other was unfamiliar, and the third—

Katherine felt her stomach do an unaccountable flip-flop as she drew nearer and entered the orbit of Peter Bradford's penetrating bright blue eyes. Katherine wondered if he and his friend had been trying to strong-arm Mr. Stuart into taking their side. Why else would they be strolling down Elm with the Taylors's attorney?

"Good afternoon, Mr. Bradford," she said politely.

"Hi," he returned, looking wary.

"Katherine," Mr. Stuart harrumphed, polishing his bifocals with his handkerchief. "Meet Mr. Morris from the town council."

"A pleasure." He nodded, his pursed lips giving him a slightly smug expression. Katherine nodded back.

"And I see you know Mr. Bradford," Mr. Stuart continued. "A man who gave up what must have been a more promising practice in the big city, to give all us small fish here in Greensdale a hard time." Both Stuart and Morris chuckled, but Peter seemed embarrassed. His eyes never left Katherine's face.

She adopted her most opaque expression for him. "Having a nice chat with Mr. Stuart?"

"We thought your attorney should be apprised of some developments that might be relevant to your . . . situation," Morris interjected.

"You can apprise him all you like," Katherine said coolly. "But I can tell you right now that we won't be selling our property to a chemical concern, in spite of what Mr. Bradford thinks is best for the well-being of the community," she added. "In fact, my sister and I have been making other plans for the house."

"Oh?" Mr. Stuart gave her a quizzical look over his bifocals.

"That's right," Lydia volunteered, although she obviously had no idea what Katherine was talking about.

"We'll come see you to discuss it," Katherine said breezily, putting her shopping bag in the back seat. "Nice to meet you, Mr. Morris." She avoided Peter's gaze, which was still riveted to her every move. She was annoyed with herself for being so aware of him. Why did she care what he thought of her? Hadn't she let him know they had nothing to discuss?

The Taylor sisters got into the car. Only when they were a good block away did Lydia turn to her. "Plans?"

"Just bluffing," Katherine said, though the glimmer of an idea had been forming in her mind since she'd left the Travis grocery. "Lydie, we want to do something with the house that Grammy would've liked, right?" Lydia nodded. "And you know what Grammy *loved*?"

"What?"

"Children," Katherine murmured. "Little children . . ."

Chapter Three

Katherine had lost all track of time, but the growling in her stomach indicated that it was probably past noon. As soon as she finished this last one of a dozen papers on the Bloomsbury group, she'd promised herself she'd take a walk on campus to stretch her legs, pick up a sandwich at the student union and see some of the beautiful weather she'd been forcibly ignoring since her return.

All about the sun-soaked lawns outside, coed couples swooned beneath trees caressed by fragrant breezes, their murmurings and breathless giggles a muted counterpoint to the singsong bells tolling from the college clock tower. Katherine was cloistered in her little cubbyhole under the stairs of the Holmes building, surrounded by stacks of paper. The work on her desk had assumed mountainous proportions. Armed with a solitary red pencil, she was doing her best to ascend its summit.

A student with a flute was heralding the start of summer out there, and lending an ear to his seductive virtuoso aria for a moment would be fatal. But soon a gentle thud on her windowsill forced her to look up gratefully from yet another term paper. Winkie the tomcat had arrived, fur sprinkled with bits of fresh-mown grass, his one eye fixed balefully on her in mute reproach.

"I know, Wink," she said. "Nobody should be inside on a day like this. But I'm behind enough as it is."

Winkie ignored this rationale, turning his upraised tail on her and disappearing out the window again. Katherine sighed, the paper blurring beneath her tired eyes. Two years ago, still numb with grief over Jeffrey's death, she'd embraced the same work load, happy to lose herself in it and turn away from June with its seemingly hollow promises of rejuvenation. And now, in the wake of her mother's demise, this pileup didn't seem so much a burden as a soothing buffer against the world. But she had to admit she felt a twinge of healthy annoyance at having to be cooped up indoors.

A breeze stirred the topmost paper on her highest stack. She hurried to clamp it down with a notebook, inhaling as she did a mind-dissolving whiff of jasmine from the trellises outside her window. Work had never seemed less inviting. She sat back in her chair, put her feet up on the desk and closed her eyes. She still hadn't regained her equilibrium since last weekend, although, she reminded herself, why should she have? She was only human, after all. And it was clearly going to take more than a few days to feel herself again.

"It doesn't matter that we all knew we had to expect this," Lydia had said, when she and Clarissa shared their last meal together that Tuesday night. "You can expect it and expect it, and think you'll be ready for it ... but I guess you never are."

It was true. They'd known Grammy's health was failing, and even her seventieth birthday celebration had been touch and go when she'd come down with the flu the week before. But they'd secretly expected Grammy to live on eternally; she was certainly strong in spirit, and always bounced back from her minor bouts of illness.

History, she told herself, *and useless to dwell on.* She knew she should open her eyes and get back to work, but she couldn't just yet. She'd gotten plenty of sleep through it all, except for that night she and Lydia and Clarissa had stayed up late, telling Grammy stories until they were able to laugh and the pain momentarily abated. But now she felt exhaustion through every nerve ending in her body.

She heard the phone ring down the hall, which was surprising on a Saturday afternoon, but she let it ring until it stopped. Even if it was for her, she didn't feel up to talking. In fact, after the slew of condolence calls from friends and relatives she'd had in her first days back at Hampshire— Grammy had touched so many lives in her time!—Katherine had taken to keeping her answering machine on most of the time.

There was another motive for that, she remembered, frowning. Peter Bradford had been calling, and she didn't want to talk to him. What did the man want with her, anyway? Hadn't she made it clear she wasn't interested in his proposition? She and Lydia had already begun formulating an exciting plan for the house, and it had nothing to do with him or his chemical plant. In fact, it was going to shut him and his town council friends up for good.

But Peter had even appeared in one of her dreams this week, which was disconcerting, because the dream had been vaguely erotic. It seemed she hadn't had all her clothes on. She'd felt exposed, vulnerable, as he'd sat down beside her and taken her hand....

Katherine opened her eyes, trying to ignore the flutter of illicit arousal the image made her feel. Dreams! Peter Bradford wasn't the idealized, sensitive man her subconscious had conjured up. Realizing that her feet were up on Jeffrey's prized mahogany desk, she quickly swung them down and inspected the wood for marks. Old habits. Even at this late date, the presence of Jeffrey Addison Cartwright hovered around her little office.

Jeffrey had detested sloppiness, vulgarity, breaches of decorum. And although she'd lived alone for some time now, she still looked out for his wishes. It was for Jeffrey's benefit that she kept her stereo volume low; for Jeffrey that she tended to walk instead of run around the campus, to speak softly instead of yell. When she thought, what would people think? she was really thinking of her late husband.

It was time to get past all that, she knew. She had to stop seeing herself as the great scholar's wife, guardian of his legacy. It was too stifling. And she sometimes sensed there was still a rebellious teenager cooped up inside her who had never had a chance to "party-hearty," as one of her students was fond of saying. Fate and her own ambition had forced adulthood on her too soon.

With Grammy gone, ghosts and spirits threatened to proliferate around her if she wasn't careful. Setting such morbid thoughts aside, she took her red pencil from behind her ear, stifled a yawn, and started on the paper. A rustling at the window suggested Winkie had returned. Not bothering to look up, she told the cat, "Just watch where you jump down, okay? Everything's in order here, for once."

"I'll try to be careful," said a voice from outside.

Startled, Katherine sat up. Her heart was pounding loudly in her ears as she stared at the smiling lips and blue eyes of Peter Bradford. He was resting his elbows on her windowsill as if it were the most natural thing in the world for him to have materialized there, like some oversize Cheshire cat.

"Hello, Katherine." His husky voice seemed to reverberate right through her as she froze, mute with surprise. "Actually," he went on, "I don't think I'll be able to jump through the window. Is that usually how your guests arrive?"

"My guests usually let me know when they're coming," she managed, having found her voice at last. "And," she added pointedly, "they're usually invited."

"I had a hard time getting through," he said, with an insouciant grin. "In fact I just called here, but someone must've been ignoring the telephone. Anyway, I figured it might be even harder for you to get rid of me, if I showed up in person. Happy June 9," he said, and with a magician-like flourish, held out a bouquet of lilacs.

Katherine gazed at the burst of color in his hand, suspended above her desk: the blue-purple, red-purple and white flowers above green stalks. "What's so special about June 9?" she asked warily, taking the flowers.

"Nothing yet," he returned. "But it could turn into something special if you'd crawl out of this closet you're in and come have lunch with me."

Katherine sat back, bouquet in lap. "Mr. Bradford—"

"Oh, please," he interrupted with a grimace. "Can't we just take this whole bit over from the top again?"

"I thought we were finished," she said wryly.

"Finished with our bad beginnings," he said. "But I have a great idea. Let's start fresh. You're not the woman who bashed up my prize BMW and I'm not the guy who offended you by making ill-timed business offers last weekend. Okay? How about it?"

"Why pretend?" she asked.

"Why hold grudges?" he countered. "What's the point? Look, I'm not here to talk about your house," he said quickly, as she opened her mouth to protest. "I'm here by way of an apology."

"You already apologized."

"Not enough to satisfy me," he said. "Katherine, I know it was bad form, coming over last Monday like that. But the truth is…" He paused, a slightly sheepish look on his face. "I wanted to see you, anyway, so I used my business reasons as a rationalization."

"Oh," she said, caught off guard and feeling suddenly all the more flustered. "Why?"

Peter Bradford shrugged. "I knew you were…going through something," he said quietly. "And though maybe it wasn't any of my business, I was a little concerned."

No, it wasn't his business, she thought defensively, but beneath it she was touched. "Oh," she repeated, aware that her usual conversational skills had a way of deserting her when she talked to him. "That's . . . nice of you."

"Rough week?" He nodded toward the stacks in front of her. Katherine absently closed the bound paper she'd been working on.

"Not one of my all-time favorites," she admitted. "But I'm doing all right." She looked at him, framed against the blue sky in the window, the wind blowing his hair about. He made a handsome picture. "Don't tell me you came all the way here just to find that out," she said wryly.

"No, I happened to be in the neighborhood."

It was a long drive from here to Greensdale. She raised an incredulous eyebrow. "Seriously?"

"Seriously," he said, brushing back a lock of brown hair from over his eye as the breeze rose outside. "A friend of mine has a summer house right outside Wilmington, and he's not in it this weekend; I am."

"How nice for you," she commented coolly, but her coolness was rapidly thawing. She didn't know if he was really being straightforward about his interest in her, but Peter had a brash kind of energy that was undeniably attractive.

"It could be nice for us," he mused. "Matter of fact, there's an ideal place for lunch right on the premises . . ."

"Us?"

"Have you eaten?"

"No, but I—"

"The way I see it, the best respite from a week of work and mourning has got to be a nice picnic lunch at a quiet spot in the sun," he said. "Don't you think?"

Picnic? That rebellious teenager inside her leaped at such a tempting prospect, but the professorial adult resisted. "No, I really couldn't," she began.

"Do I have to climb through this window after all, or are you going to come out? Katherine, it's Saturday afternoon."

"Well, yes," she said. "But I have so much work to catch up on that I really can't—"

"What you really can't do is wither and waste away in there. It's absolutely an affront to nature," he said, brow furrowed. "You like strawberries?"

"Yes," she admitted.

"Got a bathing suit?"

"Yes. No!" she quickly added. "I mean, Peter, this isn't—"

"Good," he said with a grin. "We're at least back to first names. Now, here's what you do. You take that pencil out of your hand and put it down in a safe place.... Come on, I know you can...."

One last, audible growl from her deprived stomach did the final convincing. Sure she was making a mistake, she gave in, regretting that she hadn't shown more resistance as she strode down the hall to the great outdoors. The man was probably up to something, though what, she wasn't sure. And this was going to leave her even more backed up with office work. But it *was* a beautiful Saturday....

Peter was standing by the infamous BMW, parked at the curb outside the building. The car had a new headlight, so she assumed he'd gotten her check. He was wearing worn blue jeans, sneakers and a powder-blue shirt that seemed to bring out the glimmering blue in his eyes as he smiled at her approach. "Now, here's a sensible woman," he announced, holding the door open for her. "Hop in."

Had he grown another inch or two since last weekend? she mused, then remembered she was wearing flats. As she slipped into the car, she caught a musky male scent in the interior, subtle but enough to quicken her heartbeat as she watched his lanky, muscular figure stride around the car. Exactly what was going on here? She wasn't used to men having such an effect on her, especially ones she'd been initially affronted by.

As he got the car into gear, Katherine suddenly noticed the plethora of lilac bushes ringing the building, and accounted for the bouquet. She glanced over at his cheery profile, deciding Peter Bradford was a man with no shame.

He insisted on driving her to her little apartment off campus, and waited outside while she got a bathing suit. Katherine told herself that she was merely humoring the man, since she had no intention of doing any swimming. She still couldn't quite believe she was letting him kidnap her like this.

"Where's the suit?" he inquired, as she got back in the car.

"I'm wearing it," she said, with a self-conscious glance down at her pale gray linen skirt and white sleeveless blouse. "Underneath, I mean." He nodded. She looked away, waiting for her heart to stop thumping like some adolescent school kid's. She'd been meaning to ease back into a more normal way of life. But maybe this was too much, too soon.

A sudden whirlwind car trip with Peter Bradford wasn't at all easing. The man drove like a demon. They flew over cresting hills and stomach-gripping dips in the winding road. While the sun played hide-and-seek in the arched greenery above, some folksy acoustic guitar music tinkled and hummed from his tape deck, and Peter kept up a lively conversation about the passing landmarks and the time he'd spent in both Massachusetts and Vermont.

Apparently he came this way a lot. He knew each roadside fruit stand and old inn in the vicinity. As he talked on, she realized he was purposefully taking command of the conversation, not requiring her to make much effort. Or was she imagining it? At any rate it was comforting to just sit there, watching the whizzing greenery of trees and fields, guitar notes seeming to shimmer like sunbeams on the leaves, and glide over the curves and hills at his side, time suspended.

For the first time in over a week she did feel she was getting away from it all. By the time they zigzagged down a winding dirt road and landed in front of a rustic-looking one-story cottage surrounded by white birches, she felt as though she'd taken a smooth rocket launch to land in another country altogether. Still vibrating from the speed and wind, her skin tingled from head to toe as she alighted from the car. The tape was over, but the music played on in her ears.

"Nice place, eh?" He swept an arm in the direction of the cottage. "I'll give you a tour later. Let me just load us up some lunch provisions...." He pulled an old-fashioned wicker basket from the car's trunk, slammed the lid, and favored her with that wide grin of his again. "Wait here a sec. Then we'll head for the lake."

Lake? He bounded inside, leaving Katherine to contemplate the surroundings, which were truly charming. The cottage was almost fairy-tale-like, nestled amidst sheltering birches. The chimney was covered with vines like Grammy's house. Grammy would love a place like this, she mused. She'd probably even approve of Katherine playing hooky from her work. Hadn't she been complaining just a few weeks ago that Katherine was spending too much time indoors?

"This way." Peter had reemerged, and was pointing past the house. She followed him down a path that wound its way into the woods, by now feeling not unlike an adult Alice following an attractive White Rabbit into some woodsy wonderland. But it was nice to let somebody else take charge for a change.

The white birches shone brightly in the early-afternoon sun. They walked along and suddenly a wide expanse of dark blue water was in front of her, calm and serene like a giant mirror carved into the ground. Peter hurried ahead, to a little dock where a green canoe lay overturned. He bent down to pull some rope up from the water, and produced a pair of dripping bottles from below the dock.

"You might want to strip down to your suit," he called over his shoulder. "It's going to be hot out there."

"Out where?"

"We're going to that island." He pointed toward a clump of green in the middle of the lake, stood, and tipped the canoe over, easing its end into the water by the dock. As she watched, he began unbuttoning his shirt, keeping the canoe in place with one foot. "You should at least take off your shoes," he said, noting that she hadn't made any move to disrobe.

Carefully Katherine stepped over tree roots to the dock proper. Self-conscious, she bent down to unlace her sandals. Even though her swimsuit was a one-piece that was demure by modern standards, the idea of removing her blouse and skirt in the presence of a man she barely knew gave her pause. There was a strong breeze over the lake now. She could bear canoeing fully clothed.

A few minutes later, she was seated in the rear of the narrow green boat, a paddle across her lap and Peter's wicker hamper at her feet. He'd rolled up the legs of his trousers, and bare-chested, was wading through the shallow water, pulling them out with the towrope. She couldn't exactly ignore the rippling musculature of his back, or the curls of fine dark hair on his broad chest that tapered down his flat belly to the line of his pants. She tried to ignore the rising of her pulse as he climbed back into the canoe.

For the second time that day thoughts of Jeffrey suddenly materialized. What would he think? The very idea of Jeffrey in a canoe brought a smile to her lips. Well, being in one herself was unusual enough. Peter was smiling at her, white teeth flashing as he faced her, paddle poised above the water.

"Ready?" he said. "Paddle to your right. Keep up an even rhythm and we'll move along just fine."

Katherine nodded and dipped her paddle into the cool blue water. They glided out into the lake. The sun felt wonderful on her upturned face, the breeze fine in her hair. "This is good," she said.

"It's great," he said.

"But hot," she added.

"Perfection's hard to come by," he said, looking at her with a twinkle in his eye. "Here, I'll cool you off." He dipped his paddle with some extra vehemence and a splash of water arced through the air, barely missing her face. Leaning back she laughed, then smacked the water with her paddle in return.

Peter ducked, chuckling, then looked at her again in an odd way. "There's that girl I remember," he muttered, and she wondered if she'd heard him correctly.

"What do you mean?"

"Katherine Taylor, you don't remember me, do you?"

"Remember you?" She squinted at him in the sun, confused.

"No, you wouldn't," he said, with a little sigh. "I was too many grades behind you."

"We went to school together?"

"Well, we almost did. But you left Greensdale High just as I was coming in. You never came back after winter vacation, because you went off to—"

"Andover, that's right," she said, remembering how her impatience to get out of Greensdale had led to her campaign to transfer to a private school that year. Father, seeing it all as part of a proper academic trajectory into a good college, had pulled some strings to make the switch. "I'm surprised you remember me," she said.

"The Taylors were highly visible," he said. "You know that."

Katherine shrugged and allowed herself the luxury of unbuttoning her blouse. The breeze had died, and a bead of sweat was trickling down her forehead. "What exactly do you remember?" she asked.

"Oh, nothing." He looked faintly embarrassed, concentrating on his paddling, then chuckled again. "But I'll tell you, when I was a lowly junior high student, the idea of dating a mature and sophisticated senior—one of the Taylor girls, no less—would've seemed like some kind of impossible dream. So I consider this a rare honor."

Katherine smiled. "I'm flattered," she told him. "Wait," she added in mock consternation. "You mean I'm out with a younger man?"

"'Fraid so," Peter said. "Pull a little harder there, we're in danger of going in a circle."

Katherine dutifully applied some muscle. In another minute she was sweating in earnest. Peter looked perfectly comfortable, a hint of amusement gleaming in his eyes as he watched her paddle. "If you do want to get out of those things, I've got some suntan lotion on board," he said, indicating the hamper between them.

"That's okay," she assured him stubbornly, though her blouse was sticking to her back. They were further from shore now, the island looming in the distance. She paddled harder, trying to match his stronger thrusts so as to keep them from turning.

"Need a rest?"

She opened her mouth to deny it, but his penetrating gaze made the lie seem foolish. "Well, maybe a minute."

He nodded and withdrew his paddle. She rubbed her palms, paddle at her feet, and Peter extracted one of the bottles he'd brought aboard from under the hamper. Katherine shaded her eyes, and was admiring the lush greenery on all sides of them when she heard a sudden familiar popping sound.

"Champagne?" she asked, incredulous.

Peter was already pouring it into two plastic cups, and adding a healthy dash of orange juice from a small container to each. "Mimosas," he announced.

"Isn't it sort of early in the day...?"

"You'll never convince me you're in a mad rush to get back to that mountain of papers," he said. "Just one cupful won't disable you, anyway, and you must be thirsty."

"I am," she admitted, and accepted the cup he was holding out with a nod of thanks.

Peter raised his cup in a toast. "To older women," he said, poker-faced.

"Very funny," she replied. "To old school chums."

He nodded and they both drank. The concoction was delicious. Before she realized what she was doing, she'd downed the whole cup. "More?" His bottle hovered.

"Just orange juice," she told him. "Unless you want this canoe to spin in circles for the next hour."

Peter nodded. "All right then, let's move on." He indicated the island with his raised paddle. Whether it was the effect of the mimosa or her rapidly developing forearm muscles, the canoe seemed to glide more rapidly over the water as she dug in.

"I suppose you were on the football team," she ventured, her eyes caught again by his trim physique in action.

"Co-captain," he said. "You really missed something, leaving so soon. I actually guided the notorious Green Hornets to their first season win in five years."

Katherine smiled, remembering now that their high school team had indeed been infamous for losing streaks. "Sorry," she said. "But I was never a cheerleader type, anyway."

"Oh, come on, I can just see you with pom-poms." Katherine laughed. He bent forward suddenly. "Now I'm sure you won't admit it, but you're having a good time. I can tell."

She shrugged, paddling. "All right, I admit it."

"Doesn't hurt to step out of your regular life for an afternoon."

"No," she said, instantly sobering. She watched the water whirl away from her paddle, feeling the darkness that had been hovering at the edges of her consciousness threatening to envelop her again. He was right, though. For a moment, he'd made her forget....

"Land ahoy, matey," he said, and she looked up. The island was almost upon them. Thankful for the distraction, she followed Peter's instructions as he climbed out of the canoe again to guide them in.

Katherine took his hand for assistance as the canoe wobbled beneath her. His grip was strong and warm. Why was something as casual as a handshake quickening her pulse again? Bunching her skirt carefully around her thighs—though she was wearing clothes and a bathing suit, she suddenly felt completely nude—she stepped over the edge of the boat and into the wonderfully cool water. She let go of his hand immediately and tried to look calm and collected as she followed him up the sandy shore.

At forty-three, Katherine certainly didn't consider herself entirely beyond romantic attractions, but she had been drifting into a state of remoteness where the opposite sex was concerned. She sometimes thought it was because no man she'd met since her husband's death seemed to have the stature, wisdom and worldliness of J. A. Cartwright. Sometimes she thought she was just too caught up in her own career to get involved.

But she assuredly wasn't used to feeling herself... well, vibrate, in the presence of a man like Peter Bradford. Football player physiques didn't do a thing for her, she reminded herself. But even as she thought that she knew instinctively it was something else about him she was responding to, and had noticed that first day outside the church.

What it was, she couldn't put her finger on just yet, but he was having an effect. She resolved to nail it down, this elusive attractive quality of his, and figure out if it was anything more than his sexy blue eyes. They, she had to admit, exerted a powerful pull on their own.

After he'd secured the canoe, Peter led the way through some tall grass to a knoll that overlooked the strip of beach. Katherine helped him lay out a white tablecloth and the contents of his seemingly bottomless wicker basket. He'd provided them with a mouth-watering cornucopia of food and drink. There were salmon, fresh-baked croissants and bread, cold asparagus, some Brie and sausage, even a tin of caviar.

The tall pines behind them sheltered her from the full force of the sun. The breeze rose again, lifting her hair. They ate in comfortable silence for a time, listening to the birds and the sounds of a distant motorboat. As she sipped at her orange juice, she relaxed again into a sense of well-being that bordered on the blissful. For just a moment, as Peter's eyes met hers and they exchanged a smile, she felt that all was right with the world.

"It's a beautiful place," she told him.

"Looks more beautiful now," he returned, his eyes seeming to drink in her every feature.

Katherine looked nervously away. What *did* the man want with her, anyway? What if he was only trying to seduce her into selling Grammy's house? After all, she hardly knew him, and he was being awfully attentive for a new acquaintance. "You can save the flattery," she said.

"It wasn't flattery," he said quietly. "Anything wrong with making you an honest compliment? You *are* a beautiful woman, and your being here right now is really bringing out the best in this place."

When she looked at him again it was hard to disbelieve the earnest look in those clear blue eyes. She took a sip of juice, feeling chastened for her defensive retort. "Sorry," she murmured. "And thank you, I guess."

Peter shrugged. "I guess it's the removal of that red pencil from behind your ear that does it. You look better without it."

"Are you saying I work too hard?"

"Maybe." He smiled. "Who am I to say? But I will say you don't strike me as the academic type."

"I don't?" She looked down, self-conscious again, as he scooped a second helping of strawberries onto her plate. "Well, I am."

"I've never seen an academic with a hint of freckles across their nose, and strawberry-stained lips that look so..." His voice trailed off. He seemed suddenly aware that his stare was radiating currents of sensual interest, and it took an effort for her to hold his gaze without betraying the quickening of her own heartbeat. "Let's just say you don't fit the image," he finished, now absorbed in picking out some choice strawberries for himself.

"Which is?"

"Oh, I don't know." He shrugged. "You're too young to be shut up in an ivory tower. You belong in the great outdoors."

I haven't been shut up, she thought defensively. *And what's wrong with being a good teacher?* "I'm a scholar at heart," she said warily.

"And a woman," he added, looking up again. In the suddenly electric silence between them she felt that subtle tug again. Wasn't she supposed to analyze this feeling? But her mind wasn't working properly just now. The sudden cawing of a bird in the branches right above them was a welcome distraction, and they both looked away to watch its white wings swoop off into the blue.

She got to her feet, smoothing down her skirt, feeling a little dizzy from the heat of the sun and Peter Bradford.

"Maybe you'd like to see the rest of this place," he suggested.

They fell into step together, following a path to the sandbar that fringed the island. The warm grainy sand felt good under her bare feet. Conceding to the heat at last she did take off her blouse, tying it around the waist of her black bathing suit. Peter began asking her questions about her past, present and future, and that was fine with her, as long as they avoided talking about the house. She wasn't ready to spring her idea on him yet, not until she'd returned to Greensdale and seen if it could become a reality. Avoiding the whole issue seemed the wisest. Wasn't that what he was doing?

"You were close to your father?" he asked, as they rounded another curve of tall grass and shoreline.

"Yes," she said immediately. "I mean, it's no secret that I always wanted to impress him, follow in the proverbial footsteps."

"He taught at Harvard, didn't he?" Peter said. Katherine nodded. "Does your sister teach, too?"

"Lydia? Oh, no. She runs a pet shop in San Francisco."

"Black sheep?"

"I don't think they carry sheep, no," she said, musing. Peter laughed. "No, I meant..."

"Oh!" she reddened, laughing herself. "No, Father loved Lydia dearly. It wasn't a rebellion or anything, she just wasn't interested in being cloistered in libraries like her older sister."

"That's three," he murmured, with a little smile.

"Three laughs?" she asked, remembering.

He nodded. "You have a great laugh," he informed her soberly. "I have this sense you don't let it out that often, though."

"You mean I have no sense of humor?" she inquired playfully, but at the same time feeling a little hurt.

"Not at all." He paused to look at her, arms folded. "And you certainly haven't been living through the cheeriest of times lately. But... I don't know, I just get this feeling...that you tend to hold a lot of yourself in."

He was treading on some sensitive ground here, and she could almost envision little mental Do Not Enter signs springing up on her forehead to ward him off. He was right, of course—but he didn't have any right to be! "I guess I was just brought up that way," she said testily.

"Brought up how?"

He was mocking her, wasn't he? "Properly," she returned.

Something in his expression changed. "Oh," he said. "You mean unlike us ill-bred folks from Greensdale who can't control our emotions. The rude and obstreperous sort."

She felt her face reddening. Well, she'd set herself up for that, hadn't she? She'd sounded just like one of the "high and mighty" Taylor clan. She was annoyed with herself but irked even more that Peter would be so quick to type her like that. So much for imagined sensitivities. "Maybe if you knew me better, you wouldn't say that," she said carefully.

Peter's features softened again as he nodded slowly. "I would like to know you better," he returned, holding her gaze. "Can I ask you a question?"

"I suppose."

"Did you and your mother have a falling out?"

"Absolutely not!" she said, the words so loud that she surprised herself. "What in the world makes you ask such a thing?"

"I saw you at the service in the cemetery... and you walked away so quickly—"

"I'd had enough," she said sharply. "That's all, and I don't see why I owe anyone an explanation for my behavior." It was amazing how fast her anger had risen and surfaced. It was blazing inside her like a roaring flame.

"Of course it's none of my business," he was saying mildly, still holding his ground, apparently blissfully unaware that he was in danger of being seriously scalded if he didn't just drop the subject. "But I thought you looked more, well, aloof than upset, which made me wonder—"

"I love my mother!" she cried hotly. "You have no idea how close we are! And I resent you making these insulting, ridiculous insinuations—"

"Were," he interrupted quietly. "How close you were."

"—when you don't know me or anything about me!" she barreled on. Hot tears stung the edges of her eyes as she continued, feeling her control slip away entirely. "You've got a lot of nerve, you know that! How dare you? It's bad enough what you did before, trying to take the poor woman's house away from her—"

"It's *your* house," he reminded her gently.

"—but then you have the unmitigated gall to say these things to me, which you have absolutely no right—"

"You really are angry," he said softly, so softly that for a crazy moment she thought it might be her own inner voice.

"Yes, I'm angry!" she practically yelled. "You can't—"

"But not at me," he persisted, his bright blue eyes gazing deeply into hers. "At her."

"All right, damn it!" she cried. "I am! I'm furious! How could she do such a thing, when she knew I was coming the very next day! She should've waited, she should—" Her throat was so tight she felt she was choking.

"I guess it's easier to feel that rage than to feel the pain, isn't it?"

"It's not fair!" The words burst from her lips in a childish wail. And then it happened, the terrible thing, the awful thing she'd been fighting desperately against for every day and night since . . .

The tears filled her eyes, blinding her as the pain opened up the very core of her like a bottomless chasm. The tears swelled up, a flood, wracking her body as they poured forth at last. She couldn't see, couldn't hear, knew nothing but this wrenching, rending feeling, so overwhelming she thought she might fall, fall right into that black chasm—

But then there were arms around her, holding her gently as she cried, brokenly, loudly, unable to stop. Quivering and shaking as he held her to him she felt, rather than heard, soothing words at her ear, sensed the soothing hands that patted her back, smoothed her tear-dampened hair from her eyes.

She couldn't even think to push him away, or think at all. The comfort of his arms around her, the warmth of his body against hers were like a raft she could cling to as the tears continued like a rising river. She'd been afraid that if she did start crying, it might never stop, and maybe she'd been right. She had to gasp for air as the sobs shook her body, her face contorted and soaked as she wept on, turning her face into the shelter of his shoulder.

Slowly, after what seemed like an eternity of misery that seemed to drench her, the world began to filter in again, and she was conscious of his enveloping strength, the warmth and scent of his skin against hers. Still she held on tightly, embarrassed, but afraid to let go as long as the tears still streamed down her cheeks.

His fingers gently played with her hair while his other hand made a slow, reassuring circular movement on her still convulsively shaking back. He was making a sound, she realized that was both odd and strangely familiar, one she hadn't heard in ages. "Kathy," he murmured at her ear. "Kath, it's okay."

"Kathy" was rare enough, but no one had called her "Kath" since her dad had, so many years ago. The very thought brought on yet another round of tears, but he kept on holding and comforting her and soothing her with his hands and words, until slowly, but surely, she stopped shaking.

Still the tears ran down her cheeks unabated, but now she was able to regain her balance a little and pull her face from where she'd buried it in the crook of his shoulder. She looked up at him through blurry eyes, and the gaze of compassion in his brought another knot to her throat.

Peter kissed her forehead in the tenderest of gestures. His lips were warm and soft. She gazed up at him with an instinctive trust and he kissed her face again, above each wet eyelid. Then she lifted her own trembling lips to meet his, closing her eyes, reaching out even as he held her tighter.

Their lips met in a wet and salty kiss, in a gentle and seemingly natural collision. For a long moment she lost herself in the sweetness and moist heat of his mouth upon hers, feeling that raw ache within her suddenly filled with a different kind of emotion, a less desperate longing.

His lips left hers and she opened her eyes again as he kept hugging her to him. She swallowed, blinking, at a loss, the words spilling out in a breathy gasp. "I—I'm sorry," she blurted. "I—didn't mean to—"

"Don't be sorry," he murmured, stroking her cheek. "Kathy, don't be sorry."

Chapter Four

This wasn't at all what he'd had in mind.

He hadn't even planned on this picnic, Peter remembered, busying himself with repacking the hamper while Katherine composed herself, a little ways off. Originally he'd just figured on a quick hello, maybe a snack and a cup of coffee on campus. He hadn't intended to make a day of it. But when he'd seen her holed up in that tiny dark study, looking like some kind of maiden captive in a paper-walled prison, he'd had an impulse to free her. And surprise: she'd gone along with it.

Well, it was an afternoon full of surprises. It surprised him that he was so attracted to the woman. Schoolboy crushes aside, he didn't think there was enough common ground between him and Katherine Taylor to form the basis of a—whatever sort of relationship they were forming, if they were.

What just happened hadn't just surprised him; it had completely confused him. What was he doing kissing Katherine Taylor? By all rights he was supposed to be spending his time with her finding out what harebrained scheme she and her sister were up to with their house, and then talking her out of it, whatever it was. Sudden unexpected flares of passion had nothing to do with this at all.

*Oh, admit it, Pete: you wanted to kiss her, then and ear-
lier, for no reason but that she looked so infinitely kissable.*
But such things were pure fantasy. Women as gorgeous, as
smart and coolly remote as Katherine Taylor didn't fall into
his embrace on a daily basis, if ever. But then she had, in an
unforeseen, unexpected way.

He hadn't been baiting her, really. He'd just known that
she was suffering. He'd known it since their first encounter
outside the cemetery, and he'd known as well that she was
keeping a lid on all of it, much too tightly for comfort or for
health. So one thing had led to another, and then the seemingly impossible had happened. She'd let herself go, liter-
ally falling into his arms.

Not that he'd been thinking about romance. He hadn't
been thinking at all, just feeling, feeling bad for her and
wanting to make her feel better. But strangely enough, that
kiss had seemed entirely natural. It was as if something
within both of them had reached out at the same moment
and connected, with a bittersweet intensity that had left him
pretty shaken up.

And then she'd gone back into her shell, he mused, not
entirely surprised at her retreat in the aftermath of a particularly wrenching crying jag. In fact, he ought to whole-
heartedly approve. This kind of emotional stuff was
complicating an already complicated situation. He shouldn't
have kissed her. Such behavior was downright dangerous.
What if she got it into her head that because he was still interested in her mother's house, he was willfully trying to seduce her?

The whole business was enough to give him a headache.
Peter shot a glance in Katherine's direction. She was at the
edge of the clearing, handkerchief still in hand, gazing out
at the lake, looking amazingly beautiful for someone who'd
just cried a riverful of tears.

Scowling, Peter returned to his tidying up. He'd always
been one to follow his instincts, but in this case they'd led

him right onto real thin ice. All right, he liked the woman, he'd been trying to be friendly, helpful, but it was time to backpedal, fast. *You're on opposite sides,* he reminded himself, and added firmly: *let's keep it that way, all right?*

EMBARRASSMENT did weird things to a woman. Katherine found herself making up imaginary newspaper headlines. "Tenured Faculty Member Loses Mind in Bizarre Picnic Incident" was one, "Adult Turns Infant: Possible Sunstroke?" was another.

She didn't know how she could have possibly thrown herself into the arms of a man she was barely acquainted with, but she knew one thing: if he made fun of her, or worse, assumed an intimacy with her that wasn't really there, she'd pitch him right into the lake.

Fortunately for both of them, Peter Bradford knew enough to keep his distance, and was busying himself with the cleanup of their picnic area while she attempted to collect her wits. She wasn't having a nervous breakdown. Scary as the experience had been, she'd just had herself a good cry. She was already feeling as though a weight had been lifted off her chest, a weight that had been constricting her every breath for days now, though she'd done her best to ignore it. But *he'd* known it was there, hadn't he?

She turned back to observe Peter, who was humming quietly as he folded the tablecloth. The man was a lawyer, not a psychiatrist. Nonetheless he'd managed to make her get in touch with her own buried emotions, and she couldn't help but think it had been intentional on his part. Why? Peter the Good Samaritan? Or just an unusually, craftily sensitive man with ulterior motives?

Katherine instinctively turned away as Peter glanced in her direction, apparently aware she was staring at him. She wasn't used to weeping buckets in the lap of people she hardly knew. She had an impulse to run away from the man who'd managed to turn on her inner faucet and never come back.

But she stood her ground. The sun and breeze, the gentle lapping of the water were all filtering back into her consciousness with a new color and intensity. That little dark cloud was gone, or at least banished temporarily, and if anything, she should be thanking the man who'd made it possible.

She looked over at him again as he put the last of their gear into the hamper. "Feel like heading back?" Peter's voice was gentle and casual.

"Okay," she called, then cleared her throat. Her voice sounded odd to her, not shaky, but pitched an octave too high. Hamper in hand, Peter was striding down to the canoe, leaving her alone for the moment. Giving her room, she realized, and felt her cheeks burn again. Did the man think she had to be "handled"?

Katherine managed to nip another bloom of indignation in the bud. She didn't need a degree in psychology to understand the true depth of her embarrassment. It wasn't just that she'd cried so, and shown him a part of herself hardly anybody ever got to see. It was that kiss.

Where had that come from, anyway? It struck a wholly confusing note to her, although admittedly not a dissonant one. The last time she'd allowed herself to be comforted in a time of grief had been when Jeffrey had accompanied her to Father's funeral. She'd had a good cry then in the privacy of their hotel room, but it had felt different. There'd been a paternal quality to being held by Jeffrey, she could still remember it, and it hadn't been entirely due to the difference in their ages.

He'd ordered up hot milk for her so she could sleep. And sat with her, stroking her hair. And they hadn't made love, because their usual pattern—

Katherine halted the reverie in midtrajectory. What, in God's name, was she doing musing upon her conjugal life with Jeffrey Cartwright? Maybe she was more emotionally scattered than she'd thought. But she knew why. Being held by Peter Bradford hadn't had anything paternal about it in the least. No, she'd felt as if he was an equal, a friend, and something more than that. What?

She was dawdling. Katherine pushed her hair back, untied her blouse from around her waist and put it back on, aware that her shoulders were already feeling a little sunburned. As she walked down the stretch of sandy hill to where Peter was readying the canoe for departure, she realized she was still barefoot.

"They're in here," he called, indicating her sandals atop the hamper in the canoe. Once again he'd anticipated her thoughts. Peter the Psychic, she thought wryly.

"Thanks," she said. "Need a hand?" He was wading into the water with the towrope.

"No, just climb aboard," he instructed. As he steadied the canoe, Katherine did so. She sat in the back, quickly grabbing a paddle off the other seat as he hopped in, avoiding his eyes. The sooner they left the scene of the crime— "Woman Bawls Buckets in Surprise Attack"—the better.

In a moment they were gliding over the lake's placid blue surface again. It was almost as if nothing at all unusual had happened, and she chanced a direct look at Peter for the first time in a while. The wind had blown his hair the wrong way, seeming to take a few more years off his already youthful face as he paddled on. With the sun making the tanned skin of his bare shoulders shine, he resembled one of her more mature students at a boating meet. Was this the commanding man who'd taken control of her heart and mind, disarming her completely with one devastating kiss?

But then, who'd kissed whom, anyway? At the moment she could only watch him, bemused, trying to decipher her own motives, let alone his. She'd kissed him because she'd wanted to, that was all. She'd *needed* to, was more like it. Because it had felt good to have his arms around her, to be caressed and cared for like that, and something inside her had been stirred into restless life again, a part of her she'd been keeping down for the longest time.

Need, want, the very words were anathema to her. She'd grown so used to not wanting, not needing, standing on her own and taking care of other people's problems. A mother at twenty, she'd fast grown accustomed to responsibility. If it occurred to her that she herself needed some taking care of she brushed the thought aside. But a few minutes in Peter's embrace had made her aware of a void inside that was still aching to be filled.

Scary stuff. She was overreacting, surely, still shaken up over losing her mother. Katherine stabbed her paddle more forcefully into the water, and the canoe wobbled in its trajectory. Her ever-tactful companion silently corrected her stroke with a few of his own. Did he have to do everything right? What was he thinking, anyway? Peter's poise was starting to get to her.

His eyes met hers just then. "Feel like talking?" he said.

"If it's about anything but me," she blurted, and he smiled. The hint of a dimple in his left cheek caught her eye. It was hard staying ill at ease in the presence of that smile.

"Well, we could discuss the weather, but it's perfect," observed, "so there's nothing to discuss there." He drew up his paddle, all of his attention on her now. "Are you okay?" he asked quietly.

"Fine," she said, too quickly, and as he raised a questioning eyebrow they both laughed. "All right, not completely fine," she allowed. "But a lot better, I think... thanks to you." *You seemed to know just what I needed*, she nearly added, but stopped herself.

He shrugged. "I happened to be there," he told her. His gaze suddenly felt a bit too penetrating, and she looked to her paddle for escape.

"We're drifting in a circle," she commented.

"You're closing up again," he replied.

Katherine stared at him. Peter had a way of getting directly at whatever was going on with her that was truly disorienting. "I did say I didn't feel like talking about me," she said, inwardly cringing at the stiffness she heard in her tone.

But he seemed to take it in stride, digging his paddle in again, as nonchalant as ever. "That's okay," he added, his eyes intent on the water. "This place is well suited for silence, anyway. I used to do some fishing up here, around the inlet. With my dad. He told me once that too much talk not only kept the big fish away, but it kept you from catching the big thoughts."

Katherine smiled wryly. "Smart man," she said.

Peter nodded. Silence reigned once more and they glided over the reflections of drifting clouds. Birds cawing from the greenery on the shoreline and the gentle swish of their paddles in the water were the only commentary. Some line of poetry glimmered faintly in the recesses of her mind, a favorite quote of Jeffrey's from John Donne about stirred circles in water and increasing love, but the words escaped her. A big thought that got away.

That was how Jeffrey had communicated things that mattered to him, she mused, using poetry and literature. That was how she'd fallen in love with the handsome scholar when she was young and wide-eyed in his classroom: his love of images and symbols, and the beauty of a well-wrought rhyme "that meant," the way he'd brought words to life for her, weaving powerful magic out of his own passion for them.

But in the day-to-day realities of a relationship, unfortunately, he'd been as surprisingly inarticulate as he was stunningly acute at the podium. She'd discovered way too late that he was best at dealing with human emotions when they were set down on the printed page. Getting him to own up to how he felt about things or to cope with how *she* felt, had been a major, frustrating difficulty throughout their married life.

And here was Peter Bradford, at least a decade younger than Jeffrey when he died, wisely able to deal, cope with and go right to the center of her emotions, when he'd known her only briefly. That made her uneasy.

Jeffrey had courted her with sonnets and orchids. He'd seduced her mind before even touching her skin. He'd blinded her with a brilliance she found so much sexier than the collegiate high jinks of her classmates. And only much later, long after Clarissa had been born, had that brilliance dimmed in her now worldlier eyes.

Peter was the kind of guy who stripped a lilac bush for an impromptu bouquet and sang along with rock 'n' roll songs on the radio. He wasn't a word-dazzler by any means. But he seemed to be able to touch the core of her with a look, a gesture, or a simple question. It wasn't how he said things, but what he said. He was blunt and to the point, but she had to admit she could appreciate that now. There was something to be said for not having to interpret and decipher a man as if he were a complicated piece of blank verse.

But who said Peter was courting her? Men like him didn't "court," anyway. For all she knew, he was still intent on charming her into going along with some unspoken plans for Grammy's house. As soon as he found out what Lydia and she had planned for it, his interest in her might instantly evaporate. And she was paying much too much attention to him already, she told herself, the sudden nudge of her paddle hitting bottom as they neared the shore jolting her out of such speculations.

Peter was climbing out, pants rolled up to his knees. She watched him wade in, guiding the canoe. He *was* young, wasn't he? Younger than she was. And though such things weren't supposed to matter in this day and age, it mattered to her. She had no business fantasizing and romanticizing a near stranger who most probably had political motives for pursuing her.

If pursuing her was what he was doing, of course. Katherine was irked to realize, as she alighted from the canoe without Peter's proffered assistance, that the idea wasn't entirely displeasing.

"YOU'RE NOT INVITING ME in for coffee?" Peter still had his engine running as Katherine left the car. He got out on his side, looking at her across the car's roof, struck again by how much a few hours of sun became her. Then he remembered he wasn't supposed to be thinking such thoughts.

"I'm afraid whatever coffee's left in my office wouldn't be fit for human consumption," she told him. "And I've still got that pile of papers to go through. . . ."

"Right." He himself had brought a briefcase full of office work up to Dave's cottage. He nodded, uncertain of how to proceed from here, certain only that he hadn't seen enough of her. Well, when would he think he had? Maybe when he'd found out what he was supposed to find out about her plans, he reminded himself. "What are you doing later?" he asked.

"Later?" Her expression was wary.

"I'm up here through the weekend," he said. "Why don't we have dinner together?"

"Oh, I couldn't tonight."

"Tomorrow night, then."

Katherine shook her head. "I'm really kind of busy."

He wondered suddenly if there was a man in her life. No such lucky individual had accompanied her to her mother's funeral, but here on her home turf there'd have to be someone, or someones. Hey, what did it matter to him? "Well, maybe we can hook up back in Greensdale."

She stiffened. "How did you know I'd be down there soon?"

A calculated guess. "I didn't know for sure," he answered carefully. "I was just hoping you might be. After all, you did say something about plans for your house—"

Something flashed in her eyes. She was very much on guard, and how could he blame her? *Hell,* he should drop the whole business, Randy Morgan's continual pressure be damned. After all, he really had wanted to see *her* when he'd stopped by earlier, not the deed to her land.

"Yes, I'm coming down next weekend," she said, the wariness back in her voice. "I guess that's not news."

"Look," he said. "I don't know anything about your comings or goings or what you're going to do when you come, okay? I'm just being—" Friendly? What was he being, anyway? "I just wanted to see you again," he finished lamely, annoyed at how clumsy he was sounding and disappointed that she seemed intent on returning their relationship to space one.

"I really do have to go," she said, looking at her watch and then back at him, a slight flush in her cheeks that he suspected wasn't merely sunburn. "Maybe we should just...leave on a nice and friendly note. Thanks for the lunch. It was lovely."

"My pleasure," he said evenly. If she wanted to play this way, that was fine with him. It was safer all around.

"Thank you for everything, Peter," she added in a softer tone, but before he could react to it, she'd turned on her heel and was striding back to her ivy-covered office. He watched her go, unable to keep his eyes off her retreating figure, admiring it with a pang of regret.

You figure it, Peter told himself moodily as he drove back to the summer house alone. The woman was as mercurial as the Massachusetts weather. She was warm, cool, friendly, foreboding, open, closed, beautiful...and beautiful, he reflected with a little sigh. That was one constant factor.

He kept seeing her face, the exuberant glow in her animated eyes, her clean, unlined skin, the long soft line from chin to neck and graceful shoulders. There was a tiny brown dot of a birthmark on her left collarbone, just above the collar, which had mesmerized him for a full minute. And then of course there was the sensuous fullness of her lips when they'd been dabbed with strawberry juice, and the taste of them when they'd kissed....

The whole situation was exasperating. If he was smart, he'd keep his distance. He'd been enjoying some of the benefits of a bachelor's existence for a while now, and there was no real reason to get further entangled with an uptight, unobtainable woman who was creating nothing but problems for him and all of Greensdale.

Peter called her first thing the next morning.

IT WAS SIX-THIRTY when she finally found an outfit she was comfortable with. Katherine surveyed the dress in her bedroom mirror, a simple silk shift that seemed neither too straight nor too provocative. As she wondered whether to put her hair up or leave it down, she found herself thinking that the apartment seemed unusually quiet.

Something had been nagging at her memory, and she kept glancing at the clock. Suddenly she knew what it was. Her mother's weekend call. Well, there was another little absence she'd have to get used to. Grammy had always called her at home on Sunday nights at half past six, and they'd "do the week," as Grammy put it, going over whatever news they had to share. It was just as well she was going out, she thought sadly, since going through this particular hour without—

The phone rang. Startled, Katherine stared at it, wondering for a moment. Then, irked at her own silliness, she picked it up on the third ring. "Hello?"

"Hi, Mom." Clarissa's voice sounded warm and welcome through some long-distance static. "I had a feeling you'd be there."

"You did?"

"Yeah, it's your Grammy call time, isn't it?" Katherine was too surprised to answer as Clarissa hurried on: "I figured since she couldn't call maybe I'd sort of fill in, you know?''

"Oh, honey..." She smiled, touched. "That's really sweet." For a moment she thought she might start crying again, but after yesterday's flood, the tears stayed put. "And I'd love to talk to you, but can I call you back in the morning? I'm actually on my way out. I have a date."

"A date?" Clarissa's voice lilted upward in happy incredulity. "You mean like dinner, dancing and a show?"

Katherine sighed. Her daughter always enjoyed teasing her, and she could see this was going to give her ample opportunity. "I'm not exactly over the hill," she said dryly, glancing with a little apprehension at the hall mirror as she cradled the phone in her shoulder, rummaging in her pocketbook for her hairbrush.

"No, you're in your prime," Clarissa said. "So who is it?"

"A young lawyer, if you must know," Katherine said.

"Cute?"

"Yes, cute," she admitted. "But I don't trust him as far as I could throw him." Briefly she filled Clarissa in on who Peter was and what interests he represented, then described her outing with him, touching on her emotional outburst and his behavior.

"I think he sounds neat," Clarissa said. "It's about time somebody brought you out of yourself a bit."

"Funny you should say that. He said something similar, about me holding myself in."

"Well, you do," Clarissa said promptly. "We all know that, Mom." They did? Katherine wondered suddenly if she really had any clear picture of how the world saw her. Was she that transparent? "So how come you don't trust him?" Clarissa continued.

"He could be after me for the wrong reasons."

Clarissa laughed. "But you agreed to have dinner with him," she reminded her. "Come on, you ought to go have some fun and not worry about it."

"Thanks for the counseling," Katherine said wryly.

"At least he's not another boring old academic."

"If I don't get off the phone he's going to be bored, all right. I'm already late."

"Okay, okay, I just wanted to make sure you'd send those prints down from Grammy's as soon as you get there." Clarissa had laid claim to the old lithographs that lined the walls of her grandfather's study, and wanted them for her new apartment in Manhattan. Katherine hurried through arrangements with her and then hung up, sorry she hadn't had time for a longer chat but anxious to get on the road.

She hadn't expected Peter Bradford to call, not after the way she'd acted, post-picnic. Guilt over her behavior had made for a restless night. She'd realized once she'd been sequestered in her office again that he'd made her feel better in a few hours than she had done in ages, and she'd immediately regretted letting her defensiveness scare the man away.

Not that it made much sense to see him again. They were still on opposite sides of the fence, and would be so even more firmly once she and Lydia had put their plans for the Taylor house into action. But Peter seemed sincerely interested in befriending her, above and beyond whatever business transpired in Greensdale. And maybe there wasn't anything wrong with having a friend like him.

Friend? Katherine, she warned herself as she drove down the winding road that led to Wilmington, *it's ridiculous to have anything more than that in mind.* Peter Bradford wasn't at all suited to be her suitor, and who said he was or that she needed one? Nobody. *Then why do you keep thinking about him?* she asked herself.

Sometimes the voices in her head were too persistent. She switched on the radio, and was rewarded with the slightly

Southern drawl of James Taylor, singing a perfectly appropriate song she'd always liked: "Country Road." The familiar melody fitted right in with the orangy sun through the trees that whizzed by her windshield, and those bothersome mental voices died away beneath the twanging harmonies of a well-picked acoustic guitar.

Humming along, taking curves at an adventuresome clip, it suddenly occurred to Katherine that she was...happy? She smiled at her own shying away from the big H-word. She'd been so used to feeling depressed of late that there was a trace of guilt attached to this feeling she had, of anticipation, of light-headed abandon.

Let it go. So she was being irresponsible, letting herself be seduced into a home-cooked meal at a little house buried in the woods on a summer night, alone with a devastatingly handsome man who'd already captured a small corner of her heart. Worse things had happened, hadn't they?

TURQUOISE HAD NEVER BEEN one of Peter's favorite hues, but it was now. Though he should have been shaking up the salad dressing he paused again to take in the sight of Katherine, wandering about the living room in a stunning blue-green silk that was making him reconsider his taste in color.

Something about this disarmingly simple dress was drawing his eyes away from his dinner preparation with distracting regularity. It was sleeveless, a simple cut that showed off the fresh tan on her supple arms and long legs. The neckline didn't plunge, but a glimpse of that long throat and now-familiar birthmark on her collarbone was enough to stop him in the midst of a myriad preparations.

But he had to keep his mind on the food. No gourmet, he'd gone with an easy pesto on linguine and a salad, plus garlic bread, since it seemed to him a man couldn't do much damage to such straight ahead fare. Even so, things had to be timed properly, and Katherine was making his timing go off. It wasn't her fault, it was just that she looked so good.

He still wasn't used to the idea that Katherine Taylor was here, about to eat dinner with him. The junior high student in him was trying to get over the adult's good fortune. She'd always exuded sophistication when he'd known her back then, but the older Peter could appreciate the subtleties of her style now. Just a touch of makeup, only the simplest earrings and a single band of silver on her wrist, understated perfume, all of it adding up to a masterpiece of feminine enhancement.

He had to repress an almost violent urge to leave the kitchen area and follow her around the room, inhaling her aura. But there was the pesto to attend to. And there was a subject to be broached before the evening's end that would most probably put an end to such indulgent imaginings for good.

"These yours or his?" she queried, turning from the bookshelves by the stone fireplace in the corner.

"His," he said, affecting to be absorbed again in checking the boiling water on the stove. "Dave's a real sci-fi nut."

"So I see," she murmured, then picked up a book from the table nearby with a startled exclamation. "What's this doing here?"

"It's being read," he said, lowering the flame a bit. "You mind?"

"Of course not," she said, flipping through the pages of the thick hardcover. "I just didn't realize..."

"...that I had a great love of British poets? I don't," he admitted. "Up until recently my favorite British poets have been Lennon and McCartney. But that particular critical study happened to catch my eye in the local bookshop."

"You mean, the author's name did," she said wryly.

"Jeffrey Addison Cartwright?" He feigned innocence. "Who is he to me?"

"This is one of his best works," she said, pausing at the back book flap to gaze at the black and white photo for a moment. "It actually turned a profit for the publishers. That's rare in this field, you know."

"He writes well," Peter commented. He'd only gotten through the first chapter, but he could see how the literary scholar had earned his renown. He wrote simply about complex things, in a way that wasn't pompous or off-putting. But he hadn't picked up the book by Katherine's late husband to check out the man's literary style. He'd hoped he might get an insight into what it might have been that had drawn Katherine to Cartwright. He couldn't see the beautiful woman in turquoise silk as a dryasdust academic.

"Yes, he wrote well," she said, in a resigned tone. Peter looked up from the steaming linguine, wondering what was behind her suddenly thoughtful expression. But then she put the book down and advanced toward him with a smile, her wineglass outstretched. "I think I need a refill."

"Here you go." He poured the wine, adding a drop to his own glass on the wooden counter. "Tell me something," he ventured. "You married Cartwright when you were still in college, didn't you?"

Katherine smiled. "You want to know how a young coed like me ended up with an older egghead like him."

"Exactly," Peter admitted.

Katherine sipped her wine. "Well, I fell in love with him the first time I heard him speak. A lecture on the Romantic poets from a dashing young professor with gray sideburns and beautiful, piercing eyes made quite an impression on an impressionable English Lit major. But psychologically it makes sense."

"How's that?" The linguine looked done. He pulled an experimental strand out of the pot to test.

"My father loved me, but his praise was hard to win. So having a man a dozen years my senior infatuated with everything I did..."

Jeffrey had been more than familiar with her father's work, she went on to explain. He'd even been using one of his books for the course she was taking. Naturally they had a lot to talk about, and Katherine, feeling alone, far from her family, and younger than most students in her class—precocious scholar that she was, she'd skipped a grade in junior high—hadn't made that many close friends. She found great solace in the older man's friendship.

The friendship had blossomed into a working relationship when Jeffrey hired her to proofread a monograph of his. He was a widower, captivated by the young girl who hung on his every word and was soon to become his part-time secretary. Before long they were practically inseparable, so much so that it seemed almost inevitable when they crossed the line from friendship to romance.

He was wise and worldly, but possessing a wildly romantic streak. And she was a virgin, not that she brought up that aspect of things as she helped Peter prepare their salad. She'd been "saving herself" for the right man, a rather antiquated notion in 1967, but she was a romantic, too. Jeffrey A. Cartwright had looked very much the right man to her, an Olivier-like figure who made the young men who were clumsily pursuing her seem all the more immature.

"We were married in the campus chapel," she told Peter. "In my junior year. And I'm such an old-fashioned girl," she joked, "that I got pregnant right after." Bent over a Cuisinart inspecting a container full of freshly mixed and ground green pesto, Peter nodded.

"Sounds charming. And did you live happily ever after?"

"More or less," she allowed.

"Ah. That's a provocative answer," he said. "I want the full details over dinner, which is now—pasta, bread, salad, pesto." He took stock of the many bowls around him. "Ready," he announced, pleased, "though I can't predict how it'll taste. Speaking of which..." He dipped a spoon into the pesto and proffered it to her. "You tell me. How's it seem?"

It was delicious, but a little gritty. "Maybe one more round," she suggested.

"Okay. Hold your ears while I rev up this sucker." He switched on the Cuisinart, which did have a motor of ear-splitting intensity. Almost immediately the lights in the kitchen area flickered, then died with the sputtering motor. Peter cursed. Katherine blinked in the sudden darkness.

"Great," he sighed. "I timed everything perfectly, and now an act of God..."

"Has this happened before?"

"Nope." She could vaguely make out his figure in the moonlight that was filtering through the windows as he pulled out a drawer and rummaged noisily. "I don't even know where the fuse box is in this place," he said, clicking on a flashlight that flickered too, its beam weak. "Nice," he commented.

"Anything I can do?"

"Order a pizza," he said with a chuckle. "Because by the time I figure out how to power us up again, this linguine's going to be—wait a second," he interrupted himself. "I have a better idea."

So it was that less than five minutes later, the two of them were dining alfresco by candlelight. They'd transferred the cutlery and china from his table inside to the small card table in the yard, which now, adorned with white cloth and hurricane candles, looked perfectly festive, silver and glass gleaming in the bright moonlight.

"Sure you didn't do this on purpose?" she joked, taking a piece of hot garlic bread from the basket he held for her. "It's lovely out here."

"Fate," he said, and held up his wineglass in a cheery salute. She clinked hers against it. "But no, you've caught me. I ordered the nearly full moon, the cicadas, the birds," and here he paused, listening with her to the sounds of the woods around them, "as well as the gurgling stream in the distance and this nice cool breeze, which was expensive," he admonished her, "but worth every penny. Don't you think?"

"Absolutely," she agreed. Peter was looking at her expectantly. She realized she had yet to taste the pesto, so she hurried to do so. "Perfect," she announced.

"Flattery will get you dessert," he said, smiling, and tasted it himself. It wasn't bad, he noted gratefully. Looking back at Katherine, her skin gleaming in the dappled moonlight, golden hair falling gracefully past her shoulder as she bent over her plate, he decided that perfection was in the eyes of the beholder, and he was now beholding it. Even the way she handled a fork fascinated him.

Bradford, you're a goner, he thought sheepishly. *Cut back on the wine or something, will you?* But he had a feeling it was too late. Despite his best intentions, all his inner warnings, something had started here that didn't need wine or moonlight for fuel. He could only hope he wouldn't crash-land too soon.

DINNER HAD BEEN GREAT. Dessert had been delectable. And for the past half hour, strolling along the lake with a brandy snifter in her hand and Peter at her side, Katherine had been more contented and at ease than she'd felt in a long time. Try as she might, she couldn't find anything wrong with the evening. So why was she still trying?

"What's that look mean?" Peter was looking at her inquisitively. The man certainly had reliable antennae. He seemed capable of instinctively monitoring her every mood change, somehow understanding her so well already that it made her a bit nervous.

"Nothing in particular," she replied, as they neared the spot where the canoe was moored. Moonlight bathed the lake in a silver glow. "Just admiring the view." She looked back at him. He had an odd little smile on his face. "And what's that look?" she countered playfully.

"Just admiring you," he returned.

Katherine looked away. His directness was getting to her again, but she still felt a need to maintain some distance. Her mistrust of him was wavering—and beyond that lay a kind of vulnerability she found a bit frightening. Sure, it was easy for Clarissa to say she should let herself go. But to actually do it . . .

"The thing is, you seem relaxed," he went on. "A person might even think you were having a good time."

"I am," she admitted.

"Good," he said. "That was the idea."

The whole idea? she wondered, then inwardly groaned at her own paranoia. Peter hadn't mentioned Greensdale or the Taylor house in the entire time she'd been there. It suddenly struck her that some of her reluctance to really open up to him was due to guilt—her guilt about knowing she was going to do precisely what he didn't want her to do. She and Lydia weren't going to let ConCo into Greensdale, and when Peter and his friends learned of their intentions they weren't going to be inclined to be friendly with the Taylors. Or would he think differently?

She pushed thoughts of the future from her mind. "And how did you develop this winning, be-here-now time sensibility, Mr. Attorney?" she asked. "Aren't lawyers who've spent years in New York supposed to be jaded and cynical?"

"Maybe that's why I'm not there anymore," he said with a rueful chuckle. "I didn't fit in."

He motioned her to a chairlike tree stump, easing himself down into the grass by her side, and as the moon played hide-and-seek with a bank of fleecy clouds, regaled her with tales of the cutthroat in-house competition at the Manhattan law firm he'd worked in, a place that made the academic intrigues at her school look like kindergarten squabbles.

He'd gone in idealistic, interested in *pro bono* cases that would benefit the underprivileged, but before long, the money-hungry realities of the prestigious firm he'd joined made such cases more and more difficult to take on. Though he'd respected most of his colleagues, he'd begun to lose interest in the fancier trappings of wealth and status they all aspired to.

Ultimately, a near-marriage to an associate that ended messily—he fudged on details, and for the moment she let him—in a painful breakup led to his decision to get out of the metropolitan "yuppie jungle," as he called it. Returning to Greensdale for his father's funeral, an offer from a friend of the family had cinched the move.

Despite his single-minded pursuit of matters legal, Peter had educated himself with a thoroughness that surprised her. She'd felt that little strain of snobbishness that she disliked in herself surface earlier, when she'd been startled to see Jeffrey's book in the house. She shouldn't have judged him too quickly, she realized. Just because he wasn't well versed in English literature didn't mean he wasn't extremely intelligent.

But at the moment, as if it were the most natural thing in the world, he was taking off his clothes. "What are you doing?" she exclaimed, getting to her feet.

"Time for my nightly dip," he announced. "Didn't I say you should wear a suit?"

"Well, yes," she said, and she did have one on under her dress. "I thought it was an odd request at the time, and this..."

"This is a wonderful way to cap a wonderful evening," he said, eyes twinkling. "Come on, you can just wade in. The water's perfect."

A mosquito dive-bombed her ear. She swatted it, realizing that the breeze had died down, and the warm night air was heavy on her sunburned skin. "Okay," she said impulsively. He was already down to his suit, leaving his pants folded neatly on the tree stump. Flashing her a grin, he headed into the water, with gentlemanly discretion leaving her to disrobe alone.

A few moments later she was waist deep in the fantastically cool water. Peter was a few yards out, making bizarre noises with mouth and hands. "What are you doing now?" she laughed, wading out to join him.

"Trying to talk to the loons," he said, his face comically twisted in the moonlight. "Hear them?"

She did hear noises in the distance, but Peter's pitiful attempts didn't come close to matching them. "Give it up, Bradford," she groaned. "You're offending our delicate sensibilities."

"You and the loons, huh?" he mock-growled. "All right, hot stuff, you give it a try."

Katherine cupped her mouth and attempted a loonlike call, reducing Peter to gales of laughter. She took a playful swing at him. He splashed her. She splashed back and then dived away, kicking through the silver water, feeling as if decades were dropping away from her with each kick. When was the last time she'd had such goofy—truly loony—fun?

She surfaced, sputtering, shaking her hair, heartbeat doubled. Peter had disappeared. But suddenly phantom hands made a grab for her. He was attempting an underwater tackle. Soon aquatic hysteria reigned. Laughing and choking, Katherine fended him off, deftly maneuvering herself out of his clutches.

"Hey, Professor Mermaid," he said, when they were standing in the shallows, catching their breath. "I think you've just graduated my crash course, Having a Good Time 101."

Katherine smiled, self-consciously smoothing her wet hair back from her face. As he gazed at her with undisguised interest, she was aware of how the clinging bathing suit revealed her almost nakedly in the bright moonlight. Demurely she folded her arms across her chest. "Maybe so," she admitted. "You've actually succeeded in making me forget the miles of paperwork I have waiting for me back on campus."

"Good," he said, striding closer to her. "But you know, there's one thing I haven't been able to keep my mind off." She could see the desire in his eyes now, and felt an answering flicker of heat rising within her as he closed the gap between them. "It's those delectable blue lips of yours," he murmured, and then he captured them with his.

His mouth brushed hers with tantalizing gentleness, his hands slowly urging her wet shoulders forward, bringing her body close. But even as her lips opened of their own volition to welcome his she knew she wasn't ready for this. The voluptuous swell of sensation that coursed through her body, the need rising inside her with an ache that was nearly painful—it was all too much, too soon.

"Peter..." The weak protest was torn from her in a husky whisper. Instantly he stepped back, his eyes searching hers. "No?" he asked softly.

Yes, a thousand times yes, she thought, her heart beating violently. But something inside of her, some final core of resistance and fear, was making it impossible to let go.

Peter saw the look in Katherine's eyes and immediately regretted having given in to the impulse. He sensed she wanted him to kiss her but he also sensed the fear in her, and he suddenly felt a pang of sharp remorse. What was he doing, taking advantage of her like this?

He'd mismanaged the whole evening, *damn it*. He'd wanted to diffuse the situation, have both of them put their respective cards on the table, sit down like a couple of rational adults and talk sensibly about the Taylor house business. But he'd kept putting it off and putting it off. Because he'd been enjoying her so much. *Because, face it:* he'd been starting to want her with an intensity that surprised and unnerved him.

Don't do it, Bradford! The last time he'd lost his head over a woman he'd been seriously burned. And this circumstance was loaded with not-so-hidden traps and mines, for both of them. *If you're seriously interested in Katherine Taylor,* he told himself, *stop right here. You shouldn't even be entertaining thoughts about moonlight seductions until the political heat is off and this whole messy business is behind you both.*

And so, with painful reluctance, he seized her eleventh hour moment of hesitation as a way out and forced himself to let go of her shoulders. "Sorry," he murmured. "Lost my head. We should probably move on before those lips really do turn blue."

For a moment, he thought he saw disappointment in her eyes. Then she looked past him with an enigmatic, slightly crooked smile. "I see the age of chivalry hasn't died," she murmured, and turned abruptly, wading for the shore. He watched her lithe figure in the moonlight, his insides churning with mixed emotions. Well, her facetious remark had been on target. He'd done the gentlemanly thing, the right thing.

So why did it feel so wrong?

Chapter Five

The warmth of those lips, the feel of his strong hands on her shoulders, the look in the glittering depths of his eyes...

"Kathy?"

"What? Oh!" She'd put milk in Lydia's coffee, even though her sister always took it black. "Sorry. Here, I'll pour you another."

"It's okay, we're short on cups as it is," Lydia said. "I've been buzzing on caffeine overdrive all day, anyway. I'll give this one to Betty Tyler. Can you handle those?"

"Sure." Katherine had loaded up the tray of coffee mugs for the ladies in the sun parlor, while Emily was busily transferring hot cinnamon buns from the oven to a serving platter on the counter. Katherine carefully balanced the tray and moved slowly through the kitchen, chagrined that she'd let her attention wander for the umpteenth time that day.

"The Night That Got Away," she'd labeled it, that last encounter with Peter Bradford. The irony was, she'd forced herself to stop things going any further by the lake last weekend so that she wouldn't be haunted by guilty regrets and messy complications. But the outcome was, she was haunted anyway, by regrets for having stopped things in their tracks.

Preoccupation with what she *hadn't* done with Peter Bradford was threatening to prey more heavily on her mind

than what might have if she'd given in. But now wasn't the
time to dwell on it. The first official meeting of the Taylor
House Committee, as she and Lydia had decided to call it,
was in progress. As she turned the corner of the hallway that
led into the end of the sun parlor and saw the women seated
there in readiness, Katherine reflected that she had, after all,
done The Right Thing and tried to imagine how she
might've felt, getting intimately involved with Peter and
then calling together this group of people specifically to defeat his plans.

"Who wanted the decaf?" she asked, and Barbara
Wainright, the youngest of them seated there, waved a hand.
The swell of her stomach beneath her calico shift indicated
she was due to add another number to the brood she'd
brought with her. Counting Emily, with Barbara, Betty Tyler, Sadie Travis and Marsha Rudman, there were five
Greensdale mothers attending this Saturday morning, and
their kids added up to a baker's dozen. Emily had com-
mandeered her eldest daughter and a school friend to look
after the dozen or so children now playing outside in
Grammy's yard.

The hot buns were distributed with the requisite oohs and
ahs of appreciation at Emily's baking prowess, the coffee
assigned. For a moment it was quiet in the long room.
Katherine noted that the women chattered among themselves without restraint whenever she or Lydia weren't in the
room, but tended to clam up when they were. Well, she
shouldn't really take offense. They didn't know her, and she
was only barely acquainted with them.

But that same attitude she'd sensed in Sadie Travis the
week before was prevalent here, too, and Katherine was determined to overcome it. That was part of the rationale of
this project: to break down barriers once and for all, and
have the Taylors be a part of the community at last. A good
thought, that. But looking at the five women demurely sip-
ping coffee and avoiding her gaze, Katherine had to fend off

a sinking feeling in her heart. What if everybody listened politely to Lydia and herself, thanked them for the coffee, got up and just returned to their normal lives?

Take the plunge, she told herself, and cleared her throat. "Lydia and I would like to thank you all for giving up part of your Saturday morning," she began. Five faces looked up at her with varying degrees of wary interest. "I guess Emily's told you why we wanted to have this get-together."

"Well, we didn't come here for a garage sale," Sadie cracked, and the women laughed. Their laughter was a little nervous, and the sound of it gave Katherine renewed faith. They were probably as ill at ease as she was, she realized.

"No," she said, smiling. "Although if we do go ahead with our plans for this place, I'm sure we'll need a garage sale or two to clear out some space."

"Dibs on that little table," Barbara Wainright piped up brightly, and Marsha gave her a mock swat as the women laughed again. "Really! It's just beautiful."

She was referring to an eighteenth-century antique that had probably cost Grandfather a small fortune, but now wasn't the time to call attention to that sort of thing. Each of the women had made a point of commenting on the beauty of the house's interior when they arrived, but there was a thin line between admiration and resentment. "You've got good taste," was what Katherine said.

"It wouldn't last a minute in your living room," Emily told Barbara. "Those twins of yours would demolish it in two seconds."

"Good tree house material," Sadie said wryly, and her friends chuckled.

"Like Tom's back porch steps," Marsha said. A streak of premature gray in her auburn hair gave her an air of seniority amid the group.

"And your sister's rocker," Emily chimed in. Then, noting Katherine and Lydia's confusion, she explained that an infamous project of the twins that spring had been the construction of a tree house. The kids had apparently demolished a fair amount of property getting wood together for it before Barbara's husband Tom had stopped them.

Talking about the children turned out to be the best ice-breaker for their meeting. The invisible but strong boundaries that existed between the women of Greensdale and the Taylor sisters were lowered as they traded tales of the holy terrors their kids could be. Katherine offered up her story of Clarissa's attempt to repaint their kitchen in hot pink and chartreuse at age six, when she'd first decided upon an artistic career. Everyone present except childless Lydia had similar horror stories, and Katherine began to feel that things might go easily, after all.

She opened up the discussion proper by explaining the basic idea she and Lydia had developed. They were determined not to have the Taylor house torn down. Rather than renovate it for possible sale to new tenants, they wanted to keep it in the family while opening it up to the community as a day-care center for the preschoolers of Greensdale. Since there was obviously a need for a facility like that in town, and the place had already been serving a similar purpose under Emily's guidance, why shouldn't they go all the way?

Since the center wouldn't operate for profit, it was conceivable that there might be a way to get state funding assistance, or at least avoid heavy taxation, which Mr. Stuart was looking into, and regardless, Grammy's inheritance would subsidize the renovations.

"We've already contacted Harry Settle, from Bakerston, to have an assessment of the property done," Lydia told them, and she unfolded the papers the architect had given her after his visit the day before. "The idea is to keep the entire upstairs basically as it is, for living quarters. But this room and the adjoining rooms, with a new entrance setup here—'' she pointed at the preliminary sketch the architect had drawn ''—would be converted into one large play area.''

The sketch was passed around. Katherine barreled on, anxious to share as many of their ideas as she could before the questions came. The women were being very quiet, though, and she couldn't tell what kind of reactions they were having. ''We could probably handle up to about three dozen kids or more,'' she said, ''but that would also depend on how large a staff could be put together. Emily's agreed to help with the hiring, and to organize things.''

Katherine looked around expectantly. Silence reigned in the sun parlor. The women were exchanging glances and stirring their coffee. Sadie Travis was the first to speak up. ''This is all pretty impressive,'' she said slowly. ''But it's going to take a lot of work, isn't it?''

''I'll be able to spend a lot of time down here over the next few months because summer break is coming up,'' Katherine said. ''I could supervise all of the renovations personally... if, of course, this is something you want.''

''Want!'' Marsha exclaimed. ''It's too good to be true.''

''No joke,'' Barbara said. ''It'd be like a dream come true, not having to keep shuffling the kids around like hot potatoes.''

''That's the problem,'' Sadie chimed in. ''It sounds kind of pipe-dreamish.''

''Not really,'' Lydia said. ''It will take a lot of construction and overhauling. Mr. Settle wasn't too sure about the kitchen's durability. There's some health hazards that would have to be looked into carefully. But the thing can be done.''

''Can be,'' Barbara mused. ''I hate to say it, Katherine, but if you want to know the truth, you're going to have a hell of a time getting past the resistance.''

''Resistance? But you like the idea, don't you?''

''Sure,'' said Sadie. There was a pregnant pause, and then she added, ''but my husband isn't going to.''

Suddenly a babble of raised voices erupted into the formerly quiet gathering. All the wives present were sure they wouldn't get any support from the men of Greensdale for such a project. Apparently it was already common knowledge in town that the Taylor sisters were planning to give the town council a hard time. The men wanted ConCo in. "Tom said he wouldn't mind seeing someone just drop a bomb on the Taylor place and be done with it," Barbara confided, then she added, seeing Katherine's shocked expression, "but he didn't really mean it. He's just been out of sorts..."

"...since he's been out of work," Marsha finished. "You see, that's the thing, Katherine. None of us women would have to be holding down jobs ourselves if the factory in Jefferson hadn't closed. But we've had to go out and find, well, anything, as a stopgap. I'm a part-time supermarket cashier."

"I had to break out my old RN uniform," Barbara said.

"Anyway," Marsha continued. "If we had a new chemical plant in town we wouldn't *need* a day-care center. We could go back to the way things were before."

"In a pig's eye." Emily was rising from her chair. "Come on, ladies! How many times have I heard each and every one of you confess that you didn't mind working for a living, being out of the house, having something to do instead of full-time house cleaning? If all of our husbands were suddenly pulling in their old salaries, would you really want to stop working, just like that?"

"I would," Marsha said dryly, and immediately a loud debate was raging over Emily's point.

But in the end the women conceded that whether their men were employed or not, a day-care center would be a welcome addition to the community. Besides, if ConCo didn't build in Greensdale proper, rumor had it they'd be building in Red Springs, a neighboring town within commuting distance. It wasn't a clear-cut case of choosing day care versus jobs.

"I think it sounds like a really nice idea," Barbara Wainright said, when the last coffee refills were being downed.

"I agree," said Sadie. "Though why you'd want to go to all this trouble when your own daughter's already out of college and out of town, I don't know," she said. The other women nodded. Katherine had been expecting a comment like this. She knew from talking to Emily that if there was anything the Greensdale women wouldn't take to, it was charity. She wanted to make sure they didn't think she was doing this thing to assuage some kind of snobbish liberal guilt.

"I'll be honest with you," she said quietly. "My mother loved living here in Greensdale. We don't want to let this house go, but we can't see living in it ourselves. Bringing children into it is something Grammy would've approved of. I'm doing this as much as a memorial to her as I'm doing it for your kids."

The women nodded as the meaning of her words sank in. From the yard they could hear the squeals and laughter from a game of tag in progress. For a moment they all seemed to be listening to the children play, and it seemed to Katherine that was a sound more eloquently convincing than anything.

Then one after another, excuses were being made; mothers had chores to do, and within minutes the meeting was dissolved. Emily helped Katherine clear the parlor while Lydia took a long-distance call. Apparently a few of her pet sanctuary terriers had come down with the flu. Katherine was wrist deep in sink suds when it occurred to her that the women had been vague about setting up another meeting. She wondered suddenly if things had gone as well as she'd assumed.

"I thought they seemed very interested. Didn't you, Emily?"

Emily shrugged, wrapping up the leftovers. "They're interested but they don't believe it," she said.

"Why not?" She turned to gaze at Emily, offended in spite of herself. "Why would we go to all this trouble if we weren't really planning to do this thing?"

"Don't take it the wrong way, Katherine, but talk is easy. I know Marsha and Sadie, and they may not be from Missouri, but Show Me is definitely their slogan."

"Well, we'll just have to show them, then," Katherine said, frowning. "Though I thought that's what I was doing."

"It's a start," Emily said gently. "But these are very independent women with strong opinions. You can't expect to corral them together in one fell swoop and have them on your side."

"Why wouldn't they want to be?—" She stopped herself. "Okay, I hear you. What do you think I should do?"

"Just go on doing what you're doing," Emily told her. "And keep after them. After a while, if they see you're really serious, they'll start to come around. Although Sadie'll have a problem on her hands."

"She wasn't serious about what her husband said, was she?"

"George says worse things when he's in the mood," Emily said with a knowing air. She looked up, feeling Katherine's curious gaze. "Well, what do you expect?" As Katherine didn't answer, she looked at her in surprise. "Katherine, the man's an alcoholic."

"I didn't know."

"You didn't?" Emily masked her incredulity, concentrating on wrapping up the last few cookies. "Well, of course it was the accident that did it."

"Accident?"

Now Emily turned to face her, shaking her head in wonderment. "Katherine Taylor, did you grow up in this town, or what?"

Katherine sighed. "I did and I didn't, I guess," she admitted. "Emily, I think you ought to give me a crash course in the Greensdale Who's Who."

Emily nodded. "Better late than never," she said. "Well, let's see. You know that Betty was married to the chief of police, the one who ended up going to jail himself?"

"Betty? Who was sitting right in there?" Katherine shook her head helplessly. "I'd better get a pad and paper," she said.

"YOU WOULDN'T BELIEVE the things that have gone on in this town," Katherine said. "It's better than television."

"Anything's better than television, according to you," Lydia reminded her, looking at her watch. "Well, I've got about two minutes. Calm down!" This last was directed at the rabbits in her carrier.

Katherine nodded. "Are you looking forward to going back?"

Lydia was en route to checking her bags through at the airport. "I guess," she replied. "But I'm sorry to leave."

"I'm sorry you're going," Katherine said. "I wish we could be spending more time together."

"Well, you've got your work up in Amherst, and I have my business to take care of in New York," Lydia said. "But if you think about it, we've seen more of each other over the past three weeks than we usually do in a year."

"And you'll be back next weekend," Katherine reminded her.

"Of course," Lydia said, smiling. "Sis, we're going to be sticking a lot closer from now on. I guess even the saddest of circumstances can have some happy results."

"You're right." Katherine opened her arms to envelop her sister in a warm hug. The loudspeaker above them was announcing that Lydia's flight to New York was ready for boarding. She gave her a final squeeze and let go.

"We're going to run up a nice big phone bill, right?" Lydia said. "I want you to keep me on top of every little thing."

"Absolutely," Katherine assured her. "I'll let you know as soon as we get that second estimate on the house."

"I'll phone you tomorrow," Lydia called, already backing toward the counters. One furry rabbit ear poked incongruously out of the carrier in her hand. "Go on, Sis, you're double-parked!" Lydia blew her a last kiss and waved goodbye.

Katherine turned away, feeling a sudden shaft of forlornness pierce her. She'd been getting used to Lydia's presence. It was going to be truly strange to have her go back to being three thousand miles away in San Francisco.

But Lydia was right. They had gotten a lot closer, she mused, walking back to her car in the lot. Working on the project together, they'd be in constant contact from now on. Lydia had even arranged to come back at the summer's end, to help supervise the organization of the Taylor Center, as they'd taken to calling it. Clarissa was excited about their project, too, and if she could get her own life in order by then she hoped to join them in Greensdale as well.

Thinking about that, reunions and the future, was comforting as she began the long drive back to town. Because the in-between wasn't going to be easy. She was going to face a hostile town council, oversee a major renovation at Grammy's and then begin the complicated business of establishing the center. Any thoughts she'd had a scant month or so ago about a leisurely summer vacation in Europe seemed truly ludicrous to her now.

And then there was Peter. She'd managed to avoid running into him in Greensdale so far, but she knew seeing him again was inevitable. When she'd left his friend's cottage the weekend before, she'd promised to call him when she got to town, but she'd put it off. After the meeting with Emily and her friends there'd been a conference with Mr. Stuart. Last night she and Lydia had stayed home packing up a few things to send ahead to Lydia's, and the items Clarissa wanted in NYC.

But here it was Sunday afternoon, and news of the Taylor sister's plan had undoubtedly spread around Greensdale. What would his reaction be? She half expected to see him seated on Grammy's front steps when she returned, perhaps with fellow town council members and a bucket of tar and feathers. But no, he wouldn't be like that. If he was sincerely interested in her for herself, he'd be understanding. Wouldn't he?

Walking into the house she was struck by the stillness. With Emily and Lydia gone, it was the first time she'd been totally alone there. Katherine stood for a moment in the middle of the living room, listening to the soft steady creaking of the mechanism in the old grandfather clock in the corner.

Never did get it oiled, she heard Grammy say. *What a royal nuisance of a noisemaker!*

You just like to complain about it, she answered.

Well, that's true enough, said Grammy. *If I can't complain at my age, what else can I do?*

Katherine smiled. If she didn't turn around, she could picture Grammy in the rocking chair behind her, rocking and nearsightedly tearing through the newspaper as she often had on Sundays.

Grammy, am I doing the right thing?

About which? This nice thing for the children, or the other, for yourself?

The other?

That young man! He's got a bit of a wild streak, but then so do you, thank heavens. I can't see why you always try to deny it.

The phone rang. Katherine went to answer, and knew who it would be before she picked up the receiver.

"Professor Taylor," said a familiar voice.

"I had a feeling it might be you," she answered.

"I have a feeling I'm being avoided," Peter said.

The sound of his voice in her ear was disconcerting, so close and resonant. "I've been busy," she said uneasily. "In fact, I just walked in the door."

"Have I done something wrong?" he asked congenially. "Or are you playing hard to get?"

"No to both questions, Peter," she said. "I...though maybe we might see each other the next time I'm back here in Greensdale." *If you still want to, once this day-care center is officially underway,* she added mentally.

"You're coming back soon?"

"In another ten days, I think," she said. "That's when my summer vacation starts."

"I'll live, I guess," he said wryly. "But tell me, honestly was my pesto that bad?"

"No," she said, smiling.

"The salad, then? Or was it my aquatic etiquette?"

That was closer to the mark, but she sidestepped him "It's a busy time for me, that's all."

"So I hear," he said, after a pause. Ah, so he knew Katherine steeled herself for whatever might be coming. "I hear you've been busier with plans for your house than I thought."

"This has all come together very quickly," she began defensively. "It's just an idea Lydia and I—"

"You knew you were having this meeting when we had dinner last weekend," he said. "Why didn't you tell me then?"

"It seemed we were both making it a point not to discuss business," she said guiltily.

"True," he said. "I guess I just wish you'd been able to trust me a little more."

"I'm sorry," she said, the words awkward on her tongue. "Maybe it was wrong of me, but I didn't see the point in provoking an argument."

"Might've been more like an illuminating discussion," he said lightly. "Look, Katherine, now that things are more out in the open, I've got to be honest with you. You're going to get some opposition to this project of yours, and I'm going to be part of that opposition."

"That's what I assumed." She was relieved to be talking openly about it. She was also getting a sinking feeling in the pit of her stomach.

"But if you also assumed I wouldn't want to see you again because of it you're dead wrong," he went on. "I like seeing you," he added. "If you don't mind my saying so."

Again, his directness disarmed her. "Well, no, I don't mind," she said guardedly. "You've been okay company, yourself."

Peter chuckled. "I'll take that as high praise. But where do we go from here?"

"Where indeed?"

"The way I see it, we've both got very strong opinions about this thing. You and your sister think the town would be better served by having a day-care center. I think a ConCo plant is what we really need."

"That's about the size of it."

"But we're two intelligent people and I'd like to think we're equally open-minded," he continued. "Now, maybe if we shared those opinions with each other, and had a chance to examine them..."

"I think I hear the lawyer in you talking," she said.

"True," he said. "But hear me out. There's no need for the two of us to be enemies. I'd been feeling we were becoming friends."

Friends? She supposed she could see it that way, if one were to ignore the definitely erotic charge she'd felt when he'd started to kiss her in the lake that night. Had he felt nothing at all? The idea gave her a dispirited feeling.

"We could even be closer than we are," he added. Was he reading her thoughts? "But having this difference of opin-

ion between us has made me more comfortable keeping
little distance. How about you?''

"Yes," she said, her spirits lifting again. His practice
way of smoothing over a touchy situation may have bee
lawyerlike, but it was impressive. "That's how it's been fo
me."

"Well, look, why don't we get together and talk abou
this thing?" he said. "No hidden agendas, no ulterior mo
tives—just the start of a friendly dialogue. Does that hav
any appeal?"

"It might," she said, smiling at his carefully couche
formality.

"Good! When are you free?"

"For what?" she asked carefully.

"Pure business," he said. "And philosophy. Let's say I'n
challenging you to a debate."

THE LAST WEEK OF WORK at Hampshire wasn't easy to ge
through. Her excitement over the Taylor House projec
wasn't the only distraction. Headed for the library with a
armful of overdue books, she found that although she'
successfully avoided Peter in person, he was still vividly wit
her in her mind. It was as if his seductive smile and twin
kling eyes had taken up a temporary corner in her con
sciousness, along with his husky voice whispering insidiou
suggestions.

*How can you be going into that dark library on such
sunny day?* the voice asked. *Wouldn't you rather go for
swim?*

Swim? She paused midcampus, staring at the library she'
just passed by. Since when had she ever even considere
going swimming in the middle of a working day? Since Pe
ter Bradford had insinuated himself into her life, and thoug
she knew it was silly to daydream about the man, sh
couldn't help it.

Friday came, and with it, gloriously sunny weather tha
made spending more than a minute cooped up with school

work seem insane. She kept checking her watch as she went through the last of her remaining grades. He hadn't really specified a time, but she figured she had an hour to kill before lunch. How would things have been if she'd really been infatuated with the man? She'd be a nervous wreck.

So what was she, now? In control, as always. Sensible, as she should be. Sighing, she filled in the final form of the term, then rose thankfully to her feet, nudging a dozing Winkie out from under the table. "We're done," she told him.

Katherine was taking a stroll across the quad when she noticed the blue convertible pulled up at curbside. And there he was: mischievous glint in his bright blue eyes, full lips curved in a sensuous smile, the golden-tanned skin on his inordinately handsome face gleaming. His trim torso was encased in a tight white jersey that revealed lean muscles in his downy forearm as he swung open the car door for her.

Business and philosophy, she reminded herself. "You're early," she said.

"Actually, I think I got here just in time. Your tan's already starting to fade," he observed with a frown.

"Academic life," she said wryly.

"Time to leave it behind," he announced. "We've got another perfectly beautiful day. Although Mr. Weatherman is predicting cool breezes later in the afternoon, so you'd better pack a sweater."

"Pack? I thought we were just having lunch."

"We are." His smile was mischievous. "But I've picked a real scenic spot for our great debate. No musty classrooms. The great outdoors."

"Back to your island?"

"Nope. Up to my mountain."

KATHERINE TAYLOR looked good in boots, he observed. Apparently she looked good in anything. At the moment, attired in pleated khaki pants and a simple pink button-down blouse, sweater tied round her waist, walking on the path ahead of him in the hiking boots he'd requested she bring, she reminded him of a "great white huntress" from an old Tarzan movie. She certainly had the requisite shiny blond hair and the easy, sensual stride such a role required.

"Tired?" he asked.

"No," she said, shooting him a defiant look over her shoulder. "But exactly how high is this mountain of yours?"

"We're not going for the summit," he assured her. "Just a little farther up the trail. And it's not really 'my' mountain," he admitted. "I just call it that because my dad and I used to hike around here a lot when I was a kid."

"Is this a place you take a lot of dates to?"

He could tell by the lilt in her tone that she was teasing, but he didn't mind. "Actually, you're the first," he said.

"I'm honored." She sidestepped a large tree root, then paused, looking back at him. "You're sure you don't want me to carry any of that?"

"I'm the pack horse, this trip," he said.

"What's in there, anyway?"

"Food, drink, first aid and snakebite kit..."

"What?!"

"Don't worry, it's just my Boy Scout training. Always bring provisions for any eventuality. I've got a couple of ponchos if it rains, too." And the papers he'd brought to discuss with her. "Let's bear left at that fork up ahead."

He moved ahead of her again to lead the way. She was being a good sport to go on this little hike with him. He'd been meaning to make his annual pilgrimage up the low side of Mount Toby by himself, but once he'd gotten Katherine to agree to a date, it occurred to him she might enjoy it.

He was certainly enjoying it more than usual. Even the fact that the sun was fast disappearing behind an unwelcome bank of clouds didn't dispel the beauty of the day when she was in the midst of it. The woods smelled pungently of pine and oak as they wound their way beneath a canopy of green. "Trail mix?" He held out the packet of nuts and dried fruit to her but Katherine demurred.

"I'm supposed to be saving my appetite, right?"

"Right. Okay, look out for those low branches. We're just going down this path to the overlook. Watch your step..."

The trail took a sudden curve around a bend, and Peter was rewarded with a gasp of appreciation from Katherine as a breathtaking vista of purple mountains rising above the valley below came into view. "My God," she murmured. "They make this thing we're on look like a little hill."

"It is, at this elevation," he said.

"They really are purple," she observed. "The mountain majesties, I mean."

"Just like they wrote it," he agreed, and they stood in silence a moment, basking in the glory of it. A silver snake of river glinted far below them, then seemed to disappear as the sun faded again through a sheen of graying clouds. Peter looked around him for some dead branches. The descent from here was a bit steep. In a moment, he'd fashioned a piece of oak into a good walking stick for Katherine. After foraging out one for himself, he led the way down the trail.

"Here we are," he announced, when they reached the clearing. A simple stone bench had been constructed by the trailblazers, specifically as a resting place for travelers who wanted to take in the mountainside scenery. It was one of his favorite places on the mountain, and he was happy to see no other hikers had beat them to it.

The beauty of the spot seemed to leave Katherine open-mouthed. For a while conversation was suspended as he got out the fruit salad, cheese and cold cuts, and uncorked the bottle of wine. Seeing the folder at the bottom of the pack he took it out as well. He'd stalled talking about the two appraisals long enough.

It was while he was trying to think of some suitable way into the subject that Katherine came at it herself, from left

field. "I wonder if my mother's been here," she said, gaze
fixed on the valley.

"Here?" he repeated, bemused. "Why?" By now, he
expected to be surprised by Katherine. You could rarely tell
by looking at her face where her mind might be moving to.
That was one of the things that made her a fascination to
him, the perpetual motion of her mind. But in this instance
she'd lost him.

"Grammy was a walker," Katherine said. "In fact she
hated cars, trains, never flew in an airplane in her entire life.
She used to walk everywhere in Greensdale, even the three
miles to the railroad station. And I remember that she and
Father used to take little hikes into the Appalachians. At
least she told me they had."

"Then it's possible, I guess."

Katherine nodded, looking around the small clearing with
renewed interest. "I can just see her setting off on that trail
we were on, wearing one of those funny sun hats of hers."
She smiled, shaking her head. "And I'm sure she would've
enjoyed a walking stick like this. She was fond of canes.
There's a whole collection of them back at the house."

She didn't sound as sad as she had before, talking about
her mother. Peter intuited she was getting used to the idea
that the old woman was gone, and seeing his opening,
plunged in. "Have you made plans about what to do with
them, and the rest of your family heirlooms?" he asked. "I
figure if you're planning on renovations, things like a cane
collection might be in the way."

Katherine looked at him, a faint smile playing at the edges
of her lips. "I sense the beginning of our great outdoor debate," she said wryly. "To answer your question, yes, Lydia and I have been trying to figure out who gets what and
what goes where. We'll have to rent some storage space, of
course."

"You want to clear out the whole downstairs, don't
you?"

"All but the sun parlor and the back entrance area. We want to shut that off from the downstairs proper. There's a back staircase that can be part of the separate entrance to the second floor."

"The same staircase that goes down to the basement?"

"That's right," she said and then narrowed her eyes. "How did you know that?"

"I have a confession to make," he told her, taking the folder out of his pack. I've been looking at your house very carefully, inside and out, for the past three or four days."

"You might have asked," she said, sitting up straighter with an air of indignation. "How did you get in? Has Emily?—"

"Not in person," he said. "Here, look at this."

He removed the first stapled sheaf of papers and handed them to her. Katherine flipped through the blueprint pages and typed sheets, brow furrowed. "Where did you get this? It's not the one Mr. Nettles did for us."

"No, it was done by the firm of Holbrook and Groves about six years ago," he explained. "Your mother was having a problem with the pipes in the master bathroom upstairs and the overall plumbing of the house. She had an idea that some more modern system might be put in."

Katherine vaguely remembered Grammy's complaining about this some years back, but didn't recall anything coming of it. "But she didn't modernize," she said, gazing at Peter with a renewed wariness. "How did you get this appraisal?"

"It's a very small town," Peter said apologetically. "Your Mr. Nettles used to work for Holbrook. And when we looked around for someone who might give us a second opinion on your plans for the house, Holbrook came up with these."

"What is this, a CIA operation?" Katherine shook her head. "Who's 'we,' anyway?"

"Just me, Randy Morgan and some of his friends on the council," Peter said. "It's no conspiracy, Katherine. It's merely a few people who are concerned about what's best for the town."

"And that means snooping around behind our backs like this?" She brandished the papers at him. "What's the point, anyway?"

"Look, don't get offended, but whether you like it or not, you happen to be dealing with an issue here that's affecting the whole community," he said mildly. "All we did was get a look at that early estimate to see for ourselves what kind of work you might be facing if you went ahead with the day-care center."

"*When* we go ahead," she corrected him. "So, you've looked. See anything interesting? Skeletons in the base-boarding?"

Peter sighed. "Well, in a sense, yes."

Katherine's gaze was fixed and foreboding. "I'm all ears."

"What did Harry Settle say to you about the foundations of the house? Did he mention the water table, and the way the south end's been shifting over the years?"

"He said there might be some problems, yes," she allowed. "But nothing that couldn't be overcome."

"Did he talk to you about the dry rot in the basement beams?"

"It came up."

"Did he give you an estimate on making over the kitchen?"

"A preliminary figure, sure," she began. "But—"

"It's not just a replastering job. Did you know that the ceiling is about to give in, over by the stove and pantry area?"

"Is this a debate or a courtroom cross-examination?" she said.

"Sorry." Peter held up a placating hand. "I just wanted to see if you knew the full extent of what you were getting into."

"Yes," she said firmly, arms folded. "And it still doesn't change my mind." She was omitting, of course, the plethora of doubts that Settle's first estimates had brought up, and the long talks she, Lydia and Mr. Stuart had had about them. Ultimately, even though the evidence Settle had presented them made extensive renovations a fifty-fifty proposition, let alone costly, they'd decided to go through with their original plan.

"You know that the state's going to have to give your facility a clean bill of health in order for you to open it," he said quietly. "Do you really think you'll be able to make all the necessary improvements?" Katherine nodded. "And what about alienating half the population of Greensdale? You're going to need local support to make this thing work."

"Have you ever tried to get a core curriculum approved at a progressive university?" she countered. "Peter, I thrive on adversity. You'd better get used to it."

He smiled. "You're very winning when you dig your heels in." He wasn't being facetious. Katherine Taylor had spine, and he admired her all the more for it.

"Yes, that's what I'll be," she said. "Winning."

Peter took the sheaf of papers back, chuckling. "All right," he said. "Round One to Ms. Taylor."

"It was a snap," she said, eyes twinkling. He was glad to see that she hadn't lost her sense of humor over all this—yet. The sky was graying rapidly overhead. Peter stood, gathering the remains of their main courses into his pack.

"Almost ready for dessert?"

"Sure, if I can tear my eyes away from this view." She turned to face him. "It's a wonderful place, Peter. Thanks for bringing me up here, really."

"It's my pleasure." He removed the glossy ConCo prospectus from his folder, put it on the stone bench and slid it toward her. "Why don't you give that a quick perusal before we move on?"

"Round two, so soon?" she murmured, but picked up the brightly colored folder. She flipped through the slick prospectus, with its photos of ultramodern industrial buildings nestled in immaculately landscaped greenery. ConCo had these plants down to a science, of course. They were small, pleasing to the eye in the pictures, and graphics stressed the efforts taken to have all facilities blend in with the existing topography.

She could feel Peter watching her as she read on. But then, she'd been conscious of the nearness of him all day, whether he was looking at her or not. And far from being ill at ease, she was enjoying it. Whatever differences there were between them didn't seem to matter. There was still an insidious, subtle tension of another kind that made her aware of his every move and gesture, and he seemed to react with the same attentiveness.

She'd been staring at the same page too long. Self-conscious, she shut the folder abruptly and met his inquisitive gaze. "I'll have to give it a more thorough going-over," she said.

"Did you look at this last section?" He sat beside her, leaning over to turn a few pages. "Here's a plant they built in Ohio—with a large playroom for the employees' children."

"I see," she said noncommittally.

"ConCo might be willing to allot space for a similar facility."

She shrugged. "That's nice, but . . ."

"Food for thought?"

"Not really," she said, refusing to give an inch. Then she realized he was referring to a container in his hand. "Oh." She smiled. "Well, if it really is food—"

"You like strawberries," he said, opening it. "How about fresh raspberries? Handpicked," he added. "From my backyard this morning."

"They look great," she said, and took a few gleaming berries from the handful he held out. They broke on her tongue with bittersweet freshness. She caught the look in Peter's eye as she savored the taste and sensed his pleasure at her own. It suddenly occurred to her that the man had gone to a great deal of trouble on her account. Planning this little trip, handpicking berries, no less, showed a thoughtfulness that had nothing to do with arguing a debate.

"Bringing her out of herself," that was how Clarissa had put it. That was what he was doing, all right, enabling her to enjoy some simple things, like a walk in the woods, with no thought to how she was supposed to act or who she was supposed to be. And he was doing all of this in spite of the fact that she was stubbornly refusing to go along with his proposals for her property.

She watched Peter's strong, slender fingers pop a few berries into his mouth. His eyes met hers. "Sorry I didn't hand-churn any whipped cream," he joked.

"That's quite all right," she said. "These are the best berries I've ever tasted." She was surprised at the vehemence in her own voice, but it was heartfelt. Peter smiled, and Katherine suddenly felt supremely self-conscious. She looked down at her fingertips, stained purple-red with juice. What exactly was woods etiquette? she wondered, napkinless.

"Here." The man had thought of everything. Peter was already holding a small white towel over a canteen. He handed her the moist cloth. When they'd both wiped their hands clean, he reshouldered their pack. "Ready to walk off that meal?"

She nodded, stick in hand. "Where to?"

"There's a couple of nice spots not far from here," he said, indicating the way back to the trail. "Now that you've had some food for thought, maybe you're ready for Round Two."

She looked at him blankly, then remembered. "Oh, yes, the great outdoors debate," she said with a little sigh.

"Unless you'd rather shelve the discussion until later…?"

"No, no, let's keep talking," she said, joining him on the path. Talking was actually a good idea. Because the more time she spent in the proximity of Peter Bradford, the less things cerebral appealed to her. So they'd agreed to keep things between them strictly business. But if she wasn't careful, one of the selves he was "bringing out" in her was going to be very ready for activation: a very physical self, that wanted to be touched in ways that had little to do with business at all….

Chapter Six

"We're not talking about token employment. We're talking about a job *force*," Peter was saying, as they strode leisurely down the trail. "Over a hundred slots, a hundred opportunities for men who've been living in unemployment limbo."

"I understand that ConCo's second choice is only twenty miles southeast of Greensdale," Katherine said. "If there are that many job openings, why can't Greensdale men apply for them there?"

"They can commute," Peter allowed. "But they'll be competing for each job. And it's not only the jobs. It's the business ConCo will bring into Greensdale from the outside. There'll be a boom in the local restaurant and food services, the motels . . . Just use your imagination."

"I have," she said, squinting at a root in the trail that looked suspiciously snakelike. "And that's the thing, Peter. What about quality of life? What if this big business boom you're talking about turns Greensdale into a whole different kind of community? Believe it or not, the women I've talked to actually like things pretty much the way they are."

"Maybe so, but ask their husbands if everyone's happy living in what amounts to a state of depression."

"Of course they're not," she admitted. "But if ConCo can build elsewhere and still put a lot of people in our town to work..."

"Why bother you about your property?" he finished. "It's what I've been trying to explain, Katherine. The larger picture."

"I can see your larger picture, Peter," she said calmly. "But it gives short shrift to two pretty significant special interest groups: the female population, and the children."

"No one's leaving them out," he protested. "A better economy benefits the whole family."

"Sounds like a political slogan," she said. "I have a thing about slogans. I automatically distrust oversimplifications."

"Touché," he said ruefully. "All right, I'll put a hold on all rhetoric for the time being." He suppressed a sigh, pace slowing, feeling an irritation that he knew wasn't directed at Katherine, but at himself. He was tired of arguing a position that he himself secretly had a few problems with. They'd gone over it from every angle now, and much as he hated to admit it, he was starting to see Katherine's point of view. How had he gotten into the middle of this?

He knew how. Randy Morgan's father and his had been old buddies, and though he and Randy had never been the closest friends, growing up in Greensdale, the ties still bound them. Which was why, when Peter had returned to the town, Randy had provided Peter with his first local case, talked him up to friends in local commerce, almost single-handedly helped him set up his practice. So when Randy asked for the occasional favor in return, Peter was naturally beholden.

This ConCo matter was one such favor. It wasn't the kind of litigation he'd ordinarily have been interested in doing. After all, in representing the town board in their initial negotiations with the corporation, he was acting more as a public relations go-between than as a lawyer. But for Randy's sake and the sake of the town, he'd taken it on. He just hadn't foreseen taking on the issue of the Taylor house—or the Taylor woman. Sure, it was fun matching wits with a bright and attractive adversary. But he was starting to wish they could be on the same side, and put the whole problem to bed.

To bed? Interesting choice of image, he mused, shaking his head. All afternoon he'd been finding it hard to concentrate on business when the nearness of Katherine kept bringing up memories of an elusive but vivid pleasure: the feel of her warm and vibrant body in his arms. Peter cleared his throat. "As I said earlier, ConCo can be persuaded to figure a day-care facility into their building plans. It's not in their proposed blueprint, but—"

"You're still talking to a stone wall, Peter," Katherine interrupted. "We're not letting go of the house."

They stopped on the path, squaring off face-to-face. The look in her luminous eyes was fierce. Peter held her gaze for a moment, noting that the defiant upward tilt of her face certainly did give her a stonelike demeanor. "I think I hear the bell," he said wryly. "Round Two goes to Ms. Taylor."

Her thrusting chin went down, the tightened lips relaxing in a friendly smile. "So we're even," she said lightly.

"You mean stalemated," he said. "Back to zero."

"No, we're back to nature, and I'm very happy to be here," she said playfully. "Only I hope you know where we're headed."

"In a larger sense, I haven't the slightest," he said. "But for the moment, I thought you might enjoy a little ride."

"Piggyback?" Her eyes twinkled. "Thanks for the offer. How did you know my ankles were about to give out?"

"I'm talking about a ride on that." Peter pointed ahead. In a clearing to the right of the trail she saw two ropes hanging from a huge old elm.

"A swing!" Katherine brushed past him to get a better look. It was a makeshift business formed from the side of a wooden crate. "Did you know this was here?"

"I ought to," he said. "My dad and I built it, some twenty years ago." He was taking off his pack. "Come on, I'll hoist you up."

"Wait," she protested. "Twenty years! What if it doesn't hold?"

"Well, then you go flying off through the trees and into the valley," he said. "Hey, it's a nice way to meet your maker."

"Very funny," she said. "There's no way I'm—hold it!"

Before she could stop him, he was lifting her into the air. "I'm holding," he muttered, and unceremoniously deposited her on the wooden swing.

"Seriously, is it safe?" Her heart was pounding from the sudden ascent and his confident grip on her waist. Peter tugged at the rope with his other hand, testing its strength.

"Absolutely," he said, and the next thing she knew, she was airborne. She let out a little yelp, the adrenaline rushing through her body as her feet swooped up before her. Back she came to his firm hands, and with another gentle push she was swinging forward again. Dizzy, she watched the ground sweep out from beneath her.

"This is . . . oooh," was all she could say.

"You literature professors have a way with words." Chuckling softly behind her, Peter gave her another push.

By the time her toes were clearing the treetops she was able to relax and enjoy the sight of the gray sky coming to meet her and falling away. She also enjoyed the return to Peter's touch at her back each time she swung back.

"Enough?"

"I suppose," she said, though after several glorious minutes she wished she could just remain suspended in the green and gray like that. Peter slowed the swing. Then his strong arms were encircling her as he lifted her from the wooden seat. Katherine clung to him instinctively, still dizzy as the world seemed to keep turning around them.

She tried to focus, and found herself staring into his glimmering blue eyes. His face was close to hers, and her body seemed to tingle at his touch. "Put me down," she breathed, though she couldn't say she minded being held like this.

"Are you sure?" he teased. She could feel his warm breath on her face, feel her own heart pounding quickly against his chest. The forest, no longer blurred, was coming back into focus around her, but his embrace was almost as dizzying as the swing.

"I'm sure," she murmured, though she wasn't. There was a soft sound like a rise in the wind as he smiled, slowly lowering her to her feet. Peter was suddenly looking up. A splatter of water on her forehead made her follow his gaze. The gray of the sky was rapidly turning darker. As suddenly as the flick of a switch, rain was trickling through the treetops.

"We'd better get a move on," he said, hurriedly shouldering his pack. "This way."

She let Peter pull her after him, still feeling dizzy from the swing and the excitement of his embrace. "Where are we going?"

"Shelter," he called over his shoulder. "Let's make a run for it."

They jogged down the trail, as distant thunder sounded and the rain increased, the drops coming harder and faster. In what seemed like an instant the woods around them were dark as dusk, and a strange, greenish glow lit the sky ahead. She concentrated on her footing, nearly stumbling once but saved by Peter's deft hand.

Just as the rain was beginning to pour down in earnest, they reached another clearing. There was a rustic lean-to made of logs. Katherine dashed beneath its dripping eaves. The wind had risen, whipping rain inside and she huddled against one wall. Peter was rapidly covering the dirt and pine needle floor with the ponchos from his pack. On top of them he began laying out a colorful quilted blanket.

"Prepared for anything, like I said," he told her, meeting her questioning gaze. "Here, wrap this around you!"

He handed her a second blanket, his words almost drowned by the now torrential downpour. Katherine clambered down beside him, thankful for the softness of the quilt beneath her. Peter gathered the blanket round her shoulders, huddling against the wall. She looked out, wide-eyed, as the rain became a solid sheet before them. Lightning flashed, vividly illuminating the surrounding trees.

"The great outdoors, eh?" she shouted in his ear.

Peter laughed, his arm around her as the wind rose with body-chilling force. "Just a light shower," he joked, then winced as a clap of thunder sounded, so loudly she nearly jumped.

"College Professor Perishes in Lightning Storm," she mumbled, shivering. "What fun."

"Oh, don't worry about lightning," he said, massaging her shaking shoulders. Her shivers were turning to erotic trembles at the sure touch of his supple fingers. She realized she should be telling him to stop, but it felt too good. "If you want to worry about anything," he continued, "worry about the bears."

"Bears?!"

"Well, if you were a bear, wouldn't you be looking for a lean-to in weather like this?" She turned to stare at him and saw the grin lighting up his face. "Just kidding," he assured her. "Relax."

Relax? Good luck! Huddled against him beneath the blanket, a willful prisoner in his warm arms, with a thunderstorm raging only a scant yard beyond her nose, how was she supposed to relax? It was pitch-black beyond the silvery sheet of rain. Another blinding flash of lightning made her clutch at Peter's arm. He smoothed her hair, murmuring reassurance as the thunderclap followed, seeming to shake the rafters.

"You and your big ideas," she muttered.

"Sorry you came?"

"No," she admitted, aware that every nerve in her body was responding to his closeness, the feel of his arm around her, the touch of his hand at her hair. "This wasn't at all what I had in mind, though," she said. "When we agreed to talk, I mean."

She could see his eyes in the darkness and knew he was reading the extra meanings in her words. "I didn't plan on a thunderstorm," he said mildly. "Would you feel more comfortable if I sat on the opposite side of the lean-to?"

"No," she said, too quickly, and saw the glimmer of his teeth as he smiled. "But Peter..." The words died on her tongue. She'd forgotten whatever protest she'd been about to make, distracted by the slow, soft caress of his fingers smoothing the hair back from her forehead as the thunder rumbled again.

"But what?" he asked softly.

The litany of objections failed to materialize in her mind. Yes, they were supposed to keep each other at arm's length. Yes, she shouldn't be giving in to what could only be a superficial, physical attraction to a man who, yes, was younger, not her type, arguably opportunistic— But, no. It wasn't superficial. And all the other reasons were seeming all the more meaningless. Nonetheless some protest had to be registered. Didn't it?

"We really shouldn't be doing this," she managed, even as she instinctively shifted her weight to lean more comfortably against him, her head falling back into the crook of his shoulder.

"You're right." His voice was a husky murmur, warm and breathy by her ear. "What would you like to do instead?"

His fingers grazed her cheek now, the soft palm gently caressing her softer skin. *Keep talking,* she thought, but no words came. She was too busy feeling everything, the faint spray of rain on her upturned face, the warmth of his body wrapped around hers, the desire that his touch was kindling in the very core of her. "I think..." she whispered.

"...too much," he finished for her. "We've both been thinking too much and talking too much...when there's something good going on between us that isn't about words."

She couldn't deny it. She wanted nothing more than to feel his lips on hers again, to revel in the supple strength of him enfolding her. "I know," she whispered, her hand slipping up to take his beneath the blanket.

"Professor," he said softly. "Let's call this debate on account of bad weather...."

"And spend a little time getting better acquainted?" she suggested, her own voice husky with arousal.

"Now you're talking," he said, and his lips came slowly down to claim hers. She stroked the soft bristly skin of his chin as their kiss deepened, her fingertips tingling, heat stealing through her body. Peter was slowly pulling her closer. She moved to fit herself more snugly against him, eyes closed, the rain loud in her ears. Her heartbeat was even louder as with a tender urgency his tongue gently searched the moistness of her mouth, finding her tongue, drinking in the sweetness as she savored the taste of him. She could detect the faint scent of castile soap mingled with the smell of wood and rain on his skin.

Giving herself over to his embrace was like melting. When his lips left hers to plant feathery kisses down the line of her neck she clung to him still, her mouth parted in a soundless moan of pleasure. When the lightning flashed again, she saw it through half-parted eyes and a dizzy haze of desire.

"Kath," he murmured, head nestled in the hollow of her shoulder. "Do you still think this is a bad idea?"

"No," she whispered. "To tell you the truth, I'm starting to forget why we weren't supposed to do this."

"That's excellent," he said. She could feel his voice vibrating against her flesh as he pressed his lips to the pulse at her throat. "Then I guess I won't stop...."

Stop? It was much too late. She ran her hands up his sides, feeling his firmness through the shirt's cotton. Realizing that before long he'd be removing that shirt, baring that chest, made her ache with expectation. The speed of her own arousal left her a little breathless. It was so unlike the way it had been with...

The specter of Jeffrey was suddenly hovering there, as she might have expected. But with sudden clarity she felt any unnecessary guilt fall away. This was so different, *he* was so different that comparisons seemed ludicrous.

She'd never felt this kind of desire with Jeffrey, she knew, because he hadn't really known how to draw it out of her. In fact, for all his sensitivity and knowledge, the experienced older man she'd married had been at best an affectionate but perfunctory lover. Of course, at first she'd assumed she was the one at fault, the naive virgin with only the littlest schooling in the art of love.

But as honeymoon gave way to a rarely spontaneous ritual of weekly lovemaking, she'd begun to realize that Jeffrey wasn't really all that interested in sex. He loved her, yes, and did his best to please her, but something about the romantic and literary bent of his mind resisted probing the deeper levels of physical love. Where she wanted to explore, he tended to withdraw. When she needed to prolong, he often lost his patience.

She'd reconciled herself to a bedroom life that struck her as ultimately unsatisfactory because she was in love with the man's mind and the sweetness of his soul. But she'd known for years, with a sometimes painful longing, that there was more to feel, more to experience. At the bottom line, Jef-

frey had been an old-fashioned, prudish man who never allowed himself to let go.

But she could already sense that Peter had no such reti-
cence. The way he was moving sensuously against her now,
the way his fingers seemed to delight in savoring each inch
of newly revealed skin as his hand played at the buttons of
her blouse, the urgent warmth of his lips against hers—all
of him signaled an openness and a desiring of her that made
her feel anything but inhibited.

"I could use some more lightning," he murmured, gazing up at her as his fingers deftly undid another button. "I'd
like to see more of you."

As if in heavenly answer to his request, lightning did flash
just then, and they both laughed. Impulsively she hugged
him to her, sliding down beneath the blanket to mold her
body against his. He found her lips again and this time she
arched herself against him with genuine abandon.

She felt desperate for the taste of him, for the exquisite
pleasure she felt when their tongues touched, when the soft
curves of her body molded themselves to his. No longer
concerned with rights, wrongs, do's or don'ts, she gave
herself over to the spiraling, reckless feeling of overwhelming excitement.

Returning his kiss with a breathless fervor, her arms slid
up to encircle his back, hands restlessly feeling the hard lines
of his shoulders. Peter fitted her to him beneath the blanket, a soft moan or arousal escaping his mouth as their
thighs and hips aligned in even more exquisite tightness.
"Kath," he breathed.

"Oh, Peter," she whispered back. "Why've we been
spending all our time keeping distance?"

"Temporary insanity." He chuckled deep in his throat.
"And now we've come to our senses."

He drew himself up on one elbow, one of his hands slipping beneath her shirt, gliding over the tingling nakedness

of her taut belly, caressing her hip, stealing over the soft skin of her back.

"That feels . . . heavenly . . . ," she murmured.

"Yes," he agreed. "You *do* feel heavenly. . . ." His fingertips glided over her lace-encased breasts, seeking the clasp of her brassiere. She could feel their tips swell with the anticipation of his touch. Shivers of arousal shook her as his lips, moist with the taste of her, left her lips to kiss and nibble a path to the hollow of her neck.

Katherine heard her breath come ragged and gasping as his hand glided upward, thumb tantalizingly grazing the swell of one breast. She wanted to feel his hand cup the soft mound, knowing that he'd touch her there with the surest, most satisfyingly of caresses.

Desire overtook her and she went with it, drinking in the taste of him, letting his arms encircle her, the dampness of their skins irrelevant to the heat rising up from within their melding bodies. When he lifted his mouth from hers at last, having savored and seduced every pore of her mouth into vibrant, tingling awareness, his fingers lingered over her hair, brushing a wet lock back from her cheek as he gazed at her.

Time seemed suspended. Her heart kept pounding, her breath short and ragged. "You don't know how tough it's been, not holding you," he murmured. "You could drive a man crazy, you know . . . being so desirable and distant at the same time."

"I haven't been trying to drive you crazy," she protested. *You're the one who should really be off limits,* she thought. Getting involved with Peter was bound to create problems, but she refused to think about them now, feeling a quiver of awakening arousal course through her as his forefinger gently traced the line of her cheek. Her fears were swept aside as the feeling deepened.

Her lips clamored for his kiss, already impatient to taste him again. He was driving her crazy by going so slowly.

Now *there* was a switch, after Jeffrey's impatience. Being the impatient one herself made her feel deliciously wanton. Her tongue stole out to wet her parted lips. Emboldened as she looked into the velvet depths of his eyes, she slowly guided his hand to close it gently over her breast, so he could feel the beating of her heart.

Peter let out a deep, shuddery breath. "I think we've been waiting so long it actually hurts," he murmured.

She nodded slowly. He smiled. Then his lips brushed hers with a feathery tenderness as his other arm stole around her. She felt herself arch back in his embrace as his lips found the tender hollow of her neck. Lightning danced on her half-closed eyelashes. Exquisite pleasure billowed up from deep inside her, spiraling still higher as his lips descended to the cleft between her breasts. A little growl rumbled in his throat as his fingers deftly cleared a path for his hungry lips, undoing the clasp there.

His lips sought and then found the rounded fullness of her breasts, tasting the trembling pale softness of her skin. Then, as she lay transported beneath him, he sat up, dark eyes drinking in her half nudity with a worshipful look.

"Let me see you," he whispered. "I've had only my imagination for days now...."

Transfixed, she let him guide her arms to her side, let him slide her open blouse and bra from her shoulders. His hands stole to her belt and she arched her back to help him slide the pants down her goose-bumped skin, shivering slightly in the wind and spray with more anticipation than cold.

Naked, she sighed with pleasure as his hand lightly circled the hardened tip of one breast, then traced a shivery path down her stomach. "Impossible," he muttered. "You're even more beautiful than I imagined you could be."

"Stop," she said, pleased, luxuriating in the tender touch and his awe-filled perusal. "Now you," she whispered, sitting up again and reaching out for him. Smiling, he watched her hands fly over his shirt buttons, tug at his trousers. In a few moments she was gazing at the sculpted, powerful contours of his body, the sexy thatch of hair descending to a flat trim belly, his rigid arousal.

Now it was she who slid her hands over his soft, moist skin, tracing patterns through the curls of hair on his chest, watching his nipples stiffen at her touch. Then, wordlessly, he guided her back down to the quilt, his eyes drinking in her nudity with a look of almost worshipful admiration.

Again his lips bestowed the lightest of kisses, on her forehead, nose, lips, chin. He kissed a glistening, shiver-provoking path between her breasts, over the curve of her belly. Then in a deliciously erotic slow motion that raised goose bumps on her skin, he traced a warm wet path down her trembling thighs.

She shook, tensed, relaxed and tensed again beneath the onslaught of delirious pleasure. He returned to kiss her lips, nose, cheeks.... Then, gaze locked in his, she stroked his taut belly, enjoying his shaky intake of breath as she explored each beautifully shaped plane and contour there.

"I think we're incredibly lucky," he breathed. "Lucky it happened to rain...that we happened to be here...."

"Lucky we came to our senses?" she teased.

A smile played round his lips as he drew her closer, and knelt before her, his tongue tracing the delicate whorl of her navel. He kissed a moist line to the edge of the curly hair below. Katherine shook with an arousal that seemed to inflame her every nerve ending. Inhibition was a word that obviously didn't exist for Peter Bradford, and she was overwhelmingly thankful for that.

"This is good?" he whispered.

"Better than good," she whispered back. This sensation was incredible to her. But even more so was the fact that he was talking to her, asking her what pleased her. Jeffrey had never talked during sex. But then Jeffrey had never been so knowing, so giving. So this was what she'd been missing....

The feel of Peter's lips gliding over each newly-kissed inch of her inner thighs was almost too much to bear. She shut her eyes, a low moan escaping her lips. Then, as her knees threatened to give way, he rose above her. She slid into his arms with a blissful feeling of return, gasping as she felt all of his supple length against her body.

Then they rolled together, Katherine astride him now, playfully struggling in his powerful grasp, a laugh bubbling up from deep inside her at the exhilarating release of such unbelievable tension. Pinning him beneath her...losing the mock battle to be caught by him again, until they laughed, panting in the darkness....

"Beats talking," he said, as his hands continued their leisurely exploration of her body. "Don't you think?"

"I...don't...think...," she breathed, twisting slowly beneath him, arousal coursing through her like a fiery wine in the blood.

"I'm in love with the feel of you," he whispered.

And I'm in love... she found herself thinking, and stopped the thought in its tracks. No thought, no word. Instead she covered his chest with a fiery trail of kisses, her fingers playing with the curly thatch of hair, then finding places to tickle and tease him into groans of arousal.

One kiss gave way to another. It seemed they wanted to devour each other. His luminous eyes glittered with passion as he slid his supple hands over her body in a ceaseless, endless caress. "Are you with me?" he whispered. "We're on our way."

Katherine couldn't answer this time. She could barely breathe, because his fingers had found the silken core of her, and were working an erotic magic there that made her body convulse. "I'm memorizing you, all of you," he murmured, nibbling sensuously at her earlobe. "Here," he breathed, capturing the taut rosy tip of one breast between his lips and teeth, tongue flicking and licking the sensitive skin until she cried out. "And here..."

His tongue returned to seek hers like a darting flame. His strong fingers slid over the small of her back, finding an exquisitely sensitive spot there to caress, then moving onward to cup her buttocks, gathering her tighter to him.

Her thighs parted beneath his. Lost in sheer ecstatic sensation, she clung to him, breasts crushed against the soft curls on his chest, her hands sliding eagerly over the smooth muscles of his back. His body slid over hers, poised in arched arousal. His mouth ravished hers, one hand sliding behind her head, fingers knotting the still-wet curls. She gazed up into his luminous eyes, breathless in anticipation.

"Now?" he whispered.

"Now," she answered, lips quivering as her entire body hungered to feel him merge with her. His hands guided her hips to meld with his. Lightning illuminated his body in silhouette as he entered her, and she was filled with a pulsing sweetness she'd never felt before.

Katherine held his gaze as she moved with him, finding the rhythm, pressing the silken core of her to the hardness of him. They clung together, slowly and then with gathering speed riding an incomprehensible peak of pleasure.

She heard him call her name and she answered with every breath and beat, her fingers curving to clench his buttocks as the rhythm took them faster and faster still, only to slow again for an exquisite detour of sensation.

The thunder was around her and within her, the silver rain her own sheen of sweat, the lightning these nearly unbearable flashes of sweet fulfillment that rocked her as she climbed with him to the summit, merging with him at last in a paroxysm of passion. And suddenly it was all motion and motionless, and ecstasy burst within her as it never had before.

Chapter Seven

"I still can't believe this," Katherine said.

Peter nodded, his forefinger tracing a line from her eyebrow to cheek, chin, neck. He was savoring the look of her, blond hair damp and unkempt, haloing her face as she lay beside him beneath the blanket. There was a wonderful flush to her skin that he'd never seen and a look in her eyes that went right to his heart. Her gaze was open, almost childlike in its affection and trust. He had a sudden premonition that having seen this expression once, he'd move mountains to see it again.

"It *is* hard to believe," he agreed quietly, then smiled as she caught hold of his roving finger and pressed it to her lips. "But we're really here."

She moved against him, snuggling even closer as if to confirm that fact, legs wound against his for warmth, eyes closing for a moment with a look of supreme satisfaction that made his heart give another lurch. Was it going to be like this, now—that every little thing she did, every gesture and look, was going to turn him into some kind of total mush-ball?

The thought gave him pause. But when she opened her eyes again her expression seemed to reflect some of his own trepidation. "Have we done the wrong thing?" she asked.

"Did it feel wrong?" he countered.

"No," she said, shaking her head slowly. "It felt very, very right. Righter than..." He raised a questioning eyebrow. She bit her lip thoughtfully. "Righter than I thought it would."

"Ah. So you were thinking about it before," he teased.

"Not at all!" she said, indignant. "Well, not—I certainly didn't think..."

"Right, you didn't think," he said, smiling. "That was the idea, remember? If you'd thought too much, we might not have ended up like this." He kissed her forehead and then, taken by the tip of her nose, kissed that, too. While he was there, of course, he couldn't bypass those soft full lips. But no sooner had he grazed them with his own than she was gently but firmly pushing him away. "What's wrong?"

"What about you?" she said. He stared at her, confused to see a guarded look returning to her eyes. "You haven't said..."

It took him a moment, because the idea that she might not know how he felt surprised him. "Kath, you've made me the happiest man in the known universe," he said, and was rewarded by seeing her features relax again. "Well, at least in the state of Massachusetts," he added, unable to resist another tease, then caught her hand as she took a mock swipe at his chin.

"Very funny," she muttered. "You know, this isn't the kind of thing I usually do."

"You mean, getting caught in thunderstorms with lawyers?"

"In fact, I never do," she went on. "Peter, I haven't been with anyone in...well, not since..."

He'd suspected Katherine had a passionate side to her, as well hidden as her other emotions usually were. In their lovemaking he'd felt her holding back, but then, with his urging, she'd released herself in ways that both excited and surprised him. He was flattered to think she'd given herself to him with such abandon, and no one else. "I feel honored," he told her, without a trace of facetiousness.

"And I feel . . . bewildered," she said, with a sigh. "This wasn't supposed to happen, but I'm glad it did. The thing is, as soon as I start thinking about what comes next—" She shook her head again.

"What comes next is up to us, isn't it?" he said quietly. "We're here now. Why don't we enjoy the time we have?"

He drew her closer, kissing the hollow of her neck, his arousal already rising. Her eyes widened slightly as she felt the taut pulse of him in the warm hollow of her thighs. "Really?" she whispered.

"It's still drizzling," he said, smiling.

Katherine gazed past him to the lean-to's eaves, where dwindling raindrops splashed softly on the logs below. Her body, once again dissociating itself from her rational mind, was already tingling, each inch of her skin awakening to new life as she savored the tickle of his furry chest against her breasts, the surprising vigor of his arousal against her.

Jeffrey had usually fallen into deep slumber soon after their lovemaking. Why hadn't it ever been like this with him? She knew why, and she was fast tiring of such comparisons. Peter was his own unique and marvelous person, and at the moment he was rekindling her desire with the vibrant touch of his warm, moist lips. He was such a good lover, probably because he was much more experienced than she.

The thought brought a sudden chill with it. What if she was only one more in a series of conquests? She really didn't know a single thing about Peter and women. She didn't know if he was seeing one, or many. She had no idea if he was taking this even half as seriously as she was. And it *was* serious to her, she realized, her heartbeat quickening. She was here with him like this because she was starting to really care about him, with a depth that was a little frightening. . . .

Attuned to her sudden stiffening in his embrace, Peter raised his head to look searchingly at her. "I'm sorry, but I can't seem to stop myself," he murmured. "Would you rather we talked about dead English poets or something?"

"What do you usually talk about at a time like this?"

His puzzled expression soon turned wary. "You mean, on all the other weekends when I'm bedding casual acquaintances on mountainsides? Katherine, listen to me." He took her chin in his hand. "This has been—and is—something rare and wonderful for me. I'm not used to being with anyone like this myself, if you want to know the truth. I've been used to spending a lot of time on my own."

The seriousness in his tone and the honesty in his glimmering eyes did a lot to soothe her. "I'm sorry, Peter," she whispered.

"Don't be sorry," he said, and bent to kiss her shoulder. "You're right to wonder. But not to worry. I may have been used to being alone—" he interrupted himself to plant little kisses on her earlobe and neck "—but I could really get used to being with you."

Kissing him hadn't been her intention a scant moment ago, but now she eagerly sought his lips. "Not that I could ever really get used to being with you," he murmured. "You're too exciting a woman."

All of her worries were fast evaporating again under the touch of his lips on hers. His gently probing fingertips seemed to know her every intimate pathway to pleasure. "Peter," she whispered, her breath shaky. "You know..."

"Know what?" he whispered, doing something wickedly magical to her with his hands.

I'm falling in love with you was what she wanted to say, but some last vestige of self-preservation forbade the words to leave her lips. "You're good," was what she whispered.

She felt his throaty chuckle against her breast. "Thanks," he said. "You're not bad yourself."

She closed her eyes then, surrendering to the fantastic feeling of his body joining hers again, her hands closing over the firm warm skin of his hips as they locked into a slow and sinuous rhythm. She was risking a lot, but at the moment that risk seemed worth a world of trouble. She'd face the consequences later. And later seemed an ecstatic eternity from now.

CONTENTEDLY MUNCHING on raisins and sunflower seeds, Katherine sat and watched Peter build a fire. He'd discovered some miraculously dry wood beneath a tarp in the far corner of the lean-to. She sat inside still wrapped in their blanket, feeling as if the rest of the civilized world had disappeared for good. Peter, shirtless in jeans, was lighting up a pile of kindling as the sky cleared beyond the treetops.

She couldn't help admiring the play of muscle beneath his smooth tanned skin, and the way his tousled hair kept falling over his eyes as he worked. She also couldn't help feeling oddly guilty for being so happy to be there with him.

In the aftermath of an even more deliriously satiating bout of lovemaking, all the doubts she'd been keeping at bay this afternoon were crowding in on her with renewed intensity. She'd been holding on to her independence so fiercely in the years since Jeffrey died, and now, after a few hours in Peter's arms, she was feeling more dependent, more vulnerable than she had in years. She wanted nothing more than to pull him right back into the lean-to, and let the rest of the world be gone. The intensity of this new need was scaring her.

"I've ordered up some nice weather for our descent," he said, leaning down to blow the first small flames into brighter life. "Not that we're in a big hurry. Sundown's not for another few hours. We can warm ourselves up in the meantime."

He looked over to see Katherine, a vision of loveliness in a blanket. She'd grown quiet and thoughtful, and he could guess at what was preoccupying her. Once they did make their descent, they'd be back in touch with the very things that threatened to keep them apart. He could only hope that the closeness they'd begun to share would make a difference.

"If you don't stop talking I'll never be able to get a word in," he joked, nudging a larger piece of wood toward the flickering flames.

Katherine's smile was a little wan. "Sorry, but my thinking mechanism's in full gear again," she said.

"And what's it processing?" The fire had caught well now. Satisfied, Peter brushed the soot from his hands on his jeans and joined her, sitting down on the edge of the lean-to's front log, a walking stick's length from the fire.

"You. Me," Katherine mused. "I keep thinking this is like *The Magic Mountain*, and once we're off it, we'll be back to being different people again."

"Never read it," he said. "Fairy tale?"

"No, it's Thomas Mann," she said, and her tone sounded as though he'd professed ignorance that the sky was blue.

"Oh, of course," he said dryly.

"I just thought you might've read it," she said.

"Nope," he answered. "Going to hold it against me?"

"No," she said quickly, but he was disgruntled to sense this could be an area of contention between them. Literature had never been his strong suit in college, but he liked to think that wouldn't keep the two of them from being able to get along. The very idea seemed absurd.

"Anything like 'The Magic Bus'?" he asked. She looked blank. "Famous song by The Who," he said, as if her ignorance was shocking. "You mean you've never heard it?"

She stared at him, cheeks reddening. "All right," she said. "I get the picture."

"But we were talking about you and me," he said. "And us being different people when we get back to civilization."

"Is the town council really going to give us a hard time?" she asked suddenly. "Will they play by the rules?"

"You mean, are they going to be fair, and am I going to stay on their side—right?" She gazed at him, expression inscrutable. He was disappointed that all of this was coming up again so fast. He suspected Katherine was in a desperate hurry to distance herself from what had happened between them, and he didn't want her to, not yet. Not now.

He took hold of her hand. "Look, I know things are bound to get complicated," he said quietly. "But why don't we see if we can separate those issues from our emotions? We're in each other's lives now, Katherine. We're not going to be able to deal with each other at arm's length."

"I know." She squeezed his hand, leaning her head against his shoulder, her eyes on the flickering fire before them. "Then let's not talk about it."

"We'll have to."

"Yes, but . . . you're right. Things are happening so fast. We barely know each other, Peter."

He nodded. "True. But the funny thing is, I feel as if I know the real you, the you inside, already." He slipped his arm around her, trying to find the words that would describe such an ephemeral feeling. "It's like I knew you before I met you."

"That's sweet," she murmured. "And it's true. You do know how to . . . read me, it seems. But on the other hand, we don't know the first thing about each other. I mean, really basic stuff."

"I *want* to know," he said, playing with the silken hair by her ear. "Start now, then. Tell me whatever you think is vital information, all right? We'll trade secrets."

She smiled, nuzzling his neck a moment and then moving back, turning herself around in the blanket to face him. "You start, then," she said. "You know all about Jeffrey, and the kind of life I led with him, but what about you? You never married, but that night I had dinner at the cottage, you pretty deftly avoided talking about what I guess must have been—what do they call it in the magazines?—your significant other.''

"Significant other," he mused, poking at the fire again with his walking stick. He had enough distance from it now to speak dispassionately, and had actually avoided talking about Sarah that night because he'd been genuinely more interested in hearing about Katherine. "Well, there's not all that much to tell."

"Tell me anyway," she said.

"Sarah Kinet was a junior partner at the firm I joined. She was a genuine New Yorker through and through, and I was the kid from the sticks who didn't know Manhattan chowder from New England. We dated. In fact, we dated forever, it seemed, because Sarah was leery of mixing work with romance and because she had a deep fear of getting 'tied down,' as she called it."

He threw on another piece of kindling. "After we'd been going out for about a year, things seemed serious enough to go on to the next step. I suggested living together, because the word marriage seemed to make her break out in hives. But even that created all kinds of anxieties, which we weathered, eventually, and eventually we did move in together.

"I guess you'd call it a classic reversal," he said wryly. "I was the one who was ready for a marriage, a home, a family, you know, the whole old-fashioned scenario. Sarah put her career first. I was patient, and my own career sure took up a lot of time and energy. But after a while, I began to realize that in living together, we were having even less of an intimate relationship than we'd had before. We had the appearance of being together, but when you're only seeing the person you live with at odd ends of the day, and work carries over onto the weekends..."

He shrugged. "Three years, nearly four years into the relationship I had a sense that we were going nowhere slowly.

I pushed for marriage, and we even got engaged. Then the engagement dragged on, with marriage dates being postponed. Push came to shove. When we came right down to it, Sarah didn't want to be a real partner with me. She wanted to be a senior in the firm.''

"It was one or the other?''

"It was to her,'' he said. "So we broke up.''

"What was the damage?'' Katherine asked.

Peter smiled. "Broken heart, but the rest of me was in fine shape—except I'd lost a lot of my tolerance for the fast-paced, high-pressure New York life. Then there came a point where I had a professional choice to make: step over the body of a good friend to insure a better position, or step aside. I stepped out.''

"And you've been happier in Greensdale... alone?''

"Happy's a big word.'' He looked at her. "And yes, I've been alone. I won't say I haven't had a casual relationship in all the time since Sarah. But I haven't gotten involved in anything that meant as much.''

Until now, he almost said, but he held back. He was still wary of his own depth of feeling for Katherine. It seemed to have sneaked up on him with surprising speed and intensity. He wasn't fully trusting his own emotions, and more to the point, he sensed some skittishness from her. He had a feeling it would be wise to take it one step at a time.

"So you're looking for a homemaker, then.''

Peter smiled. Katherine's face was thoughtful as she huddled in the blanket, chin resting on her knees. "I haven't been taking out any advertisements in the *Greensdale Chronicle*,'' he said. "Why—are you looking for an out?''

She bit her lip. "No, I'm just trying to get a sense of you,'' she said honestly. "I like it that you want a home and a family. I want that, too. But I've *had* that,'' she added, looking up to meet his gaze. "And for the past few years I've been pretty caught up in my own career.''

"Nothing wrong with that," he said. "But I'll take your tacit warning under consideration, Professor."

Katherine made a face, elbowing him gently in the side. "We're getting to know each other, that's all," she said. "That's all."

"Right. And now it's your turn," he told Katherine. "Got a secret to trade?"

She shook her head. "With you, I feel like an open book sometimes," she murmured. "But all right, what do you want to know that you haven't masterfully intuited already?"

"Tell me about the house."

"Grammy's? What do you mean?"

"Why, when all the evidence says you might as well let the thing go, are you holding on to it so tightly? It's not just a sentimental attachment. And I don't mean this business about the day-care center. I mean the feelings underneath it."

"Reasonable question." Katherine gazed into the fire. "Let me ask you this first. What was your house like, in Greensdale?"

He shrugged. "Nothing special. One of those tiny two-story jobs on Mulberry. It had yellow paint that was probably already peeling on the brush, shutters that banged all winter and the noisiest radiators in the world. Oh, and two things that have always struck me as amazing: a laundry chute, down which I of course tried to stuff my best friend in second grade, and one of those ironing boards that comes out of the wall, you know, a Murphy?"

Katherine nodded. "It's those little things that give a place its personality, right? Our house... Now, *there's* character."

Peter leaned forward to reposition one of the pieces of wood that wasn't burning properly. "Go on."

"The weekends were the best," she remembered. "You see, that was the only place where the whole family was ever together at the same time. Grammy and Father both home, maybe with some friends from the university over. When there were lots of people I used to go outside and look at all the windows lit up....

"It was big, but Lydia and I shared a room, maybe the nicest one in the place. At least we thought so." She smiled. "It's the one above the sun parlor in the back. It has all these eaves in it, slanted ceiling, and a blue wallpaper that made me think of the sea.... We'd have to go to bed early but we always stayed awake for a while, listening to the voices floating up from down below. You could see the lights from the parlor and the dining room shining out on the lawn, and the shadows of people moving. Grammy and Father always liked to have a full house on the weekend.

"Sometimes I'd wake up in the middle of the night because the moonlight was so bright, and I'd fantasize that we were adrift on a big ocean liner. I guess it was that wallpaper, the blue of the moonlight and the round windows. I'd go to one and watch the fireflies dancing in the yard and with my eyes squinched almost shut it was as if they were the lights of cities on distant shores, while we drifted past. It was such a safe feeling, being perched up there in my make-believe ship, sailing on a sea of grass...."

She looked at Peter, afraid he'd be ready to make fun of her. But he merely nodded, absorbed, smoothing back a curl of hair from her temple, so she went on. "And in the morning you'd smell these terrific breakfast smells, even before you were fully awake. Everyone ate together Sunday mornings. It seemed like that big oak dining room table was the biggest, longest table I'd ever seen...."

She smiled, eyes closed, seeing each room as it had been back then, filled with light and laughter. "Years later, after Dad died, we even moved back in for a few months. It was a sad time, but the house and Grammy made us feel better somehow. Clarissa was happy to play in the yard or go exploring in the rooms. There were so many! Grandfather's study, and the little rooms under the attic where Marie and her husband had stayed when they worked there...."

"Servants?"

She nodded. "Sort of all-around caretaker and cook they used to have." Peter's expression was opaque, and she wondered briefly if he disapproved of such evidence of family wealth. But she was enjoying her own stream of memories too much to ask. "Anyway, it was as if every room had rooms and rooms inside it. Closets with boxes, drawers within drawers—you wouldn't believe the kinds of things you could find in one of Grammy's drawers."

She went on, detailing the strange and wondrous stuff, from old-fashioned buttons and bows, photo albums, rosettes and paper flowers to little china figurines, souvenirs from old World's Fairs and yellowing theater programs with autographs scrawled on them. She remembered introducing Clarissa to her favorite secret hiding places, and dressing her up in Grammy's mother's old clothes from the huge steamer trunk in the attic.

"When Jeffrey died, I moved in with her again for a month or so. It was always a sanctuary for us, always like that safe ship on the sea for me." She stared into the fire. "I guess with so many people I loved leaving before they were supposed to, that house has been a symbol of better times. When I think of it, I'm thinking of those warm summer nights, with the voices in the sun parlor, when I was a child and all of us were together—Grandmother and Grandfather, my mother, Father, Mom and Dad, Lydia in her little crib...

"You take that house away, and there's nothing left. That's what I'm afraid of. All our Taylor memories live in there. Where would they go, if the house was gone?"

She looked back at Peter. His hand slid round her waist as he gently kissed her forehead. "You have them," he said softly. "In your heart."

"It's not the same."

He nodded. "I know." Katherine wriggled closer, pulling an edge of blanket around him.

"Your friends in town probably think I'm being selfish, not wanting to sell," she said quietly, head in the crook of his shoulder. "But Lord, even this garage sale we're doing is a big trauma. Lydie and I've gotten into such fights over what to keep and what we can bear to part with. We've finally settled on only selling things we really can't use at all." She looked up at him. "You can understand how it is, can't you?"

Peter nodded slowly. "Yes, I can, Kath," he murmured. He *was* understanding her, more and more, and that was the problem. Because how was he supposed to bring Katherine Taylor around to his side when he was moving around to hers? And what was he going to come back to Randy Morgan with? "Can't budge her," he'd say. "And besides, I don't want to—I'm in love."

Oh, sure, that would do it. How to lose a townful of friends and clientele in one fell swoop. The sky was a rosy pink above the trees now, and everything around them sparkled with the extra clarity a wash of rain can bring. He knew they should be getting ready to go down the mountain now. But he'd rather build the two of them a home in the lean-to and never go back to Greensdale again.

LYDIA'S RENTAL CAR was parked in the winding driveway when Katherine pulled up late that night, and another car with local plates that she didn't recognize. She'd called the house as soon as she and Peter had reached civilization because she knew Lydia was planning to meet her there that evening for dinner, and she wouldn't be back in time.

"That's all right, I've got plenty to do here," Lydia had said. "I'm still sorting through boxes and boxes of God-knows-what. Kath, what are we supposed to do with father's tie collection? And the paperweights?"

"Tag them along with everything else, I guess," Katherine had told her. Their Taylor house "garage sale" was scheduled for the following Sunday morning. Though many of the downstairs antiques were being handled by a store in Boston that had already appraised the largest pieces, there was going to be an overwhelming amount of stuff to put out on the lawn. Katherine could see lights on in the kitchen as she shouldered her bag. Lydia was no doubt tagging away with a vengeance in there.

The slate on one of the front steps crumbled as she stepped up in the semidarkness, and she nearly fell flat on her rear. One more thing that had to be repaired, she thought grimly, blowing on the chafed palm of the hand that had broken her fall. In through the ever-creaking front door—careful not to slam it because of the precarious plaster in the foyer—and down the hall she went, calling a cheery "Hello!"

One of the voices that chimed in to greet her was male. Katherine entered the brightly lit kitchen to find Lydia seated at a table overflowing with brightly tagged objects opposite a dark-haired man in a patched-elbow jacket.

"Katherine, this is Dr. Harrison," Lydia said, as the man rose politely, a china vase Katherine recognized from the living room mantelpiece in his hand. He was the doctor who'd been treating Grammy, she realized, shaking his hand.

"Good to meet you," he said.

"You look great," Lydia exclaimed, fixing Katherine with a look of openly intrigued interest. Katherine wondered what, exactly, showed in her face. Could they tell just by looking at her that she'd returned from one of the most wonderfully fulfilling romantic experiences of her life?

"How's it going?" she asked, indicating the cluttered kitchen.

"Where have you been?" Lydia countered, obviously not about to let her off the hook.

"Is there any coffee left?" Katherine said pointedly, giving her sister a don't-press-me-now-we'll-talk-later look. Dr. Harrison was still on his feet and was picking up the signals.

"Actually, I was just going," he said.

"Oh, don't leave on my account," Katherine said, heading over to the stove.

"Jake's on the run," Lydia said.

"Just stopped in to say hello," he said diffidently, putting the vase down on the counter next to a long line of such objects. "Lydia's been telling me about your plans for the house. It sounds like quite an undertaking."

"Do I detect another nay-sayer?" she asked, pouring herself a mug of coffee.

"Not at all." Jake smiled. "Since I'm not officially a Greensdalian—"

"He lives in Great Oaks," Lydia interjected.

"—I have the luxury of being a little more objective," he went on. "I think a day-care center is a great idea, if you can pull it off."

"He doesn't know the Taylor women," Lydia said, busily wrapping up the contents of a baking tin in Saran Wrap. "Nothing can stop us once our minds are made up. Right, Sis?"

"Right," Katherine said, setting down the coffee mug with a wince. "Lydia, this coffee is atomic strength."

"The better to keep us up tonight," she said brightly, and handed the wrapped tin to Dr. Harrison. "There you go. Don't eat them all in one sitting."

"That may take some self-control," the doctor said. "Katherine, why don't you have your sister turn this place into a bakery? She could make a fortune with brownies like these."

"Flattery, flattery," Lydia sighed. "Thanks for stopping by."

"Thanks for the dessert and atomic strength coffee," he said. "Good luck tomorrow, you two."

Lydia saw Dr. Harrison out and Katherine made a brief survey of the tagged items that covered every available surface in the kitchen. She stopped by a darkened windowpane to surreptitiously inspect her features. Did she look like a woman who'd been kissed to delirium? Hard to say, but she had to admit she looked . . . well, cheerier than usual.

"Start at the beginning," Lydia said, returning. "I want to hear every juicy detail."

"Of what?" Katherine guiltily turned from the window.

"Give me a break, Kath," Lydia said. "You've been consorting with the enemy, and it seems to have done you a world of good."

"Been doing a little consorting yourself, haven't you?"

Lydia looked startled, a slight blush in her cheeks. "Jake's no enemy. He's just a nice guy. He was in town visiting some friends, and when he saw the lights on at the house on his way home, he decided to see who was here."

"He's interested in you?"

"He was interested in my brownies," Lydia said.

"How do you know him, anyway? I didn't realize you'd ever spent any time in Great Oaks."

"I haven't," Lydia said. "Look, I'll tell you all about it, some rainy day. But you're the one who keeps trying to avoid the *important* subject! What's going on with Peter Bradford?"

Katherine sat down at the kitchen table, unable to suppress a smile. "Something," she admitted.

Lydia sat down opposite, clearing two vases out of the way, and fixed her sister with a stare. "You slept with him!"

"You know, the two of you would make a good match," Katherine said, shaking her head. "You're both the bluntest conversationalists I've ever met."

"You mean, because we don't use fifty-dollar, five-syllable words while we beat around the bush?" Lydia made a face. "So, how was it?"

Katherine smiled, trying to collect her jumbled thoughts and feelings, and addressed the table. "I think I'm a little in love," she said softly.

"Of course you are," Lydia crowed. "This is great!"

"Not necessarily," Katherine said. "Lydie, this is going to be nothing but trouble. We couldn't be more ill-matched, I have no idea if he's serious at all, we're going to be fighting each other tooth and nail over this ConCo thing—" She stopped herself with a rueful laugh. "I'm a mess. And I'm glad you're here," she said. "I really do need to talk about this."

"I'm glad I made an extra batch of brownies," Lydia said, and reached across the table to squeeze Katherine's hand. "Now this is my idea of a good time."

Chapter Eight

"Yes, I saw the article," Peter said, phone cradled in his shoulder as he poured himself another cup of coffee. The newspaper, in fact, was still lying spread out on his kitchen table. He'd just finished reading it when the phone rang, and he'd known immediately who it would be.

"Well, I don't know about you, but I don't like having my Sunday morning ruined in one fell swoop," Randy Morgan said. "I've already had the mayor grousing in my ear for twenty minutes and I know the only reason I don't have Tom Cormody yelling in my other ear is that I'm talking to you."

Peter eyed the reason for Randy's foul mood. "Greensdale Women Want to Give Corporation the Boot" read the big print above two thick columns on the paper's front page. "Why didn't you send this guy—" Peter frowned at the by-line beneath the headline—"Jeremy Herman to talk to me? The only reason the thing seems slanted the way it does is because he didn't get both sides of the—"

"If you'd been in town for once," Randy interrupted, his voice rising, "maybe you could have done some talking to him! But you were off on a field trip with the very uppity, cantankerous—"

"Easy, Randy."

"—lady who's started this nonsense in the first place!
Now I want to hear some good news, Bradford! Have you
gotten your bosom buddy there to listen to reason, or
what?''

Peter felt himself bridling at the way Randy talked about
Katherine, but knew now was not the best moment for
chivalrous defense. He took a gulp of coffee and cleared his
throat. "I've talked myself blue in the face, Randy," he
said. "She's just not interested in selling."

Randy swore rapidly, pounding what sounded like a fist
on Formica while Peter held the phone from his ear, winc-
ing. "Not interested? Is she on some goddamn kamikaze
mission to send this town down the toilet?''

"Of course not, Randy, she just has other ideas about
what she wants to do with the property. And from her point
of view, this day-care center is a worthwhile community
service."

"Oh, for crying out— Look, Peter: we're already losing
face here, but I can grin and bear it if we don't lose the
whole game. Now, how much higher do we have to jack up
the price? You told her ConCo's new bid, didn't you?''

Peter wasn't about to explain that his conversation with
Katherine hadn't even gotten that far. He wasn't about to
try and soothe the town supervisor's ire with tales of moonlit
bedrooms and precious family heirlooms, either. All he
could do was mollify Randy with assurances that he'd give
the situation one more shot, his best shot. But even before
he got off the phone he knew his best shot wouldn't be good
enough.

And that was mainly because he didn't even feel like fir-
ing it. Katherine and her sister were being naive and optimistic, true; the house might not be stable enough to make
it through the extensive renovations necessary without
turning into a veritable two-story money-eater, swallowing
all of their inheritance before the work was even com

leted. But financial logic was no match for Katherine Taylor's iron will, he knew that in his bones.

He was going out to the Taylor house to talk to her, but if Randy Morgan had known how little interest he really had in bringing up ConCo bids and veiled threats from the town council, he'd truly have a fit. Peter was more interested in finding out if she was free for dinner... and the rest of the evening.

Clearly, there was something seriously wrong with him. Peter downed the rest of his coffee, turning the paper over with a grimace. Staring out at the morning sunshine through his kitchen window, he found himself contemplating the dimples in Katherine's smile, going over his favorite birthmarks on the soft skin of her back. *Bradford, your priorities are completely twisted. You're over the edge,* he told himself, as he felt his features relaxing into the goofiest of grins.

Hard as it was to admit, at this point he was almost willing to concede defeat on the issue of the house. He didn't mind losing face if he knew he'd be free to contemplate *hers*. The situation was downright embarrassing, and guilt for letting Randy down hung heavy over his head. But what was a man to do when he was in love?

In the car a half hour later, it occurred to him that that particular, all-important word hadn't been spoken, either by him or by her. But it had seemed to fill the air between them, like the gazes that had lingered between each kiss. He didn't think he could have imagined what he'd seen in her eyes when they'd said goodbye the night before. And he wasn't imagining the way he felt.

The same old sights of downtown Greensdale hadn't ever looked this glowingly bright to him as he whizzed up Main Street, and that wasn't due to any miracle of sunlight. The glow was inside him. He felt a little wary of basking in it, since the sensation was so new. Maybe he was a fool to feel everything could only get better for the two of them, when

they'd only just begun to get to know each other. But th
sun was bright, the trees greener than he'd ever seen them
and the radio's blast of exuberant rock 'n' roll as he toole
down the road threatened to lift him right out of the dri
er's seat. If this wasn't love, he'd never know it.

"How MUCH for the footstool without the chair?"

Katherine peered over the table piled with kitchenware t
see the object Mrs. Haverwood was pointing at. "We real
did want to sell them as a unit," she told her. "But I tell yo
what, ask my sister Lydia over there what she thinks, and I'
go along with her decision."

"That girl with the long hair?" The white-haired woma
squinted toward Lydia, who was handing over a spun glas
paperweight to another elderly woman a few yards awa
"Oh, yes," she said, contemplating Katherine again with
little smile. "I thought you looked alike."

Katherine smiled and turned back to Emily, who wa
counting up the loose change in their makeshift shoe-bo
bank. "How're we doing?" she asked, as Emily added ar
other figure to the columns scrawled on her loose-leaf pac

"Excellent," Emily answered. "I told you most of th
good stuff would be gone by noon, and it's five minutes to.'

Katherine nodded, stifling a yawn. Emily had insisted tha
they get up at the crack of dawn, and get their goods out o
the lawn, since early morning was bound to be the busies
time. She'd turned out to be right. People who obviousl
went foraging through such sales every weekend, th
experienced hunters from out of town, came in a stead
stream at an hour when most Greensdalians were still in be
or leisurely contemplating their morning papers.

Emily was an old hand at sales like these. She'd oversee
the final taggings and helped them arrange everything, ir
cluding the placement of their most prized item of furn
ture, the oak and glass armoire, down at the end of th
driveway. "Best thing you got's the best thing to bring 'er

in with," she'd explained, and she'd been right about that, too. A couple vacationing in the Berkshires in their silver Airstream trailer had snatched the armoire up within the first hour of the sale.

"No one wants the big lamp, though." This chunky, cumbersome six-foot piece of Victoriana, complete with a monstrous yellowed fringe shade, had always been one of her favorite things in the living room, and she was secretly hoping, though Lydia despised it, that if it didn't at least fetch the high price she'd tagged on it—subject of the morning's one fierce familial argument—that they would get to keep the lamp after all.

"Can you blame them?" Emily said dryly.

"Ssh," Katherine said, as a young man in shirt sleeves and suspenders approached the lamp, inspecting it through wire rim glasses with an air of curiosity.

"One born every minute," Emily muttered, turning away from Katherine's indignant glare.

"It's quite something, isn't it?" Katherine said brightly, approaching the man as he continued his examination.

"Something, yes," he agreed, looking up with a wry grin. "When you look up the word 'eyesore' in the dictionary, they ought to have a picture of it there." Katherine's pleasant smile evaporated, but the man's eyes were widening behind his glasses. "Wait, you're Katherine, aren't you? The older one?"

Tact was not this fellow's strong suit. "Yes, I'm Katherine Taylor," she said, steeling herself. The Greensdale crowd had been predominantly women all morning, with the occasional disgruntled husband along for the ride and financial support. Though she'd gotten friendlier smiles and conversation from the women than she'd ever enjoyed before in her years of visiting, most of the local men had regarded her and Lydia with unveiled hostility. It was clear where the lines were drawn when it came to the issue of what was commonly known as "the Taylor house controversy."

"I'm Jeremy Herman," the man said, extending his hand. "You don't mind if I ask you a few questions, do you?"

"Not at all," she said. "But the prices you see on everything are pretty much what we're—"

"No, no," he interrupted, chuckling. "I'm a reporter for the *Chronicle*. Didn't you read my article this morning?"

"Oh." Katherine's smile returned. "I haven't had time to even scan the front page today," she admitted. "But enough people have told me about it. So you're the one who's trying to turn my sister and me into celebrities."

"No, just doing my job," he said. "It's a good story. I wanted to get your side of it before we went to press but you were out of town. And you weren't answering your phone up at Hampshire College, either. Where've you been?"

"Taking it easy," she said lightly, aware that if he'd had any idea of what she'd been doing and who with, he'd have had quite another kind of story.

"Miss! I want the ashtray."

"And those salt and pepper shakers—can you come down a few bucks on the two pair?"

Katherine nodded and held a hand up at the two customers who were now flanking Jeremy on the other side of the table. "Just a minute," she said. "Maybe now isn't the best time," she told the reporter. "Do you think you could wait a little while?"

Jeremy checked his watch. "Tell you what, I'll come back after lunch," he said. "Think you'll be able to take a break then?"

"My pleasure," Katherine said. From what she'd heard about the man's article, it had been tacitly supportive of the Greensdale women's group, so she'd be glad to talk to him.

"Good luck with the lamp," he said with a grin, and ambled off. Katherine watched him circulate out of the corner of her eye while she sold off some of the items on her table. She was giving in to the wheeler-dealing of a tough customer from Boston who wanted father's old carving knives when her heartbeat quickened suddenly. Peter was here.

She watched him stride slowly through the crowd, hands in his pockets, hair tousled in the breeze, his handsome features seeming spotlit by the sun as he circled closer. With an unexpectedly proprietary feeling, she watched him cruising the crowd, greeting a friend here and there, his lazily affable grin making his eyes seem to gleam a brighter blue.

When he stopped to talk to a young woman in a tight red halter over even tighter jeans, that feeling tightened in her chest. *He's mine,* she found herself thinking, and was immediately chagrined by her jealousy. Was he, really? How far gone was *she*, anyway?

The man from Pittsfield had to remind her to give him his change. When she'd corrected her error, cheeks reddening, Peter was in front of her. "Yo, Prof."

Yo, Prof? It wasn't the most romantic greeting in the world. It had neither the wit of Keats or the sweep of Byron, so there wasn't any reason why his words should have resounded so musically in her ears. Nonetheless her insides seemed to warm up at the sound and the rest of the world appeared to diminish and fade behind him as she gazed up into Peter's lazy grin.

"Yo, yourself," she said, doing her best to affect cool nonchalance. "Want to buy some dishes?"

"Only one dish here I'm interested in," he said, eyes twinkling, then added, surveying the table: "Looks like you've been putting in a full morning's work."

"Why, do I look beat?" she asked.

"No, you look great," he said. "You'd better back up a foot or I'm liable to try to kiss you."

Feeling the subtle heat emanating from his amused and affectionate eyes, she reflected that this was not the worst of ideas. But a sense of propriety asserted itself, and she took the requisite step back. "In public?" she said. "I don't know, that's a pretty radical concept." Especially, she realized, since that reporter from the *Chronicle* was still hovering around the sale area and looking in her direction.

"I'm restraining myself," Peter told her solemnly. "But I can only last so long. What are you doing when this thing is over?"

Katherine let out a deep breath. Sometimes when he looked at her in a certain way, simple things like breathing properly seemed to become oddly difficult. "I was thinking about a shower," she said.

"Sounds interesting." His smile was turning devilish.

"I'll give you ten bucks for these thingamajigs, corn on the cob holders." A woman leaned in past Peter, brandishing her money. The objects in question were marked twelve. Katherine decided to let them go.

"Deal," she said, and took the ten-dollar bill.

"We were saying," Peter went on. "Something about a shower."

"It wasn't an invitation," she said wryly.

"Well, all right, I'll invite you, then: dinner at the Red Roost Diner? Seven-thirty?"

She squinted at him as the name registered. "I thought that was sort of a kids' hangout."

"Well, it sort of is," he allowed. "But it's really for the young in spirit, all ages welcomed. Normally, of course, I'd take you some place much more sophisticated, perhaps an inn where Washington Irving had slept. But as I'm sitting in with the house band for a set tonight, I thought you might find it entertaining. You know, in a slumming kind of way."

"Sitting in?"

"Playing some guitar. They're friends I jam with now and then."

"You're a man of many hidden talents," she said, thinking that the idea of Peter Bradford "jamming" with a band made perfect sense somehow. Jeremy Herman was watching her now with evident interest and was starting to walk in their direction. "Fine," she said. "You'll pick me up?"

Peter raised an eyebrow. "Gladly," he said. "Though I can't guarantee when and where I'll put you down again."

"Cute," she said. "See you then."

Peter shook his head. "I think that's the fastest date acceptance followed by the fastest brush-off you've ever given me," he said. "Something wrong?"

"No, just busy," she said, indicating the people examining dishes at his side. Jeremy Herman was still en route, and he didn't want to risk a confrontation between all three of them right now.

"I'm out of here," Peter said. "Dress is casual, by the way."

"Good," she told him. "My blue suede shoes are at the cleaners."

Peter grinned and with a friendly wave, turned away from the table. Katherine watched warily as the newspaperman made a beeline for him. The two men stood just out of earshot, which was truly frustrating. She didn't know if Peter had seen the man's article. What kind of questions was Herman asking him?

As she watched, they walked off side by side, Peter's expression betraying no particular emotion as the reporter gesticulated, a pad and pen in hand. Then the sale of Grammy's porcelain water pitcher distracted her, and when she looked up again, Peter and Jeremy had vanished into the crowd.

"Katherine!" Emily was hurrying over, Marsha Rudman at her side. With her gray hair pinned back in a bun, a colorful shift on and a flush of excitement in her cheeks, Marsha looked younger today than her companion. She was clutching a folder of papers in her hand, eyes sparkling as she joined Katherine at the table.

"Hi," she said. "What's up?"

"A lot," Emily said. "Here, I'll spell you for a while. Marsha needs to talk to you."

Although she'd talked with the women in their little committee a few times since the first meeting, and felt she was on casually friendly footing with them, Marsha had never made it a point to seek her out. Curious, Katherine let the older woman lead her away from the lawn's activity, wondering what her air of secrecy was all about.

"Take a look at this," Marsha said, when they were close to the house. She thrust a paper into Katherine's hand.

Katherine scanned it, a copy of a news article from a paper in Des Moines. It took her a moment to comprehend the import of what she was reading, but then she looked up at Marsha, startled. "They're still in court?"

"Even as we speak," the woman told her, handing her another paper. "And that's not the only suit. Check this out."

The second article was just as volatile. Apparently the ConCo Corporation was being sued by not one, but two supervisory boards of townships in the Middle West. Rockville, near Des Moines, was up in arms because less than a year after allowing a plant to be built there, they were suddenly faced with a whopping eighty-thousand-dollar expense to expand their local sewage system. It was a "hidden cost" that had never been figured into any arrangement made with the local authorities, and ConCo had expected Rockville to foot the bill.

In Valley Springs, Illinois there was an even more provocative problem, one more recent. Although ConCo was claiming it was a mistake on the part of the town planners, an overspill from their allotted toxic dumping area had created a health hazard in a local reservoir. The county was up in arms, and ConCo was being slapped with a suit for half a million in damages.

"This is dynamite," Marsha Rudman said excitedly. "What do you think the council's going to say when they see this stuff?"

"Where did you dig it up?"

"I didn't," she said. "My older daughter Louise has a friend at college who works for the Associated Press service part-time. When she mentioned what was going on in town here, her friend remembered something about ConCo and legal suits, and she tracked the clippings down."

"It certainly puts a different light on things," Katherine said. "Who else have you shown these to?"

"Just Betty and Emily so far," said Marsha. "But I know where I'm going next. The *Chronicle*. Emily said the reporter who talked to her the other day would be interested."

"Jeremy Herman," Katherine said. "Yes, he wanted to talk to me. He's coming back in an hour or so."

"Perfect timing," said Marsha. "Why don't we see him together?"

Katherine, about to agree, paused. Shouldn't she speak to Peter before talking to the reporter? What if he didn't know about the latest suit? Marsha was looking at her expectantly. It occurred to Katherine that she and Peter were still in agreement to disagree on this issue. And it wasn't keeping them from seeing each other.

Besides, *he'd* been talking to Jeremy. Who knew what he might be telling the reporter to support his and Randy Morgan's side of things? "All right," she told Marsha. "He said he'd be back here within the hour. We'll talk to him then."

"This ought to be fun," Marsha said, and giving her a wink and a smile, she moved off into the crowd. Katherine watched her go, feeling both pleased by the older woman's friendliness and uneasy about her decision. But there wasn't much time to think it over. Lydia was waving frantically at her from Emily's table.

A long-haired man in jeans and his wife in a billowing tie-dyed shift were next to her, counting out money. Katherine's heart gave a sentimental lurch as she saw what they were about to purchase. She hurried over to bid her favorite lamp adieu.

SWEAT POURING DOWN his brow, new blisters forming on his fingers, Peter tore into the last song of the set with renewed fervor. The floorboards were shaking under his feet, the drumbeat pounding right through him and out to the dance floor, where a mass of swirling bodies in the colored lights screamed out encouragement as he dug into a searing blast of electric power chords.

The Screaming Honkers were in rare form tonight, and he wasn't too shabby himself. For the boys, a long rehearsal that afternoon was clearly responsible, but for Peter inspiration was a certain member of the audience. How could he resist showing off when the prettiest woman in the Red Roost was bopping in time to the pulsing beat, apparently mesmerized by his every move from her perch at the end of the crowded bar?

There had been some tough moments when they'd first arrived. With the good-natured but relentless ribbing from the guys in the group—they acted as if Peter's bringing a date to the gig was some historic occasion—the atmosphere particularly rowdy and the air smoke-filled this Sunday night. Since the air conditioning was temporarily on the fritz, he'd almost begun wishing he'd never had this bright idea in the first place.

But Katherine had taken it all in stride, not batting an eyelash at the jukebox pounding continuous rock 'n' roll in the background and the presence of a clientele mostly at least a decade younger than she was. She'd immediately taken to the home cooking on the menu and matched him beer for beer throughout their delicious meal, further astounding him by knowing the words to a number of songs he'd assumed she'd never heard, let alone enjoyed.

"Do you think I spend all my time listening to Schubert lieder?" she'd said indignantly. "Which was *your* favorite Beatle? I went for Paul."

When he joined the boys on the bandstand a little later, he was no longer worrying that he was about to alienate his new "main squeeze," as Terry of the Honkers had dubbed Katherine, for good. Instead he just concentrated on playing some kick-butt rock 'n' roll for the dancing fans. The set seemed to fly by on jet steam.

And every time he looked to the bar, there she was, smiling, nodding, listening and occasionally trading comments on their performance with Beano the lead singer's live-in girlfriend Lucy. The sight of Lucy's roosterish purple-tinted black bouffant brushing Katherine's demure blond bangs as the two women laughed over some private joke put a smile on his face that wouldn't quit.

Now they were closing the set with a crowd-pleasing golden oldie, Chuck Berry's "Sweet Little Sixteen," and Beano was pushing the band to its outer limits of velocity. "Peter! Come on! Do your duck walk!" he exhorted over the din. Peter shook his head but Terry joined in, urging him on.

Just as a joke, Peter had performed his imitation of Chuck Berry's famous duck walk at the rehearsal, deep-knee-bending his way across the floor in rhythm as he swiveled his guitar back and forth. Now the Honkers were egging him on in earnest to repeat the feat. Initially embarrassed, he decided to go with the flow, and bent into his best Chuck Berry pose as they hit the instrumental break.

Peter was rewarded with whoops of delight from the dancing crowd as he duck-walked down the little stage. Entirely caught up in it now, he couldn't stop himself from cranking the volume up to ten and getting down on his knees for the big finish. The Red Roost's roof threatened to fly off as cheers filled the air. And when he looked up through a sheen of perspiration to cries of "More!" a certain professor of literature was standing on her bar stool, eyes shining, hair wonderfully disarrayed. She had two fingers in her mouth and the earsplitting whistle that came from between those pert little lips would've brought any cab in Manhattan to a screeching halt.

"HERE WE ARE."

Katherine lifted her head from its comfortably snuggled position on Peter's shoulder to peer through the windshield as the car slowed. "You live in a fish and tackle store?"

Peter merely smiled, pulling into the driveway next to the cluttered window those rods and reels blinked pink and blue under the LUKE'S neon sign. "I'm not being critical, of course," Katherine added, with a yawn. "It's a perfectly charming concept."

The gentlemanly Peter was already at her door. "Charming?" he echoed, amused, as he helped her out of the car. "How many beers did you have, Professor?"

"They were *light* beers," she informed him soberly, pointedly ignoring the arm he offered her. In truth, she was a little sleepy but certainly not drunk. "Lead on, sir."

"Place is a bit on the messy side," he muttered, guiding her up the wooden stairs that ascended the side of the tackle shop. "But I hadn't planned on company."

"You're a bachelor," she said. "You're entitled to the requisite mess that comes with that kind of condition."

"Well, lady, you're about to become one of the privileged few to see what condition my condition is in," he said, opening the screen door at the top of the stairs.

"Deeply honored," she said, and walked inside. When he flicked on the lamp by the door she turned in a slow circle, smiling to herself at the no-frills, spartan masculinity the apartment displayed. One armchair which had seen better days but looked wonderfully comfortable, kept a low-slung leather couch company on an antique throw rug, with a television and VCR front and center opposite. Beyond that was practically a solid wall of record albums, with giant speakers and a rack of stereo equipment.

Katherine turned, taking in the framed photographs clustered on a little card table by the entrance to the kitchen. The other wall displayed a brick fireplace that was dwarfed by a gargantuan gray swordfish.

"Friend of yours?" she asked playfully, walking over to inspect the monstrous fish. Its wide open black eye gazed balefully at her as she ran a hand over the incredibly long snout.

"I'd love to tell you I caught that sucker, but I didn't," he admitted. "It's an old souvenir of my dad's."

"Handsome," she said, and strolled back to look at the photos. Most prominent was a silver-framed snapshot of a gray-haired man in overalls, fishing rod in one hand, his other hand tousling the hair of a beaming boy in cutoffs at his side. Peter, she realized, smiling as she made out the features of the adult in the child's innocent grin.

"Can I get you something? Coffee?"

"Do you have any tea?" She looked back at Peter, who was still hovering by the doorway with an apprehensive air, watching her every move. She realized that he hadn't been kidding; he clearly wasn't used to entertaining in his private domain.

"Iced tea," he said, and moved off toward the kitchen. "Kick your shoes off. Make yourself at home." He pointed to the screen door at the back end of the swordfish. "Porch is nice this time of night."

The long, narrow screened veranda outside overlooked Elm Street. Katherine relaxed in the wicker couch that practically filled the little space, transfixed by the view. From here, you could see half of downtown Greensdale. Since none of the buildings were more than four stories high, her eye was free to roam over the skyline.

Countless stars filled the clear night sky, and only a few lights twinkled in the quiet streets below. There was Sadie's place, dark like all the other stores that seemed to huddle together in a friendly alliance around the edges of the town green. Beyond them was the moonlit spire of the church, and the post office flag a shadow rippling in the breeze.

From Grammy's house, you couldn't even see Greensdale proper. But here she felt for the first time as if she was in the very heart of things. The orderly tree-lined streets fanned out beneath her, the warm darkness enveloping them with a distant cricket chorus. The stop light on Main blinked a perennial yellow at this hour, but instead of cars she heard the far-off toot of a train as it rumbled across the tracks at the edge of town.

"Here you go." Peter had materialized at her side, a glass of tea in hand. She sighed happily as he settled into the couch, his arm slipping round her shoulder as if it were the most natural thing in the world. Right now, it felt just like that, and she leaned back against him, contented.

"I'm glad you brought me here," she murmured.

"Me too," he said. "Good view, eh?"

"The best," she said. There was a soft buzzing in her ears that she realized came from a few hours of decibel overload at the Red Roost, but she didn't mind it. She hadn't minded anything in their long and somewhat wacky evening out, capped by Peter's trying to teach her how to lindy on the sawdust dance floor. For a moment she saw herself as someone else, a fellow faculty member, or Jeffrey might have seen her, and the incongruity of it all brought a smile to her lips.

"Share the joke," he said.

"English Lit Professor Masters Lindy-Hop," she murmured. "What are you doing to my image?"

"Nothing bad," he said. He gazed at her in the dim light, his fingers playing with a curl of her hair. "What are you doing to my heart?" he asked softly.

"Nothing bad," she assured him, and leaned forward to steal a warm, moist kiss from his lips. But when she sat back to look at him, a vague shadow flitted across the recesses of her mind. What was it? Something she'd been avoiding thinking about for hours now, that she'd meant to deal with at the top of the evening but hadn't had the heart.

Right. She'd meant to talk to him about her interview with that reporter, and ask him about those newspaper articles—but it all seemed so far away, such an unnecessary nuisance. Now, with the town spread out before them like a toy train set's scenery and her rock 'n' roll hero's arm around her, the scent of jasmine in the air, and her heart standing still like a hummingbird as ever so lightly he caressed her cheek, talking about anything so tedious as chemical plants seemed absurd.

"Listen, could you do me a favor? Stop the world for a while, okay? I'd like to stay like this for as long as I possibly can."

"I can maybe try to slow it down for you," he said, nuzzling the soft skin behind her ear. She shivered happily, feeling wonderfully wanton as her hand stole out to unbutton his shirt, fingers slipping into the soft curls of hair on his chest.

"Does this place come with a bedroom?" she whispered.

"You mean you're not running back to your mother's house?"

"Had you planned on kicking me out?"

Peter smiled. "I'll tell you what I'm planning now," he said, and with a whisper in her ear that made her pulse quicken, he began to tell, and show her. Breath becoming shaky as he kissed the hollow of her neck, Katherine began to feel the world slow down, just as he had promised.

SHE WOKE to the smell of fresh-brewed coffee and bacon and the sight of a bluebird perched on Peter's windowsill giving her a curious look. Sunlight streamed across the sheets in his big brass bed as she sat up and the bird hastily flew off. Katherine stretched, her body feeling blissfully weary of a long night's lovemaking and at the same time already vibrantly awake.

"Peter?"

There was no answer from the other room. But even as she began to wonder, the sound of footfalls on the stairs outside announced his return. She smoothed the sheet over her legs, listening to his loping strides outside with a silly grin stuck on her face. Life seemed suddenly absurdly simple: *eat dinner with Peter, sleep with Peter, wake up, eat breakfast with Peter.* Not a bad life.

"Where were you?" she called.

"Ran out of milk," he answered, leaning in the doorway, a grocery sack under his arm and the morning paper in his hand. "Breakfast is being served in the main dining room," he informed her.

"Indeed?" She looked around for her clothes, which, if she remembered correctly, had last been seen in a trail leading from porch to bedroom.

"On the door," he said, pointing to his closet, where a light terry cloth robe hung.

"Thank you," she said. "No good-morning kiss?"

"If I enter this room," he said, "our eggs will end up cold."

"You're probably right," she said, and with a wink, he disappeared from the doorway. She sat, that smile stuck on her lips again, listening to him putter around the kitchen, humming. Each little sound made her feel ridiculously happy—the milk going into the refrigerator, the squeak of a chair being pulled from the table, the crackle of the morning paper being unfolded.

Katherine got out of bed and quickly donned the robe. It was too big, of course, with sleeves that drooped over her hands, but she kind of liked being enveloped in the thing, which had Peter's scent in it. Stepping to the mirror she inspected her face. Her hair needed brushing, and there, lo and behold, was a brush. She noticed some of Peter's dark hairs twisted round the bristles, and even this gave her a little tug of pleasure.

You've truly gone round the bend, she told her reflection as she ran the brush through her hair. Then she realized that the comforting sounds from the next room, including Peter's humming, had entirely ceased. In fact, the apartment sounded strangely silent. "Peter?"

Katherine moved to the doorway. Peter was seated at his little kitchen table across the room, staring at the newspaper in his hand. The silence was all the more ominous as he slowly, too slowly, put the paper down and turned to look at her with an expression she'd never seen before on his face.

"What's the matter?"

"I think you ought to take a look at this," he said, his voice flat and cool. Katherine hurried over to the table, her heart hammering. Peter handed her the folded paper, and the moment she saw the headline, she blanched.

"ConCo a Menace to Greensdale," it read. "Corporation in Court but Council doesn't Care." "Jeremy Herman a friend of yours?" Peter asked quietly.

"No," she said, her alarm increasing as she scanned the article. "I just talked to him for a little while yesterday."

"Yes, you certainly did," he said. "You might've said something to me."

"I was going to," she said. "But we didn't get..." Her voice trailed off as she came to the next paragraph. "Oh, dear," she muttered.

"'The callous council members seemed dazzled by dollar signs,'" he quoted. "Now, that's good writing, isn't it? Really trips right off the tongue."

"'...but the unscrupulous corporation could very well become a serious health hazard to Greensdale, according to Ms. Taylor,'" she read aloud, her heart sinking.

"Nice to think you trust the *Chronicle* more than a callous council member," Peter said.

"It's not a matter of trust," she protested. "I just didn't think that you and I had to get into all this again—"

"You didn't think!" His fist hit the table and Katherine jumped. "Finish it! Did you read the last paragraph?"

She nodded mutely. The article wound up with a direct and rather snide attack on the council's spokesman, Mr. Peter Bradford, who was characterized as uninformed on the issues "—I know of one case that's in litigation now," Mr. Bradford said breezily, "but it doesn't have any relevance to our situation—" indifferent to the women's position "—Child care is important, sure, but we have a work force that's out of work—" and apparently so biased toward the corporation as to be willing to jeopardize the safety of Greensdale "—ConCo wants to make this thing work, and we want to work with them if we can."

"You knew about the suit?" she asked, forcing herself to look straight into his angry stare.

"I knew about the hidden cost case," he said. "But this chemical spill is news to me! Your pal Travis didn't mention it, either. He just used the opportunity to make me look like an idiot."

"I'm sorry," she said.

"Great," he said. "You're sorry and I'm on the front page of the *Chronicle* with egg all over my face. Thanks."

"Is it really my fault? Peter, you have your position in this thing and I have mine! We discussed it, didn't we? We said we were going to try and separate personal feelings from—"

"Separation is one thing and a knife in the back is another," he said hotly. "You should have told me about that other suit if you knew! Don't you think I might be affected by it?"

"I didn't know," she admitted, realizing with a sickening feeling that she'd secretly feared he'd laugh her off or otherwise dissuade her from making an issue of the thing. "You've been so gung ho on bringing ConCo in—"

"Yes, I *had* been," he said. "But the irony is, I was starting to feel—" He stopped himself, shaking his head. "It doesn't matter," he said grimly. "You obviously don't care about how I feel, or what kind of position I'm in."

"That's not so!" she cried. "Of course I care."

"Then why didn't you come to me?" he demanded.

She stared at him. Good question. She'd been swayed by Emily and Marsha urging her to take advantage of this news, and her own wariness over being involved with Peter had made it easier to see him as the opposition again. She'd rationalized her behavior by thinking that if she really did mean something to him, these arguments over the fate of her mother's house wouldn't matter. Now of course she realized her thinking had been muddled. "I was going to," she repeated dully. "Peter, everything's been happening so fast...."

"Too fast, I guess," he said. "And maybe what's been going on with us hasn't meant as much as I thought it did."

Stung, she drew back. "Wait a second," she said. "Just because I didn't handle this thing properly—"

The loud ring of the telephone interrupted her. "I know who that's going to be," he said with a grimace.

"Why don't you let it ring then?" she said. "Peter, we have to talk this thing out."

"We should've talked before," he said, and turning his back to her, he picked up the phone. "Yeah? Right, Randy. I know... Yes. Look, let me call you back in a few minutes, okay? No. Yes. Yes! I'll call you right back!"

He slammed the receiver down and faced her again. "I ought to take it off the hook for the morning," he muttered.

"Peter, I *do* care about your feelings," she said, alarmed to see him this upset. "But so far as I know, you're against me in this thing."

He shook his head. "Let me tell you something funny," he said, though his tone was entirely unamused. "I was supposed to talk you out of this plan of yours. And you know what happened? You talked *me* out of trying to stop you! I don't want you to sell your house, Katherine. I even came up with an alternate plan."

She stared at him, startled. "What plan?"

"There's a full five and a half acres of property between your house and the town proper that's just sitting there, unused," he said.

"You mean where the stream runs? Past that little swamp to the south of our driveway?"

"Exactly. Well, it's a parcel that used to belong to the Parkinsons, when they had a farm on it, but the point is, the town can reclaim it for next to nothing. The land isn't anywhere near as good as yours, but it's workable. If ConCo could be convinced to build there, we could still keep them in town limits."

"But that means the chemical plant would be right on the edge of our property," she said slowly.

"Not necessarily right on the edge." Peter stared at her. "Katherine, what's with you? Didn't you hear me? I'm not fighting you anymore! I'm ready to try to turn Randy around on this thing. If we can build elsewhere—"

"But it wouldn't be safe," she said. "I don't trust ConCo, especially after these suits. I don't want the children running around on property that could be ecologically unsound."

"Ecologically!" Peter's face darkened. "I don't believe I'm hearing this," he said. "Damn, I knew you were a stubborn woman, but this is madness! You're determined to make things worse for us."

"No, you are," she returned. "Why do you think ConCo is so *good* for Greensdale? You really want to turn this place into a built-up, crowded, commercial town like Jefferson?"

"I don't mean us, Greensdale—" he said tightly "—I mean us, you and me! You use every opportunity to put up obstacles between us, Katherine, and this is one more. What's the point?"

"This has nothing to do with you and me."

"It does now," he said. "We're never going to have any kind of real trust between us if you act like this."

"It's my fault?"

"Not being up front with me about those articles was, yes," he said. "I think if you'd really wanted us to be closer, you never would've handled that the way you did. But maybe you're not interested in closeness. You've got too much invested in being closed off and invulnerable."

"That's not true!" she cried as the shrill ringing of the phone chimed in.

"It certainly is," he said, glowering.

"Don't answer that," she said.

"We can have this out in a minute," he snapped, and reached for the phone.

Katherine stood for a moment, hostility seeming to zip through her bloodstream like cold fire. Suddenly the way he was acting seemed to justify all her fears. He didn't care about *them*, he cared about his friends on the town council and his precious image. And even as she registered the unfairness of that thought, she was withdrawing on the run, gathering up her discarded clothes.

"Hold on, George. Katherine!" he called from the other room. "What are you doing?"

She didn't answer, dressing in a hurry. All she wanted to do was get away from him and his temper. He was still on the phone when she came barreling through the room, and though he gesticulated wildly at her, she kept moving.

"Katherine!" he said, hand over the receiver. "Will you wait a second? Kathy!"

But she wasn't going to stick around to be yelled at. She'd known the whole situation was too good to be true. And she, as Peter might say, was out of here.

Chapter Nine

She'd known the roof was badly in need of repairs but she hadn't realized just how bad it looked. Now, perched outside the attic window, her hands gripping the sill behind her as she straddled one of the gables on the crumbling slate slope, Katherine could see that the many leaks she'd noticed already were only harbingers of the inevitable deluge. From here the roof looked like a slate sieve, and her stomach sank at the thought of yet another extra cost she'd have to add to their spiraling list.

Since she'd last seen Peter—two long days that seemed like at least a week—Katherine had thrown herself into working on the house with renewed and obsessive energy. It helped to keep her mind off him—not that he was ever far from her thoughts—and it helped prepare her for what might be a truly uphill battle in the week to come.

The town council was holding a meeting the following Tuesday to vote on the ConCo issue. Apparently the overgrown forest land and small swamp area that bordered Katherine's property was now officially being considered as an alternate location for the plant. She'd gotten a number of calls from Marsha and Betty and other women in the Alliance. They intended to lobby against ConCo.

Her feelings as much in conflict about the situation with Peter as they were already, the prospect of a public battle where their private involvements couldn't help but play a part was about as welcome to her as having this roof cave in. Which it might, she considered uneasily, gazing about the ancient ramshackle surface.

Then the sound of a car distracted her. Curious, she watched the familiar red and white of a local taxicab wend its way up the driveway. It stopped just at the edge of her bird's-eye view, which was just as well. If she tried to move forward on this gable, she was likely to go tumbling off or through it.

"Clarissa?" Katherine waved. "I'm up here!"

Her daughter shielded her eyes, peering up in confusion. "Mom?" Clarissa squinted, the cab driver pausing in the act of pulling a bag from his trunk to gaze up with her, perplexed. "What are you doing up there?"

"Housework," Katherine called. "But what are you doing here? I'm supposed to be picking you up at the station tomorrow morning."

"I had to come sooner," she said. "I'll be right up." Clarissa turned her attention to paying the driver, her newly hennaed hair glinting red in the sunlight. Katherine watched her worriedly, wondering what new wrinkle in her already overcomplicated personal life had occasioned this change of plans—and hair color. The cab driver gave her a jaunty wave before getting back into his cab and Katherine waved in return.

A good yard of the old copper gutter that lined the roof had been hanging precariously over the back door even since the last rainstorm. From the ground below there was no way of either assessing the extent of damage or doing anything about it. So Katherine, in the midst of compiling a list of house problems that would demand attention even before any renovation could get underway, had diligently marched up to the attic and climbed out of this window for a first-hand look. She was almost sorry she had.

That gutter was hanging by the merest of wire threads at various points around the gabled roof. The steady leak that had worn through the plaster in the back foyer was due, she saw now, to the fact that a whole section of gutter was missing over the south end. "Might as well replace the whole thing," she muttered, wondering how much the price of copper had gone up since World War I. The gutter was at least that old.

"Replace what?"

Katherine nearly jumped a foot at the sound of the voice behind her. She tightened her grip on the sill, heart hammering at the jolt of adrenaline. "Careful!" she croaked, turning to see Clarissa, whose face had materialized in the window.

"You're telling *me* to be careful?" Clarissa rolled her eyes. "Mom, what are you trying to do?"

"Sunbathe," Katherine said darkly, gingerly turning herself around to face her daughter as the slate crunched under her feet. "Why didn't you call me? I would've picked you up."

"Too much of a hassle," Clarissa said. "It was all very last minute, so I didn't want to make any problems for anybody."

"Have you eaten?"

"What?" Clarissa frowned, musing. "I sort of missed breakfast but I also kind of haven't had lunch, either."

"You're also sort of kind of losing your grip on the English language," Katherine said dryly. "Gangway, I'm coming through."

Minutes later she was busying herself pulling cold cuts out of Grammy's cavernous icebox, as she'd called it, a cumbersome appliance that was also a relic from decades past. "Do you like mustard?" she asked Clarissa, now ensconced at the kitchen table.

"Sure," Clarissa said, inspecting the tabletop. "I'm glad you didn't sell this. It's one of a kind, Art Deco." She looked around the kitchen with a critical air. "The place looks empty! How much stuff did you get rid of?"

"About three thousand dollars worth," Katherine said. "And there's still enough furniture and bric-a-brac in the place to furnish a whole other house."

"Good. You can unload some on me, when I move."

Katherine paused in the middle of slicing a loaf of Daisy Gardiner's stone-ground wheat bread. Daisy was a friend of Emily's who'd been showing her support for their women's group by baking breads for all the meetings. "When you move?" she repeated. "I thought you just *had* moved."

Clarissa fixed her gaze on some point a foot or so beyond her mother's head. "I don't think this is the best time to discuss the wreckage of my domestic, professional and romantic life," she said ominously. And then, her mood shifting with its usual quicksilver speed, she jumped up from the table. "That reminds me," she called in singsong over her shoulder. "I brought you a present."

Katherine stifled a sigh. She was doing her best to restrain herself from being overly motherly. Clarissa at twenty-three seemed determined to work out her personal problems by herself. It was a point of pride that she stand on her own two feet, emotionally, and in this, Katherine couldn't help but reflect, the daughter was doing the very thing her mother tended to do. So how could she criticize? All she could really do was be there for Clarissa, should the need for help arise.

"Here you go," Clarissa said brightly, reentering the kitchen with an unwrapped box that she thrust into Katherine's hand. "My friend Alicia's started working at a boutique on the Lower East Side where they have all these fabulous antiquey kinds of things, and she brought a few of them over yesterday. It's a tad big for me and not really my style, but I thought it would be perfect for you."

It was an old-fashioned white cotton nightgown, sleeveless, with a delicate appliqué of lace at the collar, which dipped low in a provocative V above a single tie. The material was light to the point of sheerness. "It's beautiful," Katherine said, touched, and held it up to check the length.

"Sexy, don't you think?" Clarissa said. "I figured you'd have more use for it these days than I would, anyway." She wiggled her eyebrows playfully. "I mean, you have someone around to appreciate you in it on these sultry summer nights...."

"Thank you, sweetheart," Katherine said, carefully folding the nightgown back into its box. "But you're wrong about that, I'm afraid. The only one who's likely to see me in this is me."

"Oh, no!" Clarissa sat down at the table with a look of great distress. "Don't tell me. What did you do?"

"What makes you think *I* did something?" Katherine said defensively.

"We had a feeling you'd try to blow it," Clarissa went on. "Mom, why couldn't you just count your blessings?"

"Who's 'we'?" Katherine demanded.

"Me and Lydie, who else? According to her, this guy is a total dreamboat." Clarissa gave a theatrical sigh. "All right, I'm going to eat this sandwich and you're going to tell me everything that happened, okay? And then we'll figure a way to work it out."

"Don't be so sure I *want* to work it out," Katherine said, amused in spite of herself.

"Sure you do," Clarissa said briskly, getting out a plate. "Now let's have all the details."

Katherine joined her at the table with a pitcher of iced tea. Though she certainly spared her daughter some of the details, she did sketch out the parameters of this Peter Bradford problem, as she termed it. The phone kept interrupting, women from the Alliance calling to arrange the details of their next meeting and estimates coming in from the plumber and electrician she'd contacted about the house, but by the end of two ham, cheese and turkey sandwiches and the full pitcher of tea, Clarissa was ready with her assessment.

"You wanted it to happen," she pronounced, fixing her mother with a shrewd gaze that reminded Katherine of Grammy.

"I wanted the man to practically yell me out of his apartment?" Katherine shook her head. "You think that's my idea of a good time?"

"No, silly, but you wanted something to come between the two of you, obviously. Why else would you have purposefully gone ahead and done something you knew would make trouble for you later?"

"If you're referring to my talk to Jeremy Herman," she said, "there was no reason why I shouldn't have given him the information I had. Peter and I had already agreed—"

"Yeah, yeah," Clarissa said, impatient. "But you knew that by not telling Peter about it you were being, well, sneaky."

"I wouldn't call it sneaky," Katherine said, but she remembered full well the misgivings she'd felt when she'd talked to the reporter without contacting Peter. "All right, I knew there might be some consequences, but . . ."

"It's just the sort of thing I used to do with Stewart," Clarissa said. "Passive-aggressive behavior, that's what Dr. Lefkowitz calls it." Katherine had been paying for Clarissa's weekly sessions with a psychologist in the city. One of the risks of helping her daughter in that way was having instant psychological insights sprung on her like this from time to time, but if Clarissa was feeling better for them, she found it hard to protest.

"All right," she allowed. "Maybe I was indirectly helping to keep barriers up between Peter and myself, I'll admit to that. But maybe that's a very healthy instinct, Clarissa. Just because the man looks like a 'dreamboat' doesn't mean he's the right man for me to be with."

"What are you so afraid of with this guy, anyway?" Clarissa asked blandly.

"I'm afraid of things getting serious when they shouldn't," she said after a moment's thought.

"Why shouldn't they?"

"Why? Because we have practically nothing in common." She could enumerate these things automatically, having thought about them often enough over the past forty-eight hours. "He's not an intellectual, he's much younger than I am, he has different values than I do, and he's not interested in a serious relationship anyway."

But Clarissa looked severely skeptical. "You asked him? About the serious relationship part?"

"Of course not. But it's written all over him. The man likes to go out Sunday nights and play in a rock 'n' roll band, Liss! He's not even sure he wants to stay in law. We're talking about someone who's not exactly rooted and secure. Besides, his last relationship was evidently a disaster, and he's not in a hurry to start another."

"According to what you and Aunt Lydie tell me, he's been relentless, pursuing you," Clarissa said. "That doesn't sound like a man who's not interested."

"It's probably just a physical thing," Katherine muttered, more to herself, then immediately averted her eyes in embarrassment at the look of startled interest on her daughter's face.

"Really?"

"No," Katherine said immediately. She didn't want even tacitly to condone that kind of a relationship before her own daughter, no matter how adult she might be. Besides, she realized, it wasn't true. Though there certainly was more than a modicum of unbridled passion between herself and Peter Bradford, that wasn't the only basis of their wanting to be together. "I think we've talked about this enough, don't you?"

"Nope," Clarissa said firmly. "Besides, I'd much rather talk about your problems than mine, any day."

"I'm sure," Katherine said wryly. "But my problem's over. I don't think I'll be seeing Peter, except at the town council meeting."

"Doesn't sound over to me," Clarissa said. "And Mom, I have to say, I haven't seen you so whipped up over anybody since Dad died."

"Whipped up?"

"You know, excited. You sounded so lively on the phone when I called that time. And Lydie says you've never been happier."

"What is it with the two of you?" Katherine asked. "Is this some kind of conspiracy?"

"Absolutely," Clarissa said calmly. "We're conspiring to make sure you're okay."

"Really?" Now it was her turn to echo her daughter's startled exclamation. "But of course I'm okay."

"That's what you always say, sure," Clarissa said. "But we know you a little better than that. You've been kind of down for a while now."

"I have not!" Her assertion sounded unconvincing even as she voiced it. Clarissa merely looked at her, chin propped in her hands. "Well, maybe from time to time I get a little blue," she said. "And certainly since Grammy died...."

Clarissa put a hand out to take Katherine's, her own eyes clouding over. Katherine squeezed her daughter's hand gently. "I miss your father, sometimes, too. I miss us all being together, like we used to."

Clarissa nodded soberly. "Me, too."

"I'm glad you found the time to come up for a visit," Katherine told her. "You know, you don't have to tell me much about what's going on, but if there's anything I can do..."

"It's good just being here," Clarissa said. They were both silent for a moment, listening to the sounds of the old house. "It's almost like she's still here," Clarissa said softly.

Katherine nodded. "Sometimes I even imagine she is," she said. "I even..." She stopped herself, self-conscious.

"You talk to her? Me, too," Clarissa said. "I have conversations with Grammy all the time."

Katherine stared at her. Clarissa smiled. "She *is* still here," she said. "As long as we keep her alive, inside."

Katherine got up and went to her daughter's side, wrapping her arms around her. She closed her eyes, hugging her warm, soft body to her. "I hate this new color in your hair," she said. "But I love you, Liss. I probably don't tell you that enough."

"Oh, come on, Mom. You always try to play down that you have any feelings at all, but they come through loud and clear," Clarissa said, and kissed her on the cheek. Katherine released her, and stood for a moment, her daughter's chin in her hand, content to study her sweet and clear-eyed expression.

"How'd you get so wise?" she asked her.

"All the best schools," Clarissa said airily, and got up. "I'm going to put my things in my room upstairs," she announced. "But listen, if you think I'm smart, you should listen to me. Maybe seeing Peter again would be good for you."

"And why is that?"

"I think it's not over," she said. "You're still all bent out of shape over it."

"I hadn't realized my posture was at stake," Katherine said.

"It's an expression." Clarissa rolled her eyes again and headed for the door. "But you know what Grammy would say?" she added, pausing in the doorway. "Always see through what you've started."

"Yes, she would say that," Katherine agreed wryly. "I haven't had a chance to put clean linens on—"

"Don't worry about it," Clarissa called, and was gone. Katherine stood in the now silent kitchen, contemplating what her daughter had said. She knew Clarissa was right; it *wasn't* over. One good rip-roaring fight hadn't put an end to the feelings she had for Peter Bradford. If anything, she was feeling his presence in her life—or the lack of it—all the more keenly.

She missed him. She wanted to be with him, if only for the simple reason that when she was she felt better than she had done in ages, more alive, more herself. That feeling was what she wanted from being with him, and if the future was uncertain and everything else about being with him problematic, so be it. Maybe it was worth the struggle.

She could see him. She could apologize for the trouble she'd unintentionally caused. She could be more direct about what she wanted from him, and find out what he wanted with her. "What have I got to lose?" she murmured aloud.

"Not a thing," Grammy whispered. Closing her eyes, Katherine could imagine the white-haired woman right behind her, stooped over as she nosed nearsightedly through the shelves of the old icebox for an afternoon snack.

"A little pride," Katherine mused.

"Pride!" Grammy sniffed. "There's an emotion with a limited use. Put a dollop of it next to love and see which weighs more on the scale of things."

Katherine smiled, then looked suddenly to the sink. "Oh! Gram, we sold your old measuring scale yesterday."

"Piece of junk," Grammy said diffidently. "Hope you got a good price for it." And shuffling out of the kitchen, she left Katherine to contemplate the clock, the phone and the man who'd been so angry when she'd seen him last.

Would he still be that angry?

"FOR THE LOVE OF—!" Peter clamped his mouth shut in midyell. Cursing the guy out was the worst thing to do just now. "Keep your eye on it, Willy!" he shouted instead, forcing a lighter, more encouraging tone into his voice.

Willy Baker, all three feet two inches of him, screwed his face up in concentration and flexed his bat. The shortest member of the Greensdale Hornets, he was usually a sure bet for an easy walk. All he had to do was stand there at the plate, and most pitchers in the league, confused by the alteration in the strike zone that his diminutive stature demanded, couldn't help but walk him. So why had Willy, despite Peter's instructions, taken a swing at a ball he couldn't have it in a million years?

The Hornets needed a walk right now, with runners on second and third, two men out, and Lennie Pike, the slugger, next up at bat. With bases loaded, Pike could bring in the winning runs—as long as little Willy did what he was supposed to do. Peter resisted gnawing on his thumbnail as another pitch swooped across the plate.

This time Willy stayed firm. "Ball three!" Ken Lewis, the portly umpire called, and Peter joined in with the yells of encouragement from the kids around him at the sidelines. He knew he shouldn't be getting so wound up over a Little League game, but then his nerves had been on edge for days, and the Hornets needed a win. They were four games behind in this year's pennant race.

"That's the eye, Willy!" Peter called. "Keep it up!"

Jonathan Penders, the pimple-faced pitcher for the Toptown All-Stars, glowered at Willy from the mound. He chewed savagely at his Bazooka bubble gum, narrowed his eyes, wound up, and threw what looked like a mean fast ball. Peter held his breath. Willy held his ground, bat erect, as the ball whizzed by—high and outside.

"Ball four!" bellowed Ken, and amid hysterical cheering from the Hornets' bench, the littlest Little Leaguer tossed his bat aside and strolled down the first baseline, head high.

Peter breathed a sigh of relief. Now if Lennie could get any kind of a decent hit, the game would be over and won.

"Go get 'em, Len!" Hearing the basso profundo roar from the bleachers, Peter knew Lennie's dad was in the stands. Ever since he'd been laid off, Matt Pike hadn't missed one of these late afternoon games, and he occasionally coached the Hornets when Peter had too much work to attend one. Peter turned to the bleachers to give him a thumbs-up hello, and froze.

One face was suddenly blindingly in focus amid the clusters of parents and school kids. The cascade of golden hair, the gleaming gaze of bright blue eyes, the pursed lips and upraised chin, riveted him with the force of a hardball pitched right at his solar plexus. What was Katherine Taylor doing at this baseball game?

Everyone else was in profile, eyes intent on the batter, but she was looking right at him. He was so distracted he barely registered the first strike Lennie took, but then cries of anguish from the dirt-and sweat-mired Hornets around him brought him back to the game. "Come on, Lennie," he called, but his attention was scattered now.

He could sense her gaze on him, and the tension he'd been feeling all afternoon threatened to knot itself into every muscle. It was bad enough that he hadn't been able to keep his mind off Katherine during a grueling few days at the office, but now, when he was supposedly relaxing, did he need this? All of his concentration should have been focused on the all-important win, but he was too busy trying not to look at her as a second strike whizzed across the plate.

After a chorus of moans from the home team and their fans, the crowd was hushed. Penders stood stock-still, glove at chest. *Come on, Lennie,* Peter prayed silently. *Get a piece of it, will you? Win this one for the guys. And for me. And for the fans in the stands, like Kath—*

Even as he registered with an inward wince that he hadn't succeeded in blocking her out of this thoughts, there was the welcome crack of ball on bat. A hit! And it was sailing out over the first baseman's head, nearly foul, almost straight down the line, and even as the Townies' fielder scrambled to get under it he knew, everyone knew, a roar going up all around the funky little diamond at the edge of the school grounds, that the Hornets had the game.

Pandemonium reigned, hats and gloves flying into the air, a ministampede of parents and peers pouring from the stands. Peter was buffeted nearly off his feet by the jubilant Hornets. For a few minutes he was able to lose himself in congratulating his team, hoisting both Lennie and little Willy aloft in an impromptu victory parade around home plate.

"You know what you oughta do with that short kid, you should teach him to bunt," Matt Pike exhorted him, after pumping his hand over the long-awaited win. Peter nodded, but he wasn't really listening. His eyes had strayed again to the stands where a solitary figure still sat patiently, watching him from across the dusty field.

He felt a tremor of excitement coupled with a sharp ache of longing as he drank in this glimpse of her. She couldn't have come here for any other reason than to see him. And if she wanted to see him . . . well, certainly she owed him an apology, didn't she? Peter went through the motions of cleaning up, with his mind and heart still in the bleachers.

He'd been hoping she'd come back. He'd long since given up on exorcising her spirit from inhabiting his heart, and if she hadn't shown up here today, he'd surely have ended up on her doorstep by tomorrow—not that he was about to let her know that, of course. No, he was going to be cool, calm, collected, a model of remote indifference. He'd hear what she had to say and then weigh it all with gentlemanly equanimity. And then, just maybe . . .

Katherine had risen and was stepping down to the straggly grass as he began to stride toward her, deliberately slowing his pace. Hands in the pockets of her skirt, she, too seemed to be affecting the most casual approach. But then she was moving faster, and somehow he was, too, and before he could even think to stop himself he was closing the last feet between them in a run, as she threw herself into his arms.

SHE'D NEVER KNOWN that a slightly unshaven face could feel so good against hers, but enveloped by Peter's strong and muscular frame she felt she'd been lifted into heaven, savoring the gentle scrape of his cheek on hers and the breathtakingly familiar musky male scent of him as he rocked her gently off her feet.

She could feel herself melting against his sweat-damp body, and far from resisting the sensation, she luxuriated in it, eagerly lifting her lips to be kissed as he eased her head back, staring down into her eyes with a wonderfully hungry look. When the kiss came, the taste of him made her blood race, and it seemed no kiss could do her emotions justice. Their mouths melded, tongues touching in a joyful, fierce yet playful dance.

The whistles and cheers of a bedraggled band of Little Leaguers were what finally brought them back to earth. Breaking apart, they found the Hornets razzing their coach with glee. Peter took it good-naturedly as he held Katherine at his side.

"You'd think they'd never seen someone get kissed before," he said, grinning as his eyes met hers again.

"Well, you certainly showed them how it's supposed to be done," she answered, her voice husky.

"I've missed you, damn it," he growled. "It's about time you showed up."

Just like him, she thought, acting as if there wasn't a reason in the world why she should've stayed away. But he was clearly so happy to see her that any lingering resentments didn't have time to flare. *Come on, Kath, do what you decided to do,* she told herself sternly. "I was busy constructing the right sort of apology," she said.

He grinned, face alight. "I see," he said. "And as a lover of great literature, what deep and high-flown kind of poetry have you prepared?"

"How about: I'm sorry?" she said.

Peter laughed, gathering her up in his arms again. "That's deep, all right," he said, and kissed her forehead, his warm moist lips sending a tremor of pure pleasure through her. "I'm sorry, too. I'm sorry whatever happened, happened." He raised an eyebrow, his dark gaze searching hers. "Want to talk about it?"

She nodded. He took her hand, and without another word, began leading her across the now deserted field. It was only a few short blocks from here to Luke's tackle shop. Katherine clung to his side, her mind teeming with all the carefully prepared sentences she'd been constructing, the things she wanted to discuss. But somehow talk didn't seem necessary, and as they neared the staircase that led to Peter's place they still hadn't said another word.

But before they reached his door she felt she had to stop him. "Peter, it's not enough to just say we're sorry and leave it at that," she said. "We still have a lot to work out."

"I agree," he said, leading her inside.

"For one thing, we should discuss—" His lips silenced her with a fiercely loving kiss. The door slowly swung shut behind her as he reached for her again, pulling her against his lean, muscled body, his hands firm but gentle as he held her there.

"What do you want to discuss, love?" he murmured. "Why you purposefully withheld information from me the other day?"

"Well, yes," she began, unable to keep from sighing shakily as his hands molded her pliant body to his tense frame.

"You were still hedging bets," he said, running one hand through her hair, his eyes aglow with a look of knowing affection. "Maybe you figured that putting a smoke screen of

ConCo controversy up between us would stop you from getting any more involved with me.''

"That's right," she said, impressed that he'd already intuited what it had taken her longer to find out. He bent to kiss the tip of her nose, fingers making magical, sensual ripples of sensation as his hands caressed her back.

"But you're here now. So I guess maybe you figure a little more involvement isn't all that bad?''

"I guess maybe," she echoed. Her hands, as if with a will of their own, were on the buttons of his shirt, fumbling with eager haste to break through that cloth barrier and feel the warmth of his flesh against her.

"We just have to be more direct," he said, his hands slipping sinuously up her sides, thumbs grazing the swell of her breasts beneath the thin material. "Communicate," he said, his voice husky with evident arousal. "Trust."

"I wasn't *ready* to trust you," she said, her voice shaky as she pulled his shirt free from his pants, sliding her hands up inside, her fingertips trailing along the smooth warmth of his chest. "With this fuss over the house going on, and you and I only starting to get to know each other..."

"It's understandable," he whispered. "Trust isn't an easy thing to come by."

"No," she agreed, and suddenly she couldn't hold back anymore. Reaching up, she sought his mouth with a desperate urgency. His passion matched her own and his hands were deft. In mere seconds, it seemed, she was standing in the circle of his arms wearing nothing but a thin wisp of silk panties.

He groaned softly as his tongue explored her mouth, hands tracing the curves of her nudity, cupping her breasts as they pressed against his still frustrating shirt front. And then his hand joined hers in practically tearing the clothing from his body.

"Yes, we have a lot to discuss," he muttered hoarsely, as her hands moved across his chest. He caught one, gliding it downward, and she gasped as she felt his raging arousal.

"So much," she breathed, moaning herself as he pressed his full nakedness to her and in one deft movement, stripped the last barrier of clothing down her thighs.

"I'm getting you all sweaty," he murmured, coming up for air at the end of a soul-melting kiss.

"I don't mind," she said, teasing his nipples into hardness and enjoying his quick intake of breath.

"Wait," he said, and with a chuckle deep in his throat, he picked her up, starting to carry her across the room. They bypassed the bedroom and he kicked open the bathroom door, only letting her down when he'd reached past the billowing shower curtain with his free arm and turned the faucets within.

"We can continue our discussion in my private chambers," he said with a mischievous grin, and pulled her under the warm cascade of water. Katherine clung to him, enjoying the wetness and the heat of his enveloping body as with soap in hand, he began to lather his skin and hers.

"The great...indoor debate?" she queried, reveling in the feel of his smooth hands spreading suds over her shoulders.

"That's right," he said. "And what was it you were so eager to talk about?"

She arched her back, a moan of pleasure escaping her lips as he cupped her breasts, teasing their rosy peaks into tingling hardness. "The women of the Alliance," she whispered.

"Oh, them," he said, his soapy hand trailing over the slick skin of her taut belly. "What about them?"

"They're still going to fight this...ConCo thing at the town meeting."

"Yes, I know." She turned to face him, the soap in her hands now, moving them over his chest, following the curls of soft hair to the thatch below, delighting in the tensing of his body as she captured him, teasing him with playful fingers.

"Even though the plant wouldn't be on my property," she continued dreamily, as he pulled her soapy body to his, "it's still close enough to make me nervous."

"Right." He turned her with him to catch the full stream of water, letting it rinse the suds from their slick skin. "And do *I* make you nervous?"

"In the best way," she murmured, closing her eyes as his hands gently massaged her back.

"Enough debate. I think we're clean," he announced. He gently maneuvered her into and out of the spray before turning it off, then faced her, dripping in the warm steam. "Towel?" he asked.

In this weather, it felt fine to be wet. "Sheets," she answered, with a provocative smile. Now it was she, emboldened, who led him across the wooden floor to the brass bed in the other room. Then, before she could protest, he rolled over onto his back on the white sheets, pulling her with him.

She lay stretched out across his body, her wet curls cascading over his upturned face. For a moment, she felt self-conscious, naked astride him in the orangy late-afternoon light. But the pitch of their emotions after so much tantalizing foreplay was too high. She let him guide her pliant limbs over his.

His firm hands caught her hips, levered her gently forward, holding her just beyond his own pulsing need for an exquisite moment as his eyes held hers. Then he pulled her down onto him, his magnificent hardness filling her to the depths.

Gazing down at him she felt brazen, all the more assured and aroused as she saw how much he enjoyed the feel of her as he arched his hips up, pulled back again, filling her each time with more and more pleasure. Her body began to shudder with little spasms of need as he kept the slow and steady pace, holding back, ever in control.

"Let go," she urged him, panting. "*You* let go." She was so close now to fulfillment that a wildness seized her, and she rode him more fiercely. At last he gave in to her almost desperate urgency, and as she cried aloud he arched even more forcefully into her. She went rigid in his arms as he followed her, breath hoarse and ragged as they reached the summit together, locked as one being in a timeless moment.

Then he was holding her shivering, damp body to his, his own hands trembling as they stroked her back and she kissed his neck, resting her cheek against his while their breaths slowed, still synchronized in the aftermath.

"Don't move," he murmured.

"I'm too heavy," she protested.

"Not for me, sweetheart." He smiled up at her, one hand lazily massaging its way up her spine. She stretched into it, as pliant and sensual as a satiated feline. Well, almost satiated. She looked into his eyes and sensed the same keen desire still stirring. She knew without asking that he, too, was in no hurry to be separated from her.

"I don't know that I ever...did that before," she admitted. "I mean, that way."

"Fun, isn't it?"

She nodded, smiling. "I have a feeling you could teach me a few things."

"And you me," he said. "That was a very...equal debate."

"But we didn't get anywhere," she said, with a facetious frown.

"Depends on how you look at it," he said. "I think we've gone far enough to have reached some conclusions." He smiled, reaching up to trace the line of her lips with one finger. "We could even go the distance," he said, and there

was an oddly serious look in his eyes then that made her
wonder.

"Meaning?"

"Meaning I'm very far in love with you, Professor," he
said.

She knew it was true. She'd felt that wonderful feeling
again, that sense of being cherished. She felt it in every look
from him, every touch and word. And she knew just as vividly what she was feeling for him. "That's good," she said,
and let out a shaky breath. "Because I'm in love with you."

"I'm glad to hear it," he said softly. "That'll make my
next question a little easier to ask."

She said nothing, only looking at him and feeling her
heartbeat quicken as he held her gaze.

"Katherine, have you ever thought about getting married again?"

Chapter Ten

It wasn't the sort of question she'd been expecting. Katherine stared at Peter, feeling a sudden chill as a breeze blew through the room, raising goose bumps on her damp skin. "I hadn't been thinking about it, no," she said, in as light a tone as she could muster as she eased herself out from his embrace.

He watched her, his expression inscrutable, as she sat up, modestly drawing his sheet around her to half hide her nakedness in the fading light. "Maybe it's a topic we could discuss," he said evenly. "Along with all the others."

After all the time she'd spent convincing herself that even if this thing with Peter was a casual fling, there was no harm in it, his unexpected raising of the stakes was disorienting, to say the least. "You're not really...serious, are you?" she asked, her voice tremulous.

Peter sat up to face her, the hint of a frown creasing his forehead. "Would you like it better if I wasn't?"

Katherine looked down, words failing her as she sought to clear her way through a tumult of conflicting emotions. "No, I just hadn't—that is, I didn't..."

She could hear the smile in his voice when he spoke. "I think I've caught the Professor unprepared," he said. "Well, hey, that makes two of us." She looked up then, to see a kindly twinkle in his eyes. "Kath, I won't say I've been thinking about this for long. Two long days ago I wondered if we'd ever see each other again, let alone end up like this. But I hoped we would.''

She nodded dumbly, feeling an odd sense of unreality. It was as if a part of her had already left the bed and was watching the scene from the doorway, ready to bolt at the slightest provocation. "Well, so did I," she began uncertainly. "But I thought we might take one thing at a time."

"Makes sense," he said. "But maybe this isn't about making sense, love. I just know what feels right. You feel right with me. And the funny thing is, you can go ahead and call me crazy, but now that we *are* here—" he held his palms upward "—it's hard for me to imagine us being apart again."

"Okay," she said. "I'll call you crazy. You're crazy."

Peter sighed and shook his head. "Crazy for you, Katherine. What's wrong with that?"

"Nothing," she said. *But everything,* she thought, all the reasons she'd so thoroughly catalogued that made Peter and herself an absolute mismatch. "But we hardly know each other."

"That's debatable." He took her hand beneath the sheet. "I'll tell you one thing I know about you. You're not the sort of woman who's used to having affairs."

"True. Is that what we're having?" she asked.

"No," he said. "That's the point. This is better than an affair. I think we could spend some serious time together. And I mean more than a few months."

Katherine took a deep, shuddering breath. This was both what she'd wanted to hear and exactly what she hadn't wanted. As long as *she* didn't take this whatever-it-was seriously, she didn't have to have anxieties about the outcome of it. "Maybe we should go one day at a time?" she suggested.

Peter nodded. "No problem. We can save any discussions about what college we send our kids to until, oh, next Friday, how's that?"

He was only being funny, she knew, but the mention of children raised her anxiety level another notch. She hadn't had the slightest intention of falling in love again, but maybe that could be dealt with. But children! Katherine cleared her throat. "Peter, I'm a little old to be planning another family."

"You're young," he said mildly. "Besides, I'll help."

Abruptly, as if on automatic pilot, she found herself getting up from the bed. "Look, don't take this the wrong way. I like you, too," she said, thinking that was an inane thing to say as she stood up, sheet wrapped around her.

"A few minutes ago it was love," he noted. "Honey, where are you going?"

She had no idea. Then a glance at the oversize antique clock hanging on the opposite wall reminded her she really did have a legitimate rationale for escape. "I have to go home and change," she told him. "I'm seeing a play tonight at the Berkshire Roundabout."

"I take it this particular topic makes you a little anxious," he said dryly.

"A little," she said. "Do you mind if I put some clothes on?"

"Yes and no," he said. "I've been enjoying you with your clothes off, but more to the point, why are you in such a rush to get out of here?"

"This play goes on at seven-thirty," she said. "It's a dress rehearsal, you see, so they start early. I have to go because the play's by a former student of mine, and I promised I'd take a look at it and tell him what I thought, so I really can't be late—"

"Whoa!" He interrupted her stream of blather and caught hold of her wrist as she passed the bed, making a beeline for the door. "You're in danger of hurting some-one's feelings here, you know that?"

"I'm sorry." She felt her face reddening under his bale-ful gaze. "Peter, I wasn't expecting this, that's all. Don't you think that us talking about marriage is a case of too much, too soon?"

"Judging from your reaction, I'd have to agree," he said. "But Kath, I *am* serious," he added quietly. "And just be-cause the idea makes you nervous doesn't mean I'm going to back off and forget about it." He was drawing her closer as he rose to his knees on the bed. Eyes even with hers now, he put his hands on her shoulders. "Unless you're trying to tell me I'm wrong to think we could have a future to-gether."

When she looked into the velvet depths of his luminous eyes, feeling the warmth of his skin on hers and the answer-ing warmth that surged up within her at his touch, it was hard to deny it. "No," she said softly. What kind of a fu-ture, she had no idea, but she wasn't about to throw this feeling away. "I guess I haven't been looking much further than the present moment," she admitted, then added im-pulsively: "But with you, the present's been pretty wonder-ful."

He smiled. "Then tell me we *will* talk about the future, when you've had some time to get used to the idea, okay?" he said. "I want to be with you, sweetheart. I'm in this thing for keeps."

The bittersweet ache of love she felt swelling in her heart at the soulful look in his eyes was almost scary in its inten-sity. She could only nod, mute, as his lips gently brushed hers with a feather-light kiss.

"Now, are you still in such a hurry?" he asked.

Conscious of his glorious nakedness and the inviting bed, she was torn. "No," she whispered. It would be so easy to sink right back into his arms, and let that all-consuming present moment continue, without worrying about any future at all. "But I do have to go."

"Maybe you'd like some company."

She brightened at the thought, then frowned, considering that Daryl MacIntosh's *Murk* wasn't likely to be the kind of theater fare that would appeal to Peter. "I would," she said. "But it's a sort of avant-garde kind of production. I doubt if you'd enjoy it."

"Try me," he said. "I'll enjoy just about anything if I'm with you."

Katherine sighed, slipping her arms around his neck. "You do say the right things, Coach," she murmured. "I'll give you that."

"NOTHING?"

"No . . . thing."

"But nothing is everything," countered the man in the top hat, feather boa and boxer shorts. He was addressing his remarks to a woman in a leotard who was suspended above the stage, hanging upside down from a trapezelike bar, bathed in a blood-red spotlight. The woman closed her eyes as some electronic music bleated briefly from unseen speakers, then clapped her hands once. A screen behind her lit up with a black and white picture of Albert Einstein.

The man in the top hat had spent the last fifteen minutes—which had seemed more like an hour to Peter—talking to the audience about God, death, and the persistence of memory and sweepstakes contests. Then this woman had come down from the ceiling, and he'd talked to her about more of the same.

Peter had started out amused and was now merely incredulous. For reasons he couldn't fathom, most of the other members of the audience seemed enthralled by this spectacle that made absolutely no sense to him. Katherine, on his right, was leaning forward, apparently intent on catching every nonsensical word. Clarissa, who'd accompanied them to the theater, seemed similarly preoccupied.

Peter sat back, taking a surreptitious survey of the other people in their section. He was thankful to see a man his age frowning at the program in his hand, and another two rows behind him who was pointedly ignoring the stage and eyeing the nearest exit. At least he wasn't alone in his befuddlement.

Back on stage, the upside-down woman had somehow gotten a gleaming revolver from somewhere and was aiming it at the man in the top hat. *Good move,* he thought. *That ought to shut him up.* His interest rekindled, he watched the man flick his feather boa at her, oddly unfazed.

"Bang," said the upside-down woman.

"But I'm already dead," the man replied, and quite suddenly, the woman was being hoisted upward again and was soon out of sight as the lights turned blue. Mr. Top Hat turned toward the audience and began talking again, his lines sounding suspiciously like an exact repetition of the ones he'd begun the play with.

Peter leaned next to Katherine's ear. "Who *was* that woman?" he whispered.

She shook her head, a finger at her lips, then gave his knee a reassuring pat. But Peter didn't feel reassured. Disgruntled, he squirmed in his seat, glancing at his watch. According to the program, they wouldn't even be allowed the reprieve of an intermission. He stifled a sigh and settled in for the long haul, wishing he'd thought to bring a transistor radio and earphone. The Mets were playing the Reds tonight in Cincinnati.

The man in the top hat had been joined by another man in a scuba diving outfit. They seemed to be arguing about the precise location of hell. "Hell is other people," said Mr. Top Hat.

"No, it's in your mind," said the diver.

"It's here," Peter murmured under his breath, and felt Katherine's elbow give him a gentle but pointed nudge as Clarissa shot him a smiling look.

A woman in the seat in front of him turned round to give him an indignant stare. "Ssh!" she said.

Most probably the playwright's mother, Peter mused. He sat back in his seat and closed his eyes. The lights on the stage had turned an electric green, and the people were painful to look at to begin with. He listened absently to the unending dialogue, his mind drifting back to the hours he'd spent with Katherine. Replaying images in his mind, such as the breathtaking beauty of her, poised above him in the orange light, was far more pleasurable than watching *Murk*.

THE NEXT THING he knew, people were clapping. Peter bolted upright, eyes blinking, and quickly added his own half-hearted applause to the respectful ovation. The actors took their curtain call and then, mercifully, he was able to stand, stretching his cramped limbs.

"Can you meet me in the lobby? I have to talk to Daryl," Katherine said.

"Sure," Peter said. Had she noticed that he'd fallen asleep? Katherine seemed a little cool to him, but he wasn't sure. Maybe she'd merely been as depressed by the play as he had, he mused, watching her hurry down the aisle toward the stage. He turned to Clarissa. "I could use some air. How about you?"

She nodded. Peter followed her out. He'd mistaken Katherine's daughter for Katherine that day in the cemetery, but now, with her hair a much redder shade of blond, cut in a severe fashion he intuited was up-to-the-minute Manhattan, it was harder to see the resemblance. Getting through the crowd took some time. At Peter's gentle prodding, Clarissa cut a quick swath through the people lingering in the lobby, where many a cigarette was being lit, and moved to the cool air outside.

"What did you think?" he asked the younger woman.

Clarissa shrugged. "Pretty tough going," she said. "Besides, Robert Wilson and Meredith Monk do that sort of thing a lot better, you know?"

He didn't know, as the names were unfamiliar. "I couldn't really follow it," he admitted.

"We noticed," Clarissa said with a grin. "Mom got a little uptight when you started snoring."

"Snoring?" Peter winced. "Was I really snoring?"

"Only toward the end," Clarissa assured him. "I stepped on your foot, though, and you stopped."

"I hope it wasn't too loud," he said, chagrined.

"Not really." Clarissa was examining him with interest. "You're taller than she is, aren't you?"

"I guess."

"You look good together," Clarissa announced. "If you don't mind my saying."

"I don't," he said, and smiled. "How long are you up here for?"

"Just through the weekend," she said. "Then I have to get back to my mess in New York."

He was about to ask her what sort of mess she'd left there when he caught sight of Katherine through the glass doors, moving slowly across the lobby with a group of people that included a wild-haired young man he assumed was the playwright, and a woman he recognized uneasily as the one who'd shushed him in the theater. Katherine was shaking her hand and saying goodbye.

"You should be proud, Mrs. MacIntosh," she was saying with a pleasant smile. *Good grief,* the woman really *had* been the playwright's mother. "Goodnight, Daryl." Daryl and Mom departed as Peter and Clarissa approached.

"You must be proud as well, Katherine." This remark came from a stooped elderly man with thick glasses who looked as if he rarely saw the light of day. "You were one of Daryl's earliest champions."

Katherine shrugged diffidently. "I just told him to keep writing," she said, and catching sight of Clarissa and Peter, hurried to introduce them. "My daughter, Clarissa, and my friend Peter Bradford—this is Cameron Whiteson, chairman of Humanities at Hampshire. And this," she went on, as Peter shook the old man's hand, "is Andrew Farron, head of the Theater Department."

With a cursory flash of teeth at Peter, Farron immediately launched into an anecdote. He was younger, possibly Katherine's age, and Peter disliked him immediately. It wasn't because of his flashy clothing and theatrical demeanor so much as the way he related to Katherine, smiling at her in a proprietary way, touching her elbow with a familiarity that set Peter's blood boiling.

He found that he couldn't follow the anecdote, not that he'd been paying much attention, and as Katherine and the older man laughed appreciatively, Farron launching right into another story, Peter drifted off to the side, watching. It struck him that Katherine didn't really have anything going on with this highbrow goofball—he could tell that by the way she kept a certain distance—but he was jealous all the same.

If these really were the sort of people she liked to hang out with, no wonder he struck a wrong note in her social score. Peter didn't know any of the names Farron was liberally dropping and didn't care to. For the first time in his pursuit of Katherine Taylor, he had a sense of just how far apart the orbits of their separate worlds really were.

There weren't many other people in the lobby when Farron and Whiteson finally departed, Katherine demurring at their invitation to join them in some brandy at the inn next door. Peter pictured the two academics floating in a vat of the after-dinner drink, and was thankful for Katherine's good sense.

"Hey, Mom," Clarissa said. "Want to go out for a cappuccino or something?" She looked from her mother to

Peter. "Or if you guys want to be alone, you can just drop me off."

"I'd rather go straight home," Katherine said, meeting Peter's questioning gaze. "If that's okay."

"Sure." Clarissa nodded and moved on ahead, Peter falling into step with Katherine behind her.

"So those are two of your esteemed colleagues."

She nodded. "I never see them outside of campus, usually," she said. "They're both a little hard to take."

He was relieved to hear this. "Andrew Farron is interested in you, in a big way," he noted.

"He's tried to pick up practically every woman who teaches there," she said dryly. "But he's a brilliant man."

Peter nodded, holding his tongue. Katherine wasn't meeting his eyes, and he sensed trouble in the air. "I hope you're not upset with me," he said. "Look, I'm sorry I fell asleep. It's been a long day." She nodded stiffly, remote and seemingly unapproachable. "You have to admit it was a little on the long side," he said. "Kind of talky."

"Talky?" she echoed, as if the word was somehow woefully inappropriate. "Just what do you mean?"

"You *liked* it?" he asked, surprised.

"Let's skip the whole discussion, okay?" Her tone was testy enough to give him pause. Peter frowned as she walked even faster toward where his car was parked. He had the distinct feeling she was overreacting for reasons other than a great love of the avant-garde theater. But even as he sensed what probably lay behind her mood, his own irritation got the better of him.

Why was she so dead set on putting distance between the two of them, whenever an opportunity presented itself? It was one thing to be wary of a man who gave a woman reason to be, but he felt he'd been perfectly straightforward with her. Hadn't he put his cards out on the table just that afternoon? So why was she so evasive?

Simmering, he matched Katherine's silence with his own as he got into the car and started the engine. Clarissa, conscious of tension in the air, did her best to keep up a monologue of casual conversation, but most of the short ride back to the Taylor house passed by in silence.

"G'night, Peter," Clarissa called gaily, hurrying out of the car the moment they were parked in the driveway. "See you 'round."

"Good to meet you," Peter said automatically, then put a restraining hand on Katherine's arm before she could leave the front seat. "Hold on a minute," he said quietly.

Katherine sighed, watching Clarissa stride quickly into the house. "Let's talk tomorrow," she said.

"No, let's talk now." He turned to face her directly. "Come on, you're not sore because I snored through that ridiculous piece of I-don't-know-what."

"It was an honest effort," Katherine asserted defensively. "It's his first play. You don't have to make fun of it. Besides, there were parts that were very good poetry."

"Poetry?" He stared at her. "You're kidding."

"Just because you don't understand something doesn't mean it has no aesthetic validity."

"Aesthetic validity?" He shook his head. "Katherine, what's really bothering you?"

"Poetry happens to be what I teach," she went on, ignoring his question. "I see a lot of these kinds of works, you know. I'm interested in language. It's my life."

"I'm interested in law," he said. "But I know legal cowflop when I hear it."

"See, that's exactly what I mean," she said. "I'm used to being with people who understand these things."

"Like that old windbag Whiteson and his foppy friend Farron?" he said, rising to the bait before he could stop himself. "Or do you mean the late great Jeffrey Addison Cartwright? Well, he may have understood poetry, but I haven't gotten a sense that he really understood you!"

From the way her face changed he knew he'd struck a nerve, but Katherine was unwavering. "I'm not going to sit here and listen to you criticize him," she said calmly.

"I'm not out to criticize anybody," he said, exasperated. "Look, you want to talk about interests? I'm interested in *you*, Kath! Why are you being like this?"

"Peter, you like to play electric guitar and baseball and go fishing," she said, turning away from him. "I don't do any of those things! Whatever makes you think that we have enough in common to stay together?"

"We have what we feel," he said.

"Yes, but what if I don't feel like having children?" she blurted.

Peter stared at her a moment, his brow furrowed. He'd known the idea of children had been upsetting to her. If she was serious about not wanting another, it *could* be a problem, and he hadn't worked out how he felt about it yet, himself. "That's something we'll have to deal with, if we ever get that far," he said.

"I'm not as young as you keep saying I am," she said. "And what's been going on between us is fine for the moment, but—"

"Katherine, listen to yourself," he said, losing patience. "You know there's more to us than this. You're making mountains out of molehills. Why?"

"No, maybe you're making the mountains," she said grimly. "Maybe all there really is to us is . . . sex, pure and simple."

Stung, he drew back, staring at her in disbelief. "You don't mean that," he said. "You know better."

"I'm not so sure," she said, and reached for the door handle.

"Katherine—"

"Look, why don't we just call it a night?" she said. "Maybe this whole thing wasn't such a good idea to begin with."

"You're making a mistake," he said evenly.

"Maybe I'm doing the right thing," she answered, and clambered from the seat. Peter stared after her, his whole body tensed in a combination of frustration, anger and pain. She was being self-destructive, running scared. Why? Did she expect him to come running after her, and convince her all over again that he really could love her the way she needed to be loved?

He wanted to. But as he watched her stride resolutely toward the house, some stubborn streak of pride kept him from making a move. If she was so hell-bent on getting away from him, *then so be it.* Grinding his teeth and grinding gears, he pulled out of the Taylor driveway in a cloud of dust and gravel.

"I DON'T GET IT," said Clarissa, putting her arm out her window and scooping in the cool dusk air with her hand as they drove. "I thought you'd just figured out you *did* want to see him again."

"I did," Katherine said, checking her makeup in the rearview mirror. She'd been late getting dressed for the town hall meeting and hadn't really had time to do anything with her hair. "See if I remembered my brush, will you?" she asked, indicating the open handbag on the seat beside her.

"Here it is," Clarissa said. "So what are you going to do when we get there? Pretend you don't know him?"

"Of course not," Katherine said, although she didn't really know how she was going to handle the encounter. "But this isn't exactly a social occasion, anyway." Far from it. Peter Bradford would be sitting in the hostile camp at the head of the room, no doubt, and she'd be with the women's alliance. Either way the informal vote went, they weren't likely to be speaking to each other.

The controversy over ConCo had continued throughout the week, with articles and editorials every day in the *Chronicle* fanning the flames. The town was so divided on the issue, everyone so vocal about their opinion, that the biweekly town hall meeting, usually attended only by a few, was due to be jam-packed. Randy Morgan, a supervisor known for listening to the people who had elected him, was opening up the final decision to the townspeople, and the Alliance had been lobbying for days to get every sympathetic person to the meeting.

"I like him," Clarissa said.

"Who?"

"Peter, who else?" Clarissa said. "I think you're nuts."

"Thank you for your support," Katherine said.

"He doesn't look so young to me," she mused.

"He's nearly five years younger than I am," Katherine said grimly. "When I turn forty-four this fall he'll still be thirty-nine."

"And in the winter he'll be forty," said Clarissa. "What's the big deal?"

"When you're as ancient as I am, you'll understand a few things. A man who's still in his mid-thirties is looking for a younger, childbearing female to be with."

"Sounds like you got that out of some magazine," Clarissa said.

"It's the voice of experience," Katherine said dryly. "And you know, as irony would have it, at first, because he was so opposed to this day-care center, I thought he didn't like children. Then I saw him with those Little Leaguers." She shook her head. "He's going to be a great father. He's a natural."

"Maybe it's not as important to him as you think," Clarissa said. "Is that the real reason you don't want to be with him?"

"It's just one among many," Katherine said. "Good Lord, look at all those people!"

There was a steady stream of them headed up the steps of the Greensdale Town Hall, casting long shadows in the yellow light from the lamps outside that were just flickering on.

Katherine recognized quite a few faces among them as she drove slowly past the entrance, and she was happy to see some of the posters Emily had been talking about were being held aloft by a cluster of teenagers joining the throng. KEEP CONCO OUT, said one, and BETTER LIVING WITH-OUT CHEMISTRY read another.

"There won't be any parking for blocks," she said, impressed. "Why don't I let you out here? Save a seat for me with Emily and the others."

"Okay," said Clarissa, as Katherine slowed down by the curb. The crowd outside showed no sign of diminishing. Watching them, she felt a sense of disbelief. She'd wanted to get involved in Greensdale, hadn't she? Well, this involvement had created waves far beyond any of her original imaginings.

Clarissa shut the door behind her, waved, and plunged into the steady stream of people. Katherine idled at the curb a moment, still a little awed. Well, her brief fantasy romance might have crashed and burned, but it was a distinct possibility that some dreams would come true.

"WHAT WE'VE BEEN TALKING ABOUT is compromise," said Randy Morgan. He mopped his brow wearily. After some speeches from other town council members, the ConCo issue had been opened up to the floor. Many women from Katherine's alliance had spoken their piece, as well as a lot of the local men. The debate had raged for over two hours now, and both sides were showing signs of fatigue within the stuffy hall, which had been equipped with some extra floor fans for the occasion.

The population of Greensdale was only a little over a thousand, and there weren't more than two hundred or so people packed into the small hall. But these were the concerned ones, who represented the many currents of opinion in the town. All of the opinions were strong and many vocal, which was why the meeting had dragged on so long.

To Katherine's surprise, a working mother with three children supported the plant, vehemently condemning the Taylor House project and Katherine as being shortsighted and selfish. To her more pleased shock, Mr. Gibbons, a middle-aged shop owner who she'd have thought would be pro-ConCo had opposed the plant, wanting to preserve what he called "the spirit of Greensdale" and not at all interested in having the place "upwardly mobilized."

Now Emily Atchins had taken the floor with an eloquent defense of the Alliance and their plans for the community. Randy Morgan, getting a little hoarse by now, was countering with a rebuttal.

"Emily, there's no reason in the world why we can't all give way a little here," Randy continued, nodding his thanks as Peter Bradford poured them both another glass of ice water from the oft-refilled pitcher on the long wooden table at the head of the room. "Greensdale can have its day-care center, and it can also get a new lease on economic life at the same time. And then everybody'll be happy. Right?"

"Wrong," Emily said stubbornly. "It's not about dollars and cents, Randy. It's the quality of life we're talking about here." The other women around her nodded emphatically. "How do we know that the same thing won't happen here that's happened in Illinois? What it comes down to is we just don't trust ConCo. And to tell you the truth, if you're more concerned with making a good deal with some corporation than making sure this community stays healthy, we're gonna start to wonder if we should trust you!"

For not the first time that evening, there were cheers and applause mingled with boos and shouts from others on the benches behind them. Katherine clapped, but her enthusiasm was tempered by a look at Peter, who'd been sitting beside Randy throughout the debate.

He looked tired and disgruntled. And he'd looked everywhere but at her ever since she'd taken her seat there next to

Clarissa. He hadn't spoken much, except for some brief remarks at the beginning, when he'd assured all present that the council had scheduled a meeting to talk to the ConCo people about the status of the two infamous legal suits in progress. He'd occasionally risen to answer questions from the floor, but seemed surprisingly detached from the business at hand.

Could he be that removed from her, sitting only a few yards away? It had been three days since their argument after the play. He'd made no move to get in touch with her. It seemed completely strange to be in such close proximity to a man who only days ago had merged with her so fiercely, held her so lovingly...and now acted as though they'd never met.

He was conferring with Randy, who was growing a permanent wince on his face from the drubbing he'd been taking all night. After a moment Randy turned to Luke Treemont on his right. Luke struck the table with his gavel and rose to his feet.

"Okay, okay, pipe down," he exhorted the crowd. "I think we've heard enough from both sides of this thing. We're going to put it to a vote from the constituents, meaning you." He surveyed the now silent faces before him. "If the count turns out to be close, we'll have to have another meeting next week, hoping some new information may come out of continued negotiations with the ConCo people to shed light on the problem and resolve it. But if we get any kind of majority, the council's going to take it under advisement." He paused, wiping the sweat from his neck with a kerchief. "Which basically means, we'll do what you want us to do."

From the grumbling tone of these last words, it was clear which way Luke himself wanted things to go. Nonetheless, he cleared his throat, continuing: "Members of the town council will cast their votes in a closed ballot up here, while we count your votes. Now, all those in favor of selling the town-owned Lots numbered 46, 47 and 47A between Haswell Road and the highway to the ConCo Corporation, raise your hands."

Katherine and the other women swiveled in their seats as one. Looking around with growing uneasiness, she saw that quite a number of hands were in the air. Two men from the council started their count, each going down the rows on either side of the center aisle. The Alliance looked on in silence.

"I got forty-seven on this side," bellowed one man from the back.

"Forty-one over here."

"Making a total of eighty-eight in favor," noted Luke, scribbling on his pad. "All those opposed to the sale?"

Katherine raised her hand high, as did the whole row of women. Looking around, she was pleased to see that a number of men, some teenagers and even some of the older men from town had their hands in the air.

"Voting age only!" Luke called, as a group of children, Emily's among them, eagerly waved their little hands aloft. Good-natured chuckles spread throughout the tense room, but then there was a lot more silence and shifting in seats as the two men counted methodically, making their ways down the aisle.

"I get forty-nine on this side."

Katherine bit her lip. That was only two more for than those against. She held her breath as the man facing their side finished up his tally. Emily caught her eye and smiled encouragingly. She felt her arm already sore with tension as she held her hand high.

"We got sixty-two here, Luke."

With a wild cheer, the women rose to their feet. A tumult of voices broke out all around her as Emily hugged Katherine, Marsha and Clarissa in turn. Only Luke's persistent gavel pounding finally quieted their jubilation. When

Katherine took her seat again, face flushed with excitement, he was holding up his yellow pad, motioning for silence.

"That's a total of eighty-three in favor and one hundred eleven opposed," he said, face impassive. "Let's see the results of the council ballot, Randy."

Randy had been unfolding little slips of yellow paper. He leaned back in his chair with a frown. "I've got ten members in favor," he said slowly. "And two opposed."

Murmurs spread throughout the room as everyone worked out the math. Katherine stared at the twelve men behind the table and Peter in particular. He was staring at the ceiling, absolutely expressionless. She couldn't help but wonder if he'd been one of the opposing votes. Randy Morgan certainly seemed to think so, from the look he cast in Peter's direction before getting to his feet.

"Well, you can see where the council stands on this, it's no secret," he said, scowling at the assemblage. "But with eighty-eight of you in favor and one hundred eleven opposed, there's still a little under two dozen more of you voters who don't want this plant built." He sighed. "As Luke said, we'll take it under advisement. And I suppose that means we're going to have to let the ConCo corporation build elsewhere."

Pandemonium surrounded her. Katherine was momentarily lost in a circle of shouting, hugging women. Emily was weeping, and the pregnant Betsy appeared likely to deliver then and there. It was only as people began filing out that Katherine looked up to see Peter Bradford standing quietly on the aisle. She felt her heart hammering as he looked at her, his luminous eyes holding hers with a strange, inscrutable intensity.

"Congratulations," he said quietly. "You got what you wanted."

And then, before she could even answer, he was walking away, and as he did an empty feeling deepened inside her. She *had* gotten what she wanted, hadn't she? Then why did she feel as though she hadn't really gotten anything at all?

Chapter Eleven

"Can't really work on the back porch with that bit of loose roof over our heads."

She had found the group of workmen sitting on the back steps. Since the wages they were being paid per hour suggested they should have at least been on their feet, Katherine was a little piqued when she sought out Edward Parker, the head of the renovation crew. But in Edward she found herself head-to-head with some real old-fashioned New England stonewalling.

"Then why not start with the repairs on the roof?" she asked him. Parker, a heavyset man in dark blue overalls, squinted up at the roof with the air of a man who'd never seen one before.

"Can't go up on that roof," he said, as if mildly astonished by her request. "I'd have a man up there but I don't trust it, Miss."

"Well, if you can't work on the roof or the porch, what are you going to start working on, then?" she asked, exasperated.

Edward Parker folded his arms and gravely nodded. "Just what we were considering," he informed her. The three men on the steps were looking on, impassive. All of them swiveled to look at Emily, who was leaning out the kitchen window.

"Trudy's here with that information about the licensing," she called.

"I'll be right in," Katherine said. Emily ducked back inside and the men turned to gaze back at her again. "Look," she said calmly. "There's a *lot* of work to be done here. You could start almost anywhere."

"We came prepared for the porch," Parker said, apologetic. "You'd said you wanted that done first."

Katherine sighed. Fine, then it was her fault. "How about the side door?" she suggested. "It's practically off its hinges and the frame around it's rotted clear through in a couple of places."

Parked nodded, head tilting to one side as he scratched an ear. "Yes, I noticed the door," he said. "I suppose we could tackle that. Boys?"

"I suppose you could," she said, with a nice smile, and hurried past him up the back steps, the men standing to let her by. The phone was ringing as she came into the kitchen. Automatically, her pulse rate rose a notch. Foolish though it seemed, any time the phone rang, there was always the possibility that *he* might be calling. She grabbed the receiver, turning off the teakettle in passing before it emitted its ear-shattering whistle. "Hello?"

"Mrs. Taylor? This is Eileen Rosdale from Saint Teresa. We talked briefly at the Town Hall meeting the other night—?"

And every time she picked it up, of course, it wasn't him at all. Why should it be? "Yes, of course. How are you?" She remembered the stout and red-cheeked nun who'd congratulated her and the Alliance on their victory. Masking her disappointment, she listened as the good sister offered her services and those of her entire staff in helping to organize the Taylor Center. Apparently the church had been wanting to put together an informal day-care program of its own for some time.

Katherine thanked Eileen for the generous offer and made an appointment to stop by Saint Teresa the next day. It wasn't until she was off the phone that she realized, with a flush of pride, that now even people she didn't know in town had taken to calling Grammy's place the Taylor Center.

"That was the church," she told Emily, entering the living room and smiling a hello to Trudy. "They want to help."

"Good," Emily said. "We need all the care-givers we can get—more than we thought we did." She indicated Trudy, who was nodding and turning over papers on her clipboard. Trudy was a young housewife, Emily's second cousin, who had volunteered to go into Boston and speak to the state licensing board about the specific requirements they'd have to fulfill.

"One staff member to three infants," Trudy said, consulting her notes. Her voice echoed oddly in the big empty room. Katherine still couldn't get used to looking at the living room without a stick of furniture in it.

"Have we got a lot of infants?" she asked Emily.

"Only a half dozen at the moment, but you see, that'll be two care-givers right there," Emily said.

"Once they're three or older the ratio isn't so close," Trudy said. "But if your total's over forty altogether—"

"Under. Two dozen plus, we think," Emily said.

"Then you'll need four additional people here full-time," Trudy concluded. "At least one with first aid training."

"Marsha's got that," Emily said. "No problem."

"And who's the manager?" Trudy asked.

"Emily," Katherine said. "I'm going to be living here full-time until I go back to work in September, and then I'll be coming down every weekend, but Em's going to caretake throughout, and she'll be interviewing all the staff members."

"You'll have to fill out these forms," Trudy told Emily, handing her some papers.

"I've already got some good people lined up," Emily said.

"Everybody over sixteen?" Trudy looked to Katherine who looked to Emily. Emily frowned.

"I guess they'll have to be," she said. "But that rules out Susie, Sadie's kid."

"Maybe one of the Saint Teresa sisters can do a shift," Katherine said, watching with some puzzlement as Trudy began moving around the room, bent over, peering at the walls and floorboards.

"Betty sent over these samples for you to see," Emily said, handing some swatches to Katherine. "She likes the tan. What do you think?"

"It's nice and thick," she said, feeling the bit of carpet. Even though the polished wooden floors downstairs had been Grammy's pride and joy, they would have to be covered wall-to-wall with soft carpeting for the coming children to play on. "But won't tan stain too easily?"

"Good point," Emily said. "How about this blue-gray?"

"You've got a problem," Trudy announced. "These outlets." She pointed at the wall with her pencil. "They're all too low and exposed."

Katherine sighed. Another hidden cost to be added to the growing list. "I suppose we'll have to have the electrician come back," she said. He'd already been over once to fix the old wiring in the kitchen, and that bill had been a real eyebrow raiser.

"Have you told her about the fence?" Trudy asked Emily.

"Fence?" Katherine turned to Emily, anxiety escalating.

"The back road to town is accessible from the driveway here," Emily explained. "Trudy says the state certainly won't license us if we don't have a fence up around the backyard proper."

She could hear Grammy's indignant gasp in her mind. *Put a fence around the yard?* It was practically blasphemous, since the very back of the yard property merged with wild state park woods, and Grammy had loved the fact that not even a stone wall created borders on the greenery for miles around. But Grammy would have to understand, as would Lydia, of course, when Katherine phoned her with the latest addition to their spiraling building costs.

"Let me make a copy of the specifications," she said, reaching for Trudy's clipboard. There was an odd snapping sound from the kitchen. Then, even as she registered it, a sudden crash froze all three women in midconversation.

"What in God's name?—" Emily began. But Katherine was already running from the room.

The scene that greeted her in the little foyer leading from the kitchen to the back porch was at first too bewildering to comprehend. One of the workmen was sprawled on the floor by an overturned stepladder, with Parker and the others crowded around him. He was grimacing in pain and oddly, covered in what looked like white paint. But then she realized, stomach plummeting, that a chunk of the plaster above him was hanging loose, and a huge gaping hole had appeared there. What was covering the injured workman was a piece of the kitchen ceiling.

"HOW BAD IS IT?"

Mr. Stuart blinked owlishly at the thick sheaf of papers in his hands, then looked over the top of his wire rims at Katherine, lips pursed. "About as bad as it can be," he said, with a sigh, and then sat back in the leather chair behind his desk, depositing the dire document on the desktop.

"Let's hear the figures," Katherine said in a small voice, steeling herself for the worst.

"Well, they're suing for seventy-five thousand," Mr. Stuart said.

"Seventy—?" Katherine gripped the side of her chair for security. "That's outrageous."

Mr. Stuart shrugged. "Well, we're dealing with a mild concussion, a bunch of cuts and stitches and that broken leg," he said. "The man's out of commission, and of course he wants compensation."

"But even half of that figure would be compensation for any medical treatment and days off the job," she said.

"True," Mr. Stuart allowed. "Problem is, Mr. Maxwell's lawyer, Mr. Proffert is claiming we're liable for a great deal more than that. It's his hypothesis that the house itself is a health risk to any workmen, period. He's claiming it's too hazardous to renovate, and the contract between you and Parker was in bad faith anyway, as you misrepresented the level of risk involved."

"I didn't," she protested. "The man even inspected the premises himself before taking on the job."

Mr. Stuart nodded. "Be that as it may," he said. "We've got a fight on our hands. I don't get the sense that Mr. Proffert is all that interested in deal-making. If we're not willing to meet that figure, there won't be any settling out of court."

"Court," she repeated dully. "That's just what we need. If this lawyer of theirs tries to prove the house is some kind of death trap, he could ruin the whole Taylor Center project."

"I'm afraid so," Mr. Stuart said. "And to be honest with you, Katherine, going head-to-head with a theatrical sharpie like Proffert is not really my cup of tea."

"But you'll do it, won't you?" she said uneasily. "Mr. Stuart, we simply can't afford to pay out that kind of money at this point."

"I'm well aware of it," he said. "But unfortunately I'm in the midst of another case as it is, with an old client of mine in Boston, and as I'm already committed to be out of town for a while, I've taken the liberty of calling upon a colleague for help."

"Mr. MacFarlane?" she asked, disappointed. Her impression of Mr. Stuart's junior partner wasn't a great one. Although he reportedly possessed one of the great legal minds in Massachusetts, he had the personality of a doorknob, and she didn't relish the idea of depending upon his performance in a courtroom.

"No, I've asked a local boy to step in. He's already made quite a name for himself here, and he used to work with a

very reputable firm in New York. I believe you know him—
Peter Bradford?''

"Oh, no," she muttered. If she hadn't been so anxiety-
stricken, she might have laughed. "He'll never take this
case," she said. "I'm the last person in Greensdale he'd be
interested in representing."

"Really?" Mr. Stuart looked at her oddly, then turned to
the door at the sound of a quiet knock. "Yes?"

His secretary, Thelma, leaned in. "Your three-thirty appointment is here."

"Send him in." Mr. Stuart turned back to Katherine,
hands folded on the rise of his stomach, an amused gleam
in his eye. "Apparently you're not quite the last person," he
said. "Because he's interested enough to have looked at the
brief and come over here." He pushed himself back from
the desk, starting to rise as the door opened. "Peter!"

"Afternoon, Oliver." He strode into the room, which
appeared from Katherine's point of view to shrink in size as
he approached. He'd had a haircut. She felt irrationally offended that he should do such a thing; didn't he know how
much she liked his hair long? And worse, he looked healthy
and happy. Shouldn't he be haggard from pining away for
her?

She watched in silence as he shook hands heartily with
Mr. Stuart. By now she was used to seeing Peter in his business clothes, but she was struck anew by the attractive figure he cut in a light tan jacket over a tieless white button-
down and black jeans, giving him just the right air of casual but serious intent. He favored her with a dazzling if
superficially friendly smile, settling into the chair opposite
hers. She attempted the same, though she was sure it was
coming out crooked or something. She was still bewildered
by his being here.

"What do you think?" Mr. Stuart was saying.

"I think they may have a case," Peter said.

"But how good a case?"

"That depends on what sort of evidence we can come up with," Peter said. "At the moment they're looking pretty strong."

"Wait a second," Katherine said, sudden paranoia seeping in. "If you're getting involved in this just to sabotage any chances we might have, and see that the house gets shut down—"

"Katherine, please," Mr. Stuart interrupted, looking abashed on her behalf. "Mr. Bradford has only the best intentions here. Let's hear what he has to say."

Peter appeared highly amused by her outburst. "Oliver, I think we'd better clear the air on something before we proceed any further." He looked from Oliver to Katherine, calm and composed. "Your client and I have had some disagreements in the recent past," he said evenly.

Katherine bit her tongue. How could he be capable of dealing with her as if she were, in fact, a client—that and nothing more? Either Peter Bradford possessed faculties of emotional self-control that surpassed her own, or he hadn't been that serious about her, after all.

"If we're going to work on this together," he continued blithely, "I'd just like to say that I'm doing it in the best interests of friendship, both to you, Oliver, and Ms. Taylor. I certainly wouldn't take on the case out of any misguided and inappropriate need for, ah, retribution."

"Then why are you doing it?" she asked coolly.

"Like I said, it's a friendly gesture," Peter answered. "And besides, I wouldn't pass up another opportunity to make a fool out of Joe Proffert in public. It's one of my favorite pastimes."

"You see, Mr. Bradford has won a few cases against Mr. Proffert already," Mr. Stuart said. "And apparently he'd like to do it again."

"The man's a shyster, Katherine," Peter said. "An ambulance-chaser. The kind of guy who occasionally makes me feel uneasy at being in the same profession with him. So if I have any vested interest here, to be honest, it's to win," he said pointedly. "Certainly not to lose."

"I see," Katherine said, but far from being mollified, she was now fending off feelings of disappointment. If only he'd said he was taking on the case to become closer to her again! That would have melted a heart that was already vulnerably soft where he was concerned. But no, he was just going to have himself some courtroom amusement on her behalf.

Men. They were an inferior breed, she reflected moodily, as Mr. Stuart and Peter compared notes on the brief—or rather some men like Peter, who apparently never completely grew up. He didn't really care about the Taylor Center. He was only interested in some sort of macho one-upmanship contest with another attorney. Typical.

"When would a good time be for that?"

She'd been so involved in her interior tirade that she hadn't realized the last question had been directed at her. "Excuse me?"

"I was wondering when I might come by to visit the scene of the accident," Peter said.

"We have photos that the insurance company took," Katherine said. Two could play at this dispassionate non-relationship game he appeared to favor.

"I know, but I really do need to go over the incident myself, in person."

Katherine shrugged. "Any time during the day is fine," she said. "There's someone there until sundown practically all the time now," she said. "Emily Atchins or one of the other women could let you in if I'm not around."

"But you were there when it happened," Peter said. "So I'd like you to be there when I look things over."

She'd be talking to Lydia from the house around eleven, since that was the hour in California her sister was still home before heading to work. Emily would be around then, too, which made her feel somehow more secure. "Before lunch-time tomorrow," she said.

"Fine. I look forward to it," said Peter Bradford, and he smiled his charming smile again.

"HE'S LOOKING FORWARD TO IT," Katherine said darkly and Lydia's tinkly laugh cut through the long-distance static.

"The two of you are simply ridiculous," she said. "It's obvious you can't keep away from each other, no matter what kind of 'final fights' you keep having."

"But I told you why he took the case," Katherine protested. Emily, hair up in a bandanna, was holding an empty cleanser bottle upside down in one hand and miming she was going out to get some more. Katherine nodded absently. "I'm telling you, it's over, and if I'd had anything to say about it—" Too late, as the front door slammed behind Emily, it occurred to her that she'd wanted Emily around for Peter's imminent arrival. "Damn," she muttered.

"What's the matter?"

"Never mind," Katherine said. "Anyway, I guess the important thing is to win this case, so I'll just grin and bear him."

"Yes, you do that, Sis," Lydia said cheerily. "What's he charging us?"

"That depends. If he wins, he costs a hundred an hour. If he loses, it's gratis."

"Now, that's a very friendly deal," Lydia noted.

"Yes, it's all just wonderfully friendly around here," Katherine said glumly. "I've never *had* so many new friends."

"Then be happy about it," Lydia said. There was a pause. "Why don't you talk to him?" she said gently. "About how you feel."

"I don't know how I feel," Katherine said. "I'm hurt that he's kept his distance instead of running after me, and I know it's a lot my fault for telling him to stay away...and the whole thing gives me a heartache. Headache," she corrected herself, too late.

"I think you were right the first time," Lydia said. "Listen, I gotta go. I have a koala bear with bronchitis."

"I'm sure you do," Katherine said, as the front doorbell chimed. "I'll call you tomorrow."

A glance at her reflection in the hall mirror as she went to answer the door showed her Katherine-at-work: scruffy jeans, paint-spattered man-tailored shirt, old sneakers, hair swept up in a ponytail. There was no way Peter could think she'd prettied herself up for this visit. It was going to be all business.

"Good morning," she said briskly, opening the door. With Peter it was less easy to tell if he was dressed for business or pleasure. In his usual combo of jeans with a suit jacket, he looked about as pleasantly casual as he had that first day when he'd appeared on her doorstep after Grammy's funeral.

Remembering that now gave a bittersweet pang of sadness. The main difference was that this time he was carrying a briefcase, and he wasn't really here to see her. He was here to investigate the scene of an accident.

"Morning," he answered her. "You look busy."

"I am," she said, and the telephone ringing inside backed her up. "Come on in," she said. "You know where the kitchen is."

Thankful for the reprieve, she took the call on the phone in the living room. It was Earl Stanley, the gardener, wanting to know if they were ready for the relandscaping appraisal.

She told him they'd have to wait on it, not mentioning the case, not wanting to admit that if they lost the case he wouldn't have any big gardening job to do, but her mind was on the man who'd walked purposefully by her and was now in the kitchen. When she got off the phone, she listened for sounds of Peter in there, but the house was so still, she might as well have been alone.

Curious, she walked through the living room and down the hall to the kitchen. Maybe he was waiting for her. Maybe this whole thing was just a pretext to see her again. Maybe he was going to beg and plead with her to give them another chance, and she'd say no, but then give in, at least for one exploratory date.

She shook her head, amazed at her own weak will. Tense with anticipation, she entered the kitchen. Peter was sitting on the floor against one wall, head in his hands, still as a statue. "Are you all right?" she asked, alarmed.

He looked up, surprised. "I'm okay," he said. "How about yourself?"

"No," she said, coloring. "I mean, I'm fine, but what are you doing there?"

"Thinking," he said. And he gazed at her a moment, as if seeing her for the first time. Katherine wanted to look away from the gently luminous intensity of those bright blue eyes, but somehow couldn't. He kept looking, transfixing her, as if he was drinking in every feature of her face.

A different kind of feeling seeped in when he just looked at her like that, openly, with what seemed like pure affection. She found resentments and apprehensions and all the other mixed emotions she had about the man slip away, and in their place, a tenderness toward him rose inside her. How could she stay cool and distant from someone who made her go all tender and caring inside just by looking into her eyes?

At last he cleared his throat. "Where were you standing when it happened?" he asked.

How could she be such an idiot? was a more logical question. Katherine folded her arms, leaning back against the doorway. It was obvious that he hadn't been thinking about her at all. "I wasn't in the room," she said evenly, evincing a sudden and intense interest in the dishes that were piled in the sink.

"That's too bad," he muttered, and rose to his feet. "So you heard the crash, and you came running in...?"

"Yes, and I saw that guy, Doug, lying on the floor there next to his ladder, and he had plaster all over him," she recited by rote, still not looking at him. Maybe if she was really crafty about it, she'd never have to look the man in the face again.

"You didn't do anything to the hole?" He was pointing to the infamous gap in the ceiling.

"Haven't touched it," she said. "Though another little chunk did come loose when we were helping him out of the room."

"Where's the ladder?" Peter asked.

Katherine shrugged. "It was their ladder. They took it with them when they left." Peter was silent. After a moment she turned to glance his way and found him scribbling in a little pad. Just before he looked up again she remembered to cross the room. Yes, those dishes certainly needed washing.

"He broke one of the ladder steps when he fell," Peter said. "That's in the deposition Parker made, as a piece of their equipment you're being asked to pay for."

Katherine shrugged. "I didn't notice," she said. "I just saw it on the floor." Peter nodded, gazing at the hole in the ceiling. Something was nagging at Katherine's memory. Now she had it. "Oh, I guess that was the kind of cracking sound I heard," she said.

"Hmm?"

"We were in here, talking, and I heard this little snapping sound from the kitchen, and then that frightening crash. I guess what I heard was his foot going through the ladder's step." Peter was looking at her with an oddly intense expression. She remembered not to get sucked in. "What's the matter?" she asked, addressing her question to the shelf of spices a few inches past his head.

"First a crack, *then* a crash?" he asked. She nodded. Peter scribbled madly on his pad. "This might be very, very useful," he said. "You'll say that in court?"

"Sure," she said. "Do I have to?"

"I'll want to talk to Emily Atchins, and that other woman, too, and if their stories corroborate yours I may have all three of you on the stand," he said.

"Why?"

He smiled faintly. "I just have a hunch about something. Can I use your phone?" She nodded, and returned to surveying her sink as he moved to the phone. So it was really capital-O Over, she mused. He hadn't taken this case as anything more than a case, period. What had he said—a friendly gesture?

Did she really want to be "just friends" with Peter Bradford? The prospect didn't thrill her, not when being with him as lovers *had* thrilled her, and shaken up her entire life. She watched his back as he talked quietly into the receiver. She could remember the feel of those smooth muscles beneath her hands. Being so near and so far from him was a sort of torture, she realized.

But if he can take it, so can I, she told herself grimly. If Peter was feeling any of the things she was, he was a better actor than she'd given him credit for. So she'd just have to follow his example and get over the whole thing. Once they'd had their day in court, their paths wouldn't have to cross again, and that was just as well.

"Okay, I have to get some research done," Peter said cheerily, hanging up the phone. "You've been a great help so far."

"Have I?" she asked.

"We might be able to really knock this thing down to size," he said, stroking his chin pensively as he gazed at the ceiling.

"I hope so," she said. "If we lose..."

"We won't," he said. "Have a little faith in me." If there was an irony intended in his remark, she chose to ignore it. Instead, she matched his cheery demeanor with one of her own. Muttering some nonsense about all the work she had to do, she was positively sunny as she hurried Peter out the door.

"...AND I UNDERSTAND you've missed a total of seventeen days of work so far, Mr. Maxwell."

Doug Maxwell, an oversize square of bandaging still conspicuously displayed on his wounded forehead, nodded at his attorney, though he couldn't face him head-on. The cast covering his right leg couldn't fit into the witness box proper, and protruded at an oblique angle. "Yeah, that's right," he said.

Joe Proffert seemed deeply saddened. "And the doctors tell us you won't be able to walk on that leg for at least another forty-five to ninety days. And then, if it hasn't healed properly, you could be forced into unemployment until, well, let's say the end of the year."

"Objection." Peter rose wearily to his feet. He was getting a bit tired of having to counter practically every other exaggeration Proffert mouthed, but he had no choice. Proffert, short, thin, dapper in his bow tie and slicked-down hair, did his "What on earth is wrong with this other trouble-making attorney?" act for the jury's benefit as Peter addressed the judge. "Mr. Proffert is leading the witness with pure conjecture. Mr. Maxwell's doctors have given us absolutely no indication that they expect any complications in the healing of his leg."

Judge Myers stroked his goatee, which was something he did as a reflex after every objection. The gray-haired judge seemed as weary of Proffert's grandstanding as he was, Peter thought. But maybe he was being overly optimistic. "Sustained," Myers said. "Have the question stricken from the record."

"Such things do happen," Proffert said, an aside to the jury with his arms spread wide, as if to say: *I'm outraged that these callous people are giving my poor client such a hard time!* Then he turned back to Doug. "I'm merely reiterating that in addition to the grave injuries you've suffered, you've been robbed of your livelihood by this untimely and avoidable accident, Mr. Maxwell. I'm sure you're regretting the day that you ever set foot in the Taylor house on Old Birch Road."

Peter stifled a sigh. It wasn't even worth objecting to this sort of melodramatic sludge, and it looked as though Proffert was done. He was. "Your witness," he said to Peter, in the same hushed and reverent tone he'd used throughout his examination of Doug, as if the man in the box behind him were a saintly martyr struck down in the midst of doing God's good work.

Peter nodded, gathering up his notepad and looking over at Katherine. She was stunning, even more so than usual, in an outfit that was the result of their last phone conversation. He'd wanted her to dress demurely, with an aura of dignity, but somehow "down-home," i.e. nothing stylish from a big-city name designer. The simple blouse and gray skirt she wore with just a little makeup created just the right impression.

Katherine met his gaze briefly, gave the merest of encouraging smiles, then looked away. Well, he was almost used to that by now. Ever since he'd taken the case on she'd avoided his eyes, steadfastly steered the conversation toward professional matters only and resisted every attempt of his to be more than superficially friendly.

Could he blame her? Not really. He hadn't come running to her with bouquets of roses, fallen at her feet with pleas of forgiveness—not that he was actually sure why he should be the one asking to be forgiven—or done anything overtly designed to get her back.

But he wasn't supposed to, *damn it!* She'd made it clear she didn't see any hope for a future between the two of them. And he wasn't going to make a fool out of himself trying to convince her otherwise. Judge Myers was looking at him expectantly. Peter abruptly terminated this counterproductive train of thought, and turned his attention to the star witness.

For the next five minutes, he went over the material Proffert had covered, doing his best to undo his opponent's damage. Proffert had turned a minor concussion, a few cuts and bruises and one broken bone into the ruination of Doug Maxwell's life. He'd managed to convey an impression of the Taylor house as something from an old Karloff horror movie, a scary and malevolent structure that might as well have been possessed by Satan for all the damage it apparently delighted in inflicting on such hapless souls as attempted to approach it.

Peter succeeded in bringing things down to a more realistic level, first by minimizing the extent of the damage Doug had suffered. Instead of treating Doug like a poor victim of menacing circumstance, he took a very direct, man-to-man approach. It worked, the male camaraderie he subtly evoked eventually making Doug downplay his injuries. "Well, sure, I've been through worse things in the line of duty," Doug said on the record at one point.

Then, by flattering Maxwell about his vivid recall of many other jobs, Peter got him to cite other houses that were in far worse shape than Katherine's. Soon Peter had defused Proffert's "mean old monster house" scenario as well. He also gained the most crucial ground: Doug Maxwell's trust. Peter was being upfront, sympathetic, not at all antagonistic. He could feel Doug relaxing on the stand.

So far everything had been by the book. He'd played fair. Now he went in for his ace in the hole. It was going to involve a little piece of trickery, but it was his best shot. "So, the other guys are outside, working on the door, and under Mr. Parker's instructions you go into the kitchen to inspect the plastering," he said, in the midst of reconstructing the incident. Doug nodded. "You take the ladder in with you, and . . . anything else?"

Doug considered. "Just the broom."

"Right, right. The broom you were going to use to poke at the bits of hanging plaster and . . . how did you put it? See how bad the situation was up there?"

"Uh-huh."

"No hat?" Peter said, all innocence.

"Excuse me?"

"No construction head covering, hard hat," Peter said.

"Oh." Doug registered uneasiness. "Well, no, you see we usually don't wear those unless we're in construction. I mean, there's no law that says you have to put on—"

"Of course not," Peter interrupted smoothly. "I'm not suggesting you were negligent in not wearing any headgear in the kitchen of the Taylor house. It seemed like a harmless enough assignment. Why would you even consider it?"

"That's right," Doug said, relieved.

"And after all, it was the *fall* that really did you the most damage, not that bit of plaster."

"Well, yeah," Doug allowed. Peter nodded, secretly pleased. He'd raised Doug's doubts, allayed them, and at the same time driven home two underlying themes: one, Doug's job had been a piece of cake, not a dangerous mission, and two, the plaster—i.e. the menacing Taylor house— hadn't been the only major element in the accident.

"Okay, so you set up the ladder—" Peter paused as if struck by a sudden thought. "Your *own* ladder, not Ms. Taylor's."

"It's Ed's," Doug said.

"A trusted tool."

"You could say that, sure, we've been using it for years."

"Any idea how many years?" Peter appeared to be just making conversation, but Proffert, smelling danger, was on his feet.

"Objection! Your honor, I don't see how this question has the slightest bit of bearing on the—"

"I will prove to the court's satisfaction that this line of questioning is extremely relevant to the case," Peter said.

"Overruled."

"Thank you." Peter saw that Proffert was nervous, which was a good sign, and he saw that Katherine Taylor was just as nervous, but that was all right. He gave her an encouraging little nod and turned back to Doug. "Now, Mr. Maxwell, we've heard a lot this afternoon about how old the Taylor house is, and the dangers of working on such a creaky old building, as you called it, but how do you feel about working with a ladder that's older than you are?''

Doug looked momentarily startled. Peter saw a telltale glint of uncertainty and fear, and in that instant, knew his hunch had been correct. "Well, I never really gave it much thought.''

"Well, I happened to do a little homework on that ladder after I examined it, and you know, it was purchased by Ed Parker's brother when he worked with Ed, in 1949. Let's take a look at Exhibit Four, shall we?''

"Objection!" Proffert called out, but the judge was intrigued.

"Overruled," he said, and from a side door, the deputy brought in the ladder in question. As the jury members exchanged puzzled looks and the spectators buzzed, Peter helped him set it up.

"This is the ladder you fell from," Peter said. "And this is the step you broke, going down.''

"Yes," Doug said, now visibly uneasy.

Peter gave the ladder a push and watched it wobble. He prodded one side while holding the other to show how flimsy and ancient a piece of equipment it actually was. "Looks a little unsafe to me," he noted. "But you're used to using it.''

"That's right," Doug said.

"Must've shocked you when that step gave way, then.''

"Uh-huh." Doug's voice had dropped in volume.

"I mean, you're standing there, poking around with a stick at some loose plaster, and the step goes out from under you—didn't have anything to grab onto, did you?''

"No," Doug said. "Wait a—''

"Objection!" roared Proffert, but he was too late. Doug Maxwell had already, so to speak, put his foot in it.

"Overruled.''

"Mr. Maxwell, I'm a little confused. Do you mean to say that the step gave way *first*, and then you fell?''

"I never said... Wait, no, that's not the way it happened," Doug said. "No, I already had some plaster and dust in my eyes, and a good chunk of that plaster had just winged my head!" he said indignantly. "*That's* when..." He stopped.

The silence was very loud as Doug sat there, Peter fixing him with a steady stare. This was where the true trickery came in, but he had to play it out. "Mr. Maxwell," he said, holding up a sheaf of papers. "I have the sworn testimony of Katherine Taylor, Trudy Davis and Emily Atchins here." He didn't. He had Katherine's, true, but the other two women hadn't remembered hearing the noise. It was a bluff, and if Proffert called him on it he'd be in big trouble. But Proffert wasn't saying a word, which only added to his certainty. He could feel in his bones that he was on the money, so he went with it.

"All three of them concur that they heard the breaking of this ladder's step a good three or four seconds *before* you fell."

Doug didn't say anything, merely looking to Proffert for help. But his lack of protest was the most eloquent admission imaginable. Proffert had his head in his hands. And the judge was rapping his gavel for silence in the court as pandemonium reigned in the spectators' section.

Peter turned to look at Katherine. And when he saw the beaming smile on her face, the brightness in her eyes as she looked up at him, the feeling that welled up inside him was so jubilant that he could have died and gone to heaven on the spot. A man would do a lot to see those beautiful eyes gleaming at him with gratitude. He reflected briefly what a shame it was he'd never get to see such a welcome sight again.

Chapter Twelve

"Make some noise," Emily hissed.

Betty elbowed Sadie, who immediately gave out a whoop of laughter, and Katherine, following Marsha's example, clapped her hands. She couldn't even hear the quiet pop of the champagne cork as Emily worked it loose, so they were safe from prying nurses for the moment.

"Plastic cups!" Betty commanded, and Marsha hurriedly unpacked them from her bag.

A hospital room wasn't the most festive place for a celebration, but Barbara Wainright had just been delivered of her eight-pound, ten-ounce baby boy the night before. So the Alliance women had trooped over to Boston in Sadie's roomy station wagon, armed with presents for the baby and a bottle of champagne to be smuggled in.

"Fifteen minutes or so, okay?" the nurse had said worriedly, seeing the five of them, packages and balloons in hand, preparing to invade Barbara's room. She'd have been more upset to see the sparkling bubbly Betty was pouring out for each of them now, but it was all harmless fun.

"First of all here's to—what's the little sucker's name, Barb?" Betty asked, occasioning another gale of laughter in the small white room.

"My beautiful young son, if you please," said Barbara, her paleness already giving way to a healthy red glow in her cheeks, "will be christened Zachary Robert Wainright." Her small frame dwarfed by the covers, with the little mound of presents piled at her feet and the colorful balloons Marsha had brought tied to one bedpost, she looked as though she herself were the birthday girl in this celebration.

"To Zack," Betty said, plastic cup raised high.

"To Zack," they echoed, and drank.

"This is the good stuff," Marsha noted.

"You bet," said Sadie. "We don't even stock it at our store. Too expensive."

"Katherine's treat," Marsha said. "Speaking of which, here's to our other grand cause for celebration: we've won our case—" she paused for applause "—and work resumes tomorrow on the Taylor Center. Here's to it—and to the lady who really got the ball rolling to begin with: Katherine Taylor!"

Katherine flushed with pride as the other women saluted her. This particular gulp of not-so-chilled champagne in a plastic cup tasted like the finest ambrosia to her. "I couldn't have done a single thing alone," she said, and raised her own cup. "Here's to the women of the Greensdale Alliance!"

All the cups went up as one. Looking around at Barbara, Betty, Sadie, Marsha and Emily, Katherine realized that any last traces of that outsider feeling she'd always had were gone. They were an unbroken circle of smiling faces, at least for that moment truly united. She made a silent vow with herself not to let the circle be broken as time went by.

"Another toast," Emily announced.

"Then you'll have to pour us all another glass," Marsha said, and the others nodded encouragement.

"Just a teensy bit for me," said Barbara from the bed. "I'm still woozy enough as it is."

"Child's portion for Mom," Marsha said, passing the cup to her. "And a grandmother's portion for me." She held her thumb and forefinger wide apart.

"Who's driving? Sadie? Go easy on Sadie's."

"I've got no excuses," Emily said, filling her own with a healthy amount of champagne. "All right. Now here's to the help we all got from an unlikely source. I'll say this, I never thought any man in Greensdale would lift a finger to assist the Alliance—" murmurs of assent filled the room "—but if it wasn't for him, we wouldn't be celebrating. To Mr. Peter Bradford, attorney at law."

"Here, here!" crowed Marsha, and everyone downed their glass. But Katherine only sipped at hers, her high spirits suddenly in danger of inflating. She hadn't seen Peter since their victory in the courtroom, and though she planned to stop by his office that afternoon to give him the fee he was owed, the prospect filled her with sadness.

"Although we should thank Katherine again for that," Emily added.

Katherine looked up. "Why?"

"Well, he didn't really do it for the Taylor House Alliance," Marsha said wryly. "He did it for you."

"He did it to win another case from Joe Proffert," Katherine said. Betty and Barbara were exchanging a knowing look, and Emily was shaking her head. "What?" she demanded.

"Oh, come on, Katherine," Sadie said. "There's no need to keep it a secret, at least not from us."

"You *can't* keep a secret from us, it's impossible," Betty said, and the others laughed.

"No, seriously," Katherine protested. "There's nothing going on between Peter Bradford and myself." Emily rolled her eyes heavenward. The other women looked equally unconvinced. "Well, there was... we did have a little... involvement," she said, embarrassed. "But it's over."

"She is in a hospital," Sadie said to Emily. "Maybe while she's here we can have her head examined."

"No, really!" Katherine said, and the others laughed.

"Give it up, Katherine," Marsha said. "All a person has to do is see the two of you in a room together. If that's what you call 'over,' then I'm Vanna White."

"You dress almost as well," Betty teased, amidst whoops of laughter.

"Well, it's Katherine's business," Emily said. "A private, personal matter that isn't for us to discuss." Sadie and Betty nodded gravely, and for a moment all were silent. Katherine studied her shoes, feeling immensely self-conscious. Then Barbara's high voice piped up from the bed.

"But he's so-o-oo cute!"

A nurse had to come in and quiet them, and Katherine couldn't help reflecting that he certainly was.

GOOD LOOKS NOTWITHSTANDING, Peter Bradford wasn't at his office, a little two-room suite over the barbershop on Main. He wasn't at home either, and Luke himself hadn't seen him when she inquired downstairs at the tackle shop.

On an impulse, she decided to stop back at Mr. Stuart's, to see if her attorney had heard from him. "Ah, Katherine," he said, when she arrived. "There you are."

"The question is, where is Peter Bradford?" she said, plopping herself down in the comfortable chair before his desk. "I don't like carrying around a check for nearly five thousand dollars."

"Well, then give it back to me," Mr. Stuart said. "Because Mr. Bradford doesn't want it."

"He what?!"

"He's waiving his fee," Mr. Stuart said, sitting back in his leather chair. "He called this morning to say there was no need to send a check."

"But that's not the agreement we made," Katherine said, confused.

Mr. Stuart shrugged. "I suppose victory was its own reward for the sterling young counselor," he said, with a smile. "I would've thought you'd be pleased."

"Well, I'm..." She paused, frowning. "No, I'm not pleased," she muttered, more to herself, and rose slowly from her chair.

"Do you have the check with you?" Mr. Stuart asked. "We can dispose of it right now."

"Yes, but no," Katherine said. "I'm going to get him to take it." She looked defiantly at Mr. Stuart.

"Well, that's your choice, Katherine, but he was very firm when he spoke to me. And besides, if you want to speak to him, you'll have to wait a while. He said he was going out of town."

"Where?"

"He didn't say, specifically. Just something about his last weekend in a summer house."

"Wilmington," Katherine said. "Mr. Stuart, I'm going to deliver it to him in person." He was looking at her curiously. Katherine wondered what he was thinking. Were her emotions as evident to him as they were to the women in the Alliance? It didn't matter at the moment. "I don't want to be in debt to the man, for anything," she told him. "That's all."

"THAT'S NOT ALL."

Katherine sighed, her eyes glued to the road as she gripped the wheel. "Yes, it is," she countered. "The man just wants to be one up on me, somehow, so I can feel guilty about rejecting him."

"Which you do."

"Yes, I already do," she admitted. "So why make things worse?"

"Worse or better? Seems to me you wouldn't be driving all this way—and pushing the speed limit, by the by—if you didn't really want to see the man again."

"I just want to give him the check and be done with it," Katherine said, but she lacked conviction.

"I don't think you want to be done with it, at all. Now you listen to me, young lady. Life's too short. You can come up with a million reasons why things won't work out, but it's an awful waste of time. The man's crazy about you. You love him, too, but you're still stuck holding on to silly images you have about who Katherine Taylor's supposed to be, and who Katherine Taylor's supposed to be with—''

"Enough, Grammy."

"And it's all a terrible bore! Jeffrey's gone, and you can curse me for saying so, but it's just as well. You *are* young, and being with Peter Bradford's making you younger. It's about time you let yourself be who you are inside, anyway."

"Grammy, please!" Katherine exclaimed, and the car was silent. She could no longer hear the old woman's warm raspy voice in her ear, but she couldn't dismiss what she'd been hearing. Why *was* she so determined to see Peter Bradford face-to-face again? Merely to prove a point, that she wouldn't be beholden to him, that a deal was a deal?

"Right," she said aloud, and then, annoyed that she was talking to herself again, switched on the radio. The music was oddly familiar, and she realized with a start that it was one of the songs Peter had played with the Honkers that night at the Red Roost. She smiled, thinking about the figure he'd cut duck-walking across the stage, and then the smile faded. She switched stations.

Affairs were like this, she told herself. When they were over, everything reminded you of the person involved, but after a while, that stopped. How did she know this? Mainly from books and the movies. Her life hadn't exactly been affair-ridden. And that was the only reason Peter seemed to matter so much, of course. She hadn't been with another man since Jeffrey, and then Peter had come along, and so it was only natural....

Natural, yes. Everything had felt wonderfully, exquisitely natural. Odd that for two such disparate personalities it had seemed so easy to fall in love. Easy? Looking back now, she felt as though after a hesitant beginning, she'd hurtled headlong into it. Falling for Peter had been something entirely new, so different from the slow building of friendship and trust she'd experienced with Jeffrey.

Funny, but she hardly thought about Jeffrey at all these days. She'd never thought the time would come when such a large figure in her life would diminish, and take his place truly in the past, but apparently that time was here. And that was Peter's doing, too. He'd somehow helped her put things in perspective, made her see that Jeffrey really was the past, and that he, flesh and blood and vivid in the present, could really be a new future.

But he wasn't, she thought grimly. She hadn't let that happen. Passing another car as she zoomed up the highway, Katherine, for the umpteenth time in days, tried to convince herself that she'd been right. But her heart wasn't really in it. The closer she got to the turnoff for Wilmington, the faster her heart was beating.

PETER HOISTED THE CANOE off its stand and dragged it down the stretch of beach, humming off-key with an air of good cheer that was patently false. He stopped himself in midhum as he set the canoe down at the water's edge, and frowned at his surroundings.

The late-afternoon sun was burnishing the blue waters with a golden cast. The bright green that ringed the lake stirred in a warm breeze under a cloudless sky. Out there the island beckoned, its peaceful solitude awaiting him. And the whole scene looked about as inviting to him as a dark closet on a rainy day.

Peter nosed the canoe into the water, then climbed in, paddle in hand. It was a good thing this was his last weekend at Dave's place, but not because the weather would be getting colder now. He'd lost the spirit for it, that was all. As long as the lake, the boat, the house, even the sun itself continued to remind him of Katherine Taylor, having a fun weekend here was a lost cause.

He couldn't even revel in the satisfaction of having won his case. Joe Proffert had been a sitting duck, once Peter had gotten a look at Parker's ladder and put two and two together. He was happy that an equitable settlement had been reached, with Katherine's house declared safe for re-construction, and Parker and Maxwell only getting a tenth of what they'd asked for in damages. There was some sat-isfaction in all of that, but it wasn't quite enough.

Peter paddled listlessly, first to one side and then the other, remembering that he should try to enjoy himself. But he kept seeing Katherine's smile, hearing the sound of her voice in his mind, as vivid and real as—

"Peter!"

He shot up in his seat, convinced for a moment that he'd lost his mind. He could've sworn he had actually heard Katherine Taylor's voice come floating out over the lake. Then the call came again and he whipped around in his seat. There was a woman on the shore, waving at him, and un-believable as it seemed, he could tell by the blond hair and the look of her that Katherine Taylor really was there.

Peter turned the canoe to face the shore. She stopped waving, and stood patiently waiting, arms folded, as he glided in toward her. The sun seemed to light up her hair, bring out the pinkness in her blouse, the sheen of her gray jeans. It wouldn't do to betray his excitement at seeing her, so he did his best to keep paddling slowly.

Nonetheless when he touched shore, he practically leaped over the canoe's side before straightening up to face her. He couldn't help wondering if the fool woman had finally come to her senses and wanted to make things up with him. "Well," he said, wading up the sand to meet her. "What brings you out to these parts, Ms. Taylor?"

Katherine extended her hand, and when he saw what was in it, Peter's face fell. "Your check," she said.

He didn't take it, but shook his head. "Don't want it," he told her.

"And why not? You earned it. We had a deal," she said.

Peter gazed at her, seeing something beyond the defiant tilt of her chin, a glimmer of emotion in her eyes that re-kindled his hopes and made him wonder. "We had a lot more than that," he said evenly. "Money doesn't really matter when it comes to you and me."

"I thought this didn't have anything to do with us," she said. "You just wanted to show up the prosecution."

"I said it was a friendly gesture."

"That's true," she said. "But especially between friends, a deal is a deal."

"Look, forget about that money," he said. "I did it because I wanted to help you out, all right? And I did, and you don't owe me anything. End of story."

Katherine looked at him a long moment. She was wondering if this really could be the end, and the prospect alarmed her. He seemed almost angry. "I'd feel better if you took it," she said quietly.

"And I'd feel better if you ripped the damn thing up," he said. "It's no big deal."

"But we are," she blurted out. "Peter, we can't leave things like this, can we? I mean, are we friends? Or are we . . . what are we?" she said helplessly.

He gave her a rueful smile. "Now that's a good question," he said. "What do you think?"

"I think we've still got a lot of feelings for each other," she said carefully. "Things seem unresolved. Maybe if we could talk things out, we really could be friends."

Peter shook his head. "I don't think so," he said. "That's not really what I want."

"No?" she said, stung. Maybe she shouldn't have come, and she was only making a complete fool of herself. She could feel tears welling at the corners of her eyes and she ordered them to stay put. "Well, then, what do you want?"

"I want you to marry me."

Katherine stared at him, disbelieving. "You do? Still?"

Peter sighed. "Katherine, it's only been a couple of weeks since you turned me down," he said wryly. "And that wasn't even a straightforward proposal. You didn't give me half a chance."

"But that's because..." She paused uncertainly. What had happened to all her well-thought-out reasons why it wouldn't work?

"Maybe you thought I was being too hasty," he said. "And maybe in a way I was. Maybe it took being away from you for a while for me to understand that my instincts had been right in the first place."

"What do you mean?"

"I mean I've been finding out the hard way that I can't really live without having you around," he said, in a tone that sounded almost annoyed. "Now if you haven't been feeling the same way, you just tell me right now and we can have this thing be over and done with, okay?"

"No," she murmured, and he saw to his surprise that her eyes were filled with tears.

"No?"

"No, I don't want it to be over and—" But her last words were cut off as he pulled her into the shelter of his arms, his mouth seeking hers with a blind intensity. They kissed, and the feeling was dizzying, overpowering. She lost herself in the bittersweet, rough tenderness of his lips pressing so forcefully against hers as he enveloped her in his embrace. She was hazily aware of his heart beating as fast as hers against her breast.

She could only answer the urgent passion of his kiss with a desperate eagerness of her own, willingly surrendering herself to his powerful passion. Her hands seemed to slide up around his neck of their own accord, as he pulled her closer, molding her body to his, and when they broke apart at last, she had to struggle to catch her breath.

"How could you stay away so long?" he asked. "Have you felt better, not seeing me?"

"No, I've been miserable," she murmured. "Trying to pretend that I'd done the right thing and that I could get along without you and I didn't care—"

"But you do care," he said gently.

"I love you, Peter." She stared up into his eyes, surprised that the words had come so easily to her. "I wasn't prepared to fall in love again, and not . . . this way, but—"

"You mean with an unacademic younger person such as myself?"

"Don't tease me," she said. "I've been confused and afraid of my own feelings—"

"Kath, Kath," he said, shaking his head. "How can you be afraid of something that feels this good?"

This time his kiss began with an aching gentleness, his lips just brushing hers in the lightest of sweet caresses. But in a moment neither one of them could hold back their surging desire. His tongue found hers, engaging it in a languorous, sensual swirling dance. Her blood rose, the tips of her breasts swelling to aching arousal against the hard planes of his chest. His musky, masculine scent, the familiar taste of him, the taut muscles that held her in willing captivity—all of it combined to sweep all doubts away. She wanted him so much it hurt.

When at last they broke apart again, and she leaned back in his strong arms, gazing up in wonderment at blue velvet eyes that were hooded with passion, she could only weakly shake her head. Peter's face glowed with amusement and affection as he gave a deep, throaty chuckle.

"Now you're supposed to tell me this is just a physical attraction," he said. "Right?"

"Wrong," she said. "I know it goes deeper than that."

"Deep as a river," he said, still smiling, but there was a seriousness in his gaze that made her heart beat all the faster. "Katherine, I don't even want to try to analyze it. I just know that when I'm with you, it seems like all's right with the world."

"That's it!" she cried. "I couldn't put it better myself."

He lifted her chin with his thumb and forefinger, gently caressing the line of her cheek. "I know who you are in there," he said softly. "Underneath that woman-alone-against-the-world pose you've been hiding behind, I know you're still a teenager somehow, who likes to laugh and cut loose and kick out the jams—''

"Peter, I don't even know what the jams are," she protested.

"And I don't know what you see in that godawful poetry theater you dragged me to," he said. "But I don't care."

"I didn't like that play myself," she admitted. "I was being generous to Daryl, and defensive about it."

He let out a mock groan. "Now you tell me."

"But I'd rather read a scholarly text on Yeats than watch the Yankees play the Cubs."

"The Yankees don't usually play the Cubs, darling; they're in a different league," he said, grinning.

"You see? We'll never get along."

"Oh, stop," he said. "We've got a lot we can share with each other, and you know it as well as I do." A cloud seemed to cross her brow then. "What is it, Kath?"

She bit her lips, looking away. "Peter, there is one thing I don't thing we can share," she said, throat tightening. "I know how much you love children. I saw it when I watched you with your Little Leaguers. But I'm forty-three years old, and I don't know if I can really have another child." She looked up at him, tense and anguished. "I mean, I might be willing to try, if it was what you wanted, but . . ."

"Sweetheart." He stroked her hair tenderly and shook his head. "Don't you think I've given that some thought? Look, I'll admit that when we first talked about it, and you reacted the way you did, I felt a little upset. But I've had time to make my peace with it and Kath, you're the most important thing. I don't have to have a child with you."

"No?" Her eyes widened in surprise.

"I'd like to think that Clarissa could be mine as well as yours, within time," he said. "We seemed to have hit it off all right so far."

"She likes you a lot," Katherine said eagerly.

"And I like her. I might even start to love her, if she's anything like her mom." He smiled, and kissed the tip of her nose. "Besides, we're going to have about thirty-odd kids to look after once your mother's house is fixed up. Isn't that so?"

"You mean you'd help?"

He looked offended. "Haven't I so far?"

She kissed his hand. "Yes, you have," she said. "I'm just surprised you'd want to stay involved."

Peter sighed. "You know, for such a smart woman you've got a pretty thick head sometimes." He put a hand on each of her shoulders and looked her straight in the eye as he held her at arm's length. "I want to be involved, period! I want our lives to get all put together and intertwined. You know, like love, honor and cherish till death us do part, et cetera?"

"I like the sound of that," she admitted, smiling.

"Now can we get any other objections out of the way, as in speak now or forever hold your peace?"

She nodded, silent, feeling too dizzy with excitement to really think straight. "We do everything so fast," she said.

"I guess we want to," he said. "Now, I love you, you love me, we got that part straight. Do I make you happy?" he asked.

She'd never been made so happy by a man in her life. She couldn't deny it as she looked at him. And the thought of a future with Peter, a future she hadn't thought was possible, filled her with an excitement that was overwhelming, even as her head whirled crazily with questions.

"Of course," she said. "But—"

"Wonderfully happy?"

"Yes," she admitted, feeling a blush coming on as she saw the erotic implications gleaming in his eyes. "But, Peter—"

"Can you imagine us separating for good?"

"No," she said immediately. "But that doesn't mean—"

"Wouldn't you like to be able to spend more time doing the sorts of things we've been stupidly depriving ourselves of?"

"I guess," she said, snuggling up to him, limbs once more comfortably entwined with his. "I'm sure there's a hundred things we'll have to figure out to make it work."

He sighed. "I'm sure."

"Like how we're supposed to have a relationship when we live nearly two hours away from each other."

"Absolutely insurmountable," he said, with a mock frown. "You're right. It's hopeless."

"Well, I do have a sabbatical coming to me," she mused. "And I don't have to teach full-time, if I don't want to. I was planning to be in Greensdale this fall, to oversee the Center...."

"And there's no room in my place for you to live," he said sternly. "So I guess we can't live together."

"Well, I don't know if I could live with that swordfish," she said. "But there's plenty of space upstairs at Taylor House."

"And deal with a houseful of kids all day? Absolutely not. You're going to have a helluva time convincing me," he said. "Let's forget about this whole idea."

"All right," she said, taking a playful swat at his mockingly sorrowful countenance. "I'm getting your point."

He caught hold of her hand and smiled, playfully kissing the soft skin of her palm. "Then are you persuaded?"

She shook her head. "Not yet. So maybe you ought to start convincing me harder."

"Convincing you?" He looked at her, bemused. Then his eyes glimmered with a knowing look. He bent to savor her lips again, possessing her with a tantalizing sureness that made her blood simmer. "Like that?" he murmured.

"Like that," she sighed. "Convince me some more, Peter. I think I like this part the best."

"My pleasure," he whispered.

"Umm," she murmured. "And mine..."

Epilogue

The house, all things considered, had never had it so good. Shiny with a new coat of sparkling white paint, it took in the sun, complacent and proud as an elderly matron bedecked in a brand-new outfit. Even the moss-covered back wall of stone seemed to gleam a brighter gray and green, and the repaired roof's new slates glimmered amid the old ones, catching the light like so many jewels. The clean back windows twinkled as a wind rose, sprinkling them with autumnal leaves like so much confetti.

The yard was abuzz with excitement. Two dozen children were everywhere at once, running in and out of the open back door and all over the grass. Happy cries and screams filled through the air as the newly-installed swings were tested, along with the silver slide and little wooden merry-go-round. Along with their periodic exclamations could be heard the steady murmur of admiring adults. Today was the official opening of the Taylor Center, and Greensdale was here to take a look.

"There's no ribbon to cut," Emily Atchins said anxiously, when she caught up with Katherine at the little table set with refreshments by the back porch. "How do we have any sort of an opening ceremony without a ribbon?"

"Maybe we should just break a bottle of champagne against the side of the house," Clarissa suggested.

"It's not a bridge or a boat," Katherine said, laughing. "Besides, we don't need any speeches. The kids have already taken over the place. It's open already, no matter what."

"I've got just the thing," said Lydia, and smiling mysteriously, she hurried off into the house, calling over her shoulder: "I'll be right back! Tell everybody inside to come out here."

"I'll go." Barbara Wainright, baby strapped to her side in a sling, headed for the new sliding doors by the back porch. Katherine turned to Clarissa.

"I'm so glad you could come," she said. "What do you think?"

"I think it's fantastic, Mom." She turned around, scanned the crowded yard. "Speaking of which, where's my stepfather-to-be?"

"Over here!" Peter called. He was arm in arm with a disgruntled man in overalls, who was trying to pull away as Peter dragged him closer. Katherine suddenly realized it was Luke, of the fish and tackle store. "Kath, Luke here wants to tell you something."

"Bradford, you toad!—"

"Come on Luke, just repeat what you said to me when we were in the main playroom just now."

A few of the other Greensdale husbands and wives had followed the men over, and more came in their wake, probably alerted by Barbara that some announcement was going to be made. Luke looked around him, supremely embarrassed, then grimaced at Katherine. "I said it looked like the ladies had run out of beer," he said, and the onlookers laughed.

"No, you don't," Peter said, not relinquishing his grip on Luke's shoulder. "Tell my fiancé here what you said about the Taylor House day-care center."

Luke sighed. "I said, if it weren't for those silly clouds you got painted on the walls in the crib room, the place wasn't half bad-looking."

"All right!" Peter crowed amid applause, as Luke slunk away. "How's that for an endorsement, eh?" He joined Katherine, slipping his arm around her waist, and speaking close to her ear. "What'd Clarissa say?"

"She thinks we did a great job," Katherine said.

"No, about the ring," he said, frowning.

Katherine smiled, and held up her hand to examine the engraved silver band with a purple rhinestone in it that adorned her finger. "She thought that your giving me your high school ring as an engagement present was completely corny," she told him, then added quickly, as his face fell: "And completely lovable."

"Hmph," he said, which she knew was his sound of being pleased about something when he didn't want to let on he was. "So what's going on? Why is Sadie pushing everybody out of the house?"

"I don't know exactly," Katherine said, craning her neck to see over the heads of the various parents who were now gathered in a semicircle around them. "Lydie went running off to—here she is."

Lydia was pushing her way to the front. Bounding to her sister's side with a brown paper-wrapped parcel in her hand, she put two fingers to her lips and blew a piercing whistle that caused the people to quiet down and Jeremy Travis's dog to start barking. "Hear ye, hear ye!" she called gaily. "I want to present Ms. Katherine Taylor—and the town of Greensdale—with this, on the fifth day of October 1988."

She tore off the brown paper and held up a framed piece of paper for Katherine to see.

"What is it?" Katherine asked, unable to make out the writing as the sun hit the glass.

"It's our daycare license from the state of Massachusetts!" Lydia exclaimed, and held it over her head. "I now proclaim the Taylor Center officially open for business!"

A good-natured cheer went up across the lawn, mixed with applause that made Katherine feel as though her heart might swell right out of her chest. "More beer!" Clarissa called from the kitchen window, and the applause continued.

Katherine turned to look up into Peter's eyes. *I love you,* he mouthed above the tumult, and she kissed him, beaming. She hugged him tightly to her, reveling in the warmth and strength of his unfolding arms, not really wanting to let go, ever, until she felt a tugging at the edge of her skirt.

"Miss Taylor?" Katherine looked down to see the cherubic Michael Travis gazing up at her.

"Yes, Mike?" He kept looking, biting his lip shyly. She bent down to be level with him. "You like the house?"

He nodded. "Yup," he said. "And so does Grammy Taylor."

Katherine stared at him. "Well, that's . . . I'm sure she would if she could see it," she said, bemused.

"She did," he said. "She does like it."

Katherine glanced up to see Lydia close by, watching Mike with a peculiar expression on her face. "Michael, you know Grammy isn't here," Katherine said gently.

"But I saw her," he protested. "Over by that big weeping willow tree, where the fence is."

"Maybe you saw Mrs. Kavelson," Katherine suggested. The elderly lady was here with her grandchildren, and her silver hair and height had reminded Katherine of Grammy when she'd met her.

Michael shook his head. "I know what Grammy looks like," he said, in that tone children use when they're disgusted by the stupidity of adults. "She was standing there in that funny hat she used to wear, smiling at the house. And she waved at me."

Clarissa was at Lydia's side now. Sister and daughter looked at each other, then at Katherine. Sadie had been hovering behind her and she stepped forward now. "Michael, really," she said, clucking her tongue.

Lydia and Clarissa didn't say anything as Katherine patted Michael's head. "Thank you for telling us," she said, and the boy went scurrying off to join his friends. Katherine straightened up.

"That boy of mine has the wildest imagination," Sadie said. "I'm sure he was only trying to be nice." She smiled, and moved off as Katherine nodded absently, her eyes roving over the greenery in the yard and distant willow, swaying in the wind. She could feel Peter watching her, and she was glad he was there, but she moved away to join Clarissa.

Wordlessly she took Lydia's hand, and the three Taylor women turned as one to face the house for a moment. Red, yellow and orange leaves danced across the green lawn as the jubilant cries of children playing echoed all around them.

"Well," said Katherine softly. "I'm glad she likes it."

Harlequin American Romance

COMING NEXT MONTH

#269 LYDIA'S HOPE by Leigh Anne Williams

Lydia Taylor had come back home to Greensdale, Massachusetts, to help her sister Katherine with the Taylor House day-care center and to find out if she still had a home in the heart of Dr. Jake Harrison. Don't miss the second book in the Taylor House trilogy.

#270 CAPERS AND RAINBOWS by Jacqueline Diamond

Brite Cola president Jonas Ameling and heiress Whitney Graystone didn't share the same priorities, but that didn't stop her from secretly loving him. Could the California socialite prove that with the right woman in his arms, Jonas would have no problem getting his priorities straight?

#271 SIMPLE WORDS by Modean Moon

Victoria Tankersley had experienced too many changes in her life. Now she wanted to live a life of normalcy, but that wasn't her destiny—Phil Wilcox was a sure indication of that. Nine years ago he'd changed her life, and he was determined to do it again—but this time there was much more at stake.

#272 HEART'S DESIRE by Margaret St. George

When she won $6 million, small-town girl Ivy Enders found herself living a dream. When he won $5 million, Eric North lived out a fantasy. Both searched for the mate of their dreams, but when fantasy became reality, would they find their heart's desire?

ATTRACTIVE, SPACE SAVING BOOK RACK

Display your most prized novels on this handsome and sturdy book rack. The hand-rubbed walnut finish will blend into your library decor with quiet elegance, providing a practical organizer for your favorite hard-or soft-covered books.

Only $9.95

Approximately 16" x 8" when assembled

Assembles in seconds!

To order, rush your name, address and zip code, along with a check or money order for $10.70* ($9.95 plus 75¢ postage and handling) payable to *Harlequin Reader Service*:

Harlequin Reader Service
Book Rack Offer
901 Fuhrmann Blvd.
P.O. Box 1396
Buffalo, NY 14269-1396

Offer not available in Canada.

BKR-1A

*New York and Iowa residents add appropriate sales tax.

Taylor House

by Leigh Anne Williams

One house . . . two sisters . . . three generations

Harlequin American Romance introduces the TAYLOR HOUSE trilogy in October 1988

The Taylor family of Greensdale, Massachusetts, had always been "the family on the hill." Grammy Taylor and her two daughters, Katherine and Lydia, were admired more than they were known and loved. But the passing of the matriarch brought with it a unique test for the two sisters—could they save Taylor House . . . and save the town?

—Meet Katherine, who is determined to bring her dream to life.

—Meet Lydia, who hopes to keep that dream alive.

—And meet Clarissa, Katherine's daughter, whose wish is to carry on the traditions of Taylor House for a new generation.

A story of family, home and love in a New England village.

Don't miss the stories of these three women in the October, November and December Harlequin American Romances for 1988:
#265 *Katherine's Dream*, #269 *Lydia's Hope* and #273 *Clarissa's Wish*